BURIED DEEP WITHIN

Detectives expose a small town's secrets
in this artful mystery

CHERYL REES-PRICE

THE
BOOK
FOLKS

Published by The Book Folks

London, 2025

ISBN 978-1-80462-276-6

www.thebookfolks.com

Buried Deep Within is the tenth title in a bestselling series of standalone mysteries set in the heart of Wales.

Prologue

The heavy backpack dug into Eira's shoulders, and her arms ached from carrying the additional equipment. The mountain grass was uneven beneath her boots, and rocks jutted out, waiting to trip her up. She pressed on without complaint as she knew her five companions would be feeling the same. They had been hiking for hours but were close to their destination. Eira's excitement kept her pushing on.

Alex was leading the group. He had a compass in one hand which he periodically checked. He had memorised the coordinates. Eira was still amazed at how he had found this place. This would be the group's third visit, and she doubted she would have been able to find it alone.

'Here we are,' Alex said.

Eira put down the bag she carried and joined Alex. She looked down at the hole between two rocks. It would be easy to walk by if you didn't know of the cave's existence.

The hole was only wide enough for one person to climb through at a time. They put on their helmets, switched on the torches, and went in one by one. The last person handed down the equipment to pass along in a chain. Eira was third in. She inhaled the damp, earthy air and felt the drop in temperature as she descended. It wasn't a steep drop down, so they didn't need rope at this stage. Next was a slow crawl through a narrow passage which was made all the more difficult by having to push and pull their heavy bags and backpacks through. The passage then widened so they could stand but the taller ones in the group still had to stoop. Finally, they emerged onto a loose stony bank that sloped down into the first cavern.

They all stood in silence for a moment. The only sound came from the plink plunk of water falling from the ceiling, and the distant sound of the underground stream.

Eira looked around. Her headlamp illuminated the stalactites, and the ceiling glittered with thousands of tiny crystals. She had seen this part of the cave on the last visit, but she still felt a thrill. Today, they would explore further by splitting into two groups and laying more guidelines through the sumps.

Bits of rock tumbled down the bank as the group carefully made their way down. The lights from their torches cast tall shadows on the walls. Beyond the pool of light was inky darkness.

After a drink from her flask, Eira moved away from the others to change into her wetsuit. She listened to the chatter among the group. There had been something off about them all morning. It was so subtle that she couldn't work it out. When she thought about it, it was more about the demeanour of one of them. She looked across and saw that the person was already kitted up and ready to go.

Eira shook off the unsettling feeling. They would be diving into the unknown and there wasn't room for distractions.

Her fiancé came to stand next to her. In the light from her head torch, she could see concern in his eyes.

'I'll be fine,' she said.

He nodded. 'I just feel bad that I'm not going with you.'

Only she knew why he had chosen to go with the other group. 'Please don't worry about it. Just think how exciting it is. It's only us that have ever been in this cave. And now we're going to explore further. We'll swap stories later.'

The others called out to him, and he kissed her. 'See you later.'

Eira watched him walk away. He took the left-hand passage with his group and slowly their lights faded away.

'You ready?' Alex asked.

'I need a pee first,' Ceri said.

Eira waited while Ceri disappeared and returned a few moments later. 'I should have gone before I put my wetsuit on,' she said.

Eira laughed. She slipped on her harness and clipped it in place, then grabbed her swim fins. There was a more relaxed atmosphere now that the other group had gone. They carried their equipment down the right-side passageway. Here, a stream ran past them before disappearing beneath the surface. The passage opened into a small chamber and revealed the source of the stream, a deep resurgence pool. On the right-hand side of the pool, the ground gently sloped upwards to meet the wall of the cave. Eira sat down on the slope and put on her fins.

'This is not my SPG,' Ceri said. 'Mine has a compass. Someone has taken mine.'

'You've got the right harness, haven't you?' Alex asked.

'Erm… I'm not sure now.'

'Mine would have been too loose on you,' Eira said.

Ceri looked back. 'We'll have to go after the others.'

'They'll be in the water by now,' Alex said. 'Chill. It's just a gauge. Probably the wrong one was attached when the tanks were replaced. The only gauge you have to worry about is the pressure. You're not going to get lost.'

Eira could see the worry on Ceri's face. The younger woman was a less experienced diver than herself and not as confident. 'You can have mine,' she offered.

'You're not switching SPGs down here,' Alex said.

'I'm not thick,' Eira said. 'Just change over the harnesses. Same equipment.' She unclipped her harness.

'Thank you,' Ceri said. 'I know I'm being pathetic.'

Eira shook her head. 'You need to feel comfortable. That's what matters.'

With the harnesses changed and adjusted, Eira pulled up her hood, put on her goggles, and placed the regulator in her mouth. She gave the thumbs up and slipped into the water. The first thing she felt was the strong pull of the undercurrent. She kicked her feet as hard as she could while trying not to stir up any silt from the bottom. Rock ledges jutted out on either side of her, and she knew the dangers of getting trapped under one.

As Eira moved into the passageway, the current slowed. There was an other-worldly feeling as she glided through the water. She could hear her rhythmic breathing through the regulator, and the popping sound of the air bubbles. The water was clear, with dancing particles. She pulled herself forward using the guideline that they had placed on their last visit. Ceri was in front of her and Alex behind. Their lights bounced off the cave walls and Eira drank in the details. They came to a tricky U-bend and squeezed themselves through before ascending to the surface.

The second chamber was larger than the first and they rested for a moment before wading through the water to the next sump. This was unexplored territory. They would be laying another guideline and hoped to find a third chamber.

'Ready?' Alex asked.

Ceri bit her lip. 'I'm not sure about taking the lead.'

'It's your turn to name the next cavern we find,' Alex said.

Ceri looked at Eira. 'Do you mind doing it?'

'Tell you what. I'll lead but you can stay next to me when it's wide enough. When we come to the next surface, I'll hold back, and you can be the first to set eyes on the place.'

Ceri smiled. 'Thanks.'

'No problem,' Eira said. She held her hand out for the reel.

They returned to the water. This time was different as there were no guidelines. Eira moved slowly and looked around. She stopped now and again to secure the line before moving on. The passage widened and Ceri glided along next to her for a while. Up ahead, the passage split into two. More exploring opportunities, Eira thought. She signalled to take the left. This was a narrow passage with just enough room for one person to manoeuvre. The passage sloped up, and Eira was sure it would lead to the surface. She moved faster now, excited to reach the next chamber. She planned to stop before breaking the surface to let Ceri move past, but at the top, the passage turned sharply downwards. Eira's air tanks caught on the top of the rock and loosened a chunk. It dropped on her back and stirred up the water. She was attempting to wriggle her hands to loosen her harness when Ceri collided with her.

Eira felt the impact and pitched forward so her front half was leaning down. A sharp tug on the line caused her to drop the reel. She could feel the water thrashing around her body. She guessed that Ceri had panicked and probably got caught in the line. Eira knew it was best to keep calm. Panic in this environment was a killer. She lay still, keeping her breathing even. She checked the time and calculated her air. There was plenty. She wouldn't have used up a third yet. She always kept to the rules. A third in, a third out, leaving a third spare.

The water started to settle, and she could no longer feel movement behind her. Being alone didn't worry her. One of them would come back for her. It would more than likely be Alex. Both of them would have returned to the wider section. Alex would send Ceri back to go after the others, in case he needed more help, then he would come back and stay with her.

It didn't take long for Alex to return. Eira felt his weight on her legs as he pulled at the stone on her back. It loosened, and she was able to wriggle free. Visibility was poor, and as much as she wanted to continue the exploration, she knew it would be foolish. She backed out of the passage until she had room to turn around. She signalled for Alex to go ahead. A few moments later, it became difficult to breathe through the regulator. This meant that she was running low on air. She reached down for the gauge and saw it was still showing full. She knew she should have used a little over a third of the air.

She stopped and reached behind her back to feel for the valves. The isolator switch between the two tanks might have been switched closed when she was shunted. The valve was open. She was nearly out of air but thirty minutes from the chamber. She wouldn't make it. It was then that she panicked.

Chapter One

Six years later

Detective Inspector Winter Meadows was sitting in his garden enjoying the last rays of the autumn sun. It had been the first dry day in over a week, and he wanted to make the most of being outdoors. His wife, Daisy, his mother, Fern, and his brother, Rain, had joined him, and he felt a deep sense of contentment. He threw another log on the fire and inhaled the woody scent. It reminded him of his childhood in the commune.

Beyond the garden, fields stretched out and met the edge of the Black Mountain. Trees moved in the gentle breeze and sent russet leaves scattering like confetti. The Welsh valley felt still and peaceful.

'Ah, this is nice,' Rain said. He took a drag of his joint and blew out a long plume of smoke.

'You better finish that quick,' Daisy said. 'The gang will be here soon.'

'Yeah,' Meadows said. 'I wouldn't put it past Edris to arrest you.'

Rain laughed. 'Edris loves me.'

The garden gate squeaked on its hinges and Rain stubbed out his smoke. DC Reena Valentine appeared. She wore a pair of cropped jeans, and with sunglasses pushing back her black glossy hair, she brought back the feeling of summer.

'There you all are,' she said. 'Am I the first?'

'Yes,' Meadows said. 'Come and grab a seat.'

'Can I get you something to drink?' Daisy asked.

'I'm on call,' Valentine said.

'I've made some lemonade,' Fern said. 'Help yourself.'

'Thanks.' Valentine poured herself a glass, then settled next to Daisy. 'It's nice not to be in the office. This is what Sunday afternoons should be like.' She put her head back and let the sun fall on her face.

'Your boss works you too hard,' Daisy said.

'Yeah, you couldn't get a worse one,' Valentine said. She looked at Meadows and laughed.

The gate opened again, and DS Tristan Edris poked his head around the corner.

'There he is,' Fern said. She patted the chair next to her. 'Come and sit next to me, Tristan.'

'Hello beautiful,' Edris said. He planted a kiss on Fern's cheek before sitting down. 'How are you?'

'All the better for seeing you,' Fern said.

Valentine shook her head. 'Don't flirt with him. He doesn't need any more encouragement.'

'I'm a changed man,' Edris said.

'I did hear that you've got a new lady friend,' Fern said.

'Yeah, she's—'

Valentine held up a hand, cutting him off. 'No, you don't. You know the rules. We don't want any info until you've been seeing this one for at least two months.'

'Oh, leave him alone,' Fern said. 'He's got a lot of love to share.'

'No kidding,' Daisy said.

Meadows laughed. 'I have to agree. He's almost been through the alphabet.'

'What are we going to talk about, if not Tristan's love life?' Rain asked. 'It's the highlight of my visits.'

'You don't have to work with him,' Valentine said. 'He gets a new one, is all loved up for a couple of weeks, introduces us, and then dumps them. They come crying to me. I'm the one left persuading them that he's a dick, and they are better off without him.'

'Oh, don't be mean,' Fern said.

'It's nearly been two months,' Edris said.

'Well, until then, we don't want to hear another word,' Valentine said.

Meadows' phone rang and there was a collective sigh.

'Don't answer it, bro,' Rain said.

Meadows grabbed his phone from the table, and the group around him fell silent as he talked. 'On my way,' he said and ended the call. 'Missing baby in Garnant.'

'I'll come with you,' Edris said.

'You're not on call, are you?' Daisy asked.

'We'll all be called in for a missing child,' Valentine said.

Meadows nodded. 'Sorry, guys.' He kissed Daisy. 'See you later.'

'I hope the little one is found safe,' Fern said.

'I hope so too,' Meadows replied.

* * *

Edris travelled with Meadows, and Valentine followed in her car. It was quiet as they drove in and out of the small villages. There was the occasional dog walker, but most people were indoors enjoying a relaxing evening before the start of the week. This all changed when they reached their destination. People were scurrying around, looking in dustbins, and under bushes.

'Looks like the whole village has come out to help,' Edris commented.

Meadows pulled into a large driveway where two vehicles and a police car were parked. Valentine parked behind him. The house was a large, detached property sitting near the River Amman. It had a grand Georgian porch with vines growing up the pillars and looked to be newly built.

'Bit pretentious for this area,' Edris said.

'If you've got the money and it makes you happy, why not?' Meadows said.

They got out of the car and were met by PC Matt Hanes.

'What have you got for us?' Meadows asked.

'Missing baby. Six-week-old Cora Hendon. The parents are Gareth Hendon and Jenna Ford. It was Cora's christening this morning. The family and friends came back here to celebrate. Around 6 p.m. Gareth's parents were leaving and taking his granny with them.' Hanes checked his notes. 'Olwen Hendon. She has Alzheimer's. They couldn't find her in the house. There was a bit of a commotion when they looked for her. That's when Jenna noticed that Cora wasn't in her crib. Initially, they thought Olwen had taken Cora and gone walkabout. Olwen was found on the cycle path, but no sign of the baby. They called us at 6.45 p.m. I got a description of the pyjamas she was wearing. A woollen blanket was also taken.

'As you can see, gardens are being checked in case she put the baby down somewhere. Uniform have made a start searching the cycle path. There are a lot of trees and bushes, and some parts are quite dense.'

'How long has the baby been missing?' Meadows asked.

'I haven't been able to pin that down. They were all having a very good time by the sounds of it. Most of the friends had left before anyone noticed the absence of Olwen and the baby. It's mostly family left now. It was bedlam when I arrived. Given the age of the child, I thought it best to call you in.'

Meadows nodded. The last missing child case in the area had not ended well, and he expected that it was at the forefront of all their minds.

'Even if it was just before six that the baby went missing, that's still over an hour and a half,' Valentine said.

'The temperature has dropped,' Meadows said. 'If she's out in the open, we don't have much time.'

DS Stefan Blackwell arrived while they were talking. He had the physique of a bulldog, small beady eyes, and rarely smiled.

'You'd think someone would have heard a baby crying by now,' Blackwell said. 'Unless…'

No one wanted to finish the sentence. They knew too well that if the baby had been placed face down, it may already be too late.

'I take it the front door was unlocked,' Meadows said.

Hanes nodded. 'Cora was in the nursery.' He pointed up to the last window on the left.

Meadows turned to Blackwell. 'Call in every resource we have. I'll leave you and Valentine to coordinate the search. Better initiate Child Rescue Alert. We need all the help we can get. Edris and I will talk to the parents and the grandmother. If we can get a better estimate of the time the child went missing, we can at least narrow down the search radius.'

'I'll take you in,' Hanes said. 'The parents are in the front room. Olwen and her daughter-in-law, Beth, are in the conservatory.'

Meadows and Edris followed Hanes through the front door into a large hallway. In the centre was a wide wooden staircase with glass panels running up each side and along the landing.

Four doors led off the hallway. A fifth door at the back opened into the kitchen where they could see a couple of children, four women, and a man. Meadows noticed that Edris' attention was on this group of people. He had an odd expression on his face.

'What is it?' Meadows asked.

'Nothing. They all look fairly relaxed considering the circumstances,' Edris said.

Meadows looked. Three of the women were leaning against the worktop. A man had just taken something out of the fridge and was stuffing it into his mouth. One of the women giggled.

'They've been in and out searching,' Hanes said. 'I imagine they are trying to keep calm for the children's sake. The young girl and little boy are Cora's brother and sister. There is an older brother. Jamie. He's a teenager. He's gone out to join the search.'

'I think it's a good idea to ask everyone that is not immediate family to leave,' Meadows said.

Hanes nodded. 'I'll take you to the parents and then clear the house.' He knocked on a door on the left, opened it, and introduced Meadows and Edris.

'About bloody time,' Gareth Hendon said. 'We've been told to wait here when we should be out searching.'

Meadows judged Gareth to be in his early thirties. He had dark-blond hair, and a beard, which was trimmed close to his square jawline. He was pacing back and forth. His pupils were dilated and the whites of his eyes were bloodshot.

Jenna Ford was sitting on a brown leather corner sofa. Her chin-length red hair was flat on one side and sticking out on the other. She had a pale complexion with a smattering of freckles across her nose and cheeks. Mascara was smudged under her eyes, and she had a faraway look.

Both of them were smartly dressed, but Jenna's navy dress was badly creased.

'I'm sorry to have kept you,' Meadows said. 'There are a few questions we need to ask you. In the meantime, I assure you that everything is being done to find Cora. We have activated the Child Rescue Alert. This means that as well as the police, search and rescue, and the media, we'll be seeking help from the local community. Cora's details will be sent out across all media channels. A lot of people will be looking for her.'

'I should be one of them,' Gareth said.

'It is vital at this stage that we establish a timeline of events. It will help us narrow down the search area.'

'Fine.' Gareth sat down next to Jenna. His legs jiggled up and down.

Meadows noted that Jenna had not yet spoken. She sat slouched, with an almost dreamy expression on her face. He took a seat in an armchair and waited for Edris to take out his notebook.

'We understand you had a celebration here today,' Meadows said.

'Cora's christening,' Gareth said. 'I've already told that copper all this. We were all at the church this morning.'

'What time did you get back?'

'Around one.'

'How many of you?'

Gareth shrugged. 'About thirty.'

'Can you talk me through the afternoon?'

'We all went out in the garden. Had some food, a few drinks, and took photos.'

'Was Cora out in the garden with you?'

'Most of the time, yeah. She was passed around.'

'Who put Cora in the nursery?'

'Jenna.' Gareth gave her a nudge.

Meadows looked at Jenna. 'What time was that?'

Jenna shrugged. 'Dunno.' Her voice was barely above a whisper.

Gareth looked at Jenna. 'It must have been after Andrew left because I remember him making a point of saying goodbye to you. That was just before four.'

Jenna nodded.

Meadows addressed Jenna. 'Was it just you that went upstairs?'

'Yeah,' she said. 'I went for a lie-down as I was tired.'

'Did you hear anyone come up after that?'

Jenna shook her head.

'I went up not long after, to see where she was,' Gareth said. 'She was out for the count. It's the first time she's had a drink since Cora was born.'

'I wasn't drinking,' Jenna said. Her voice rose. 'Why would you say that?'

'You were laughing a lot, and you looked unsteady on your feet,' Gareth said.

'I told you. I was tired.'

Jenna appeared to be coming out of her stupor, and Meadows noticed she was agitated. Her hands were clenched and her eyes narrowed.

'OK, so you put Cora in her crib around four. Did she wake up after that?' he asked.

'No.' Gareth said. 'We have monitors in here and the kitchen. My mother also had a portable unit. We would have heard her crying.'

'It looks like it has been switched off,' Edris said and pointed to the monitor on the table.

'Someone probably switched it off to stop the noise of us searching echoing around the house,' Gareth said.

'When did you discover that Cora wasn't in her crib?' Meadows asked.

'Half six, something like that,' Jenna said. 'People coming up the stairs shouting for Olwen woke me up. I thought at first that someone had taken her downstairs to give her a bottle.'

'Is there any reason, other than the fact she was missing at the same time, that you believe Olwen took Cora?'

'Olwen's cardigan and shoes were in the room opposite the nursery,' Jenna said.

Gareth looked at Meadows. 'Are you thinking someone else took her?' He shook his head. 'It has to be Gran. No one else here would have taken her.'

'Do you mind if we take a look upstairs?'

'What for?' Gareth asked.

'Just to see the layout. Forensic officers will also need access to the room.' Meadows saw the look of horror on Gareth's face. 'This is standard procedure. We would ask that in the meantime, no one goes into the room.'

'Fine. Can I go now? I want to look for my daughter.'

'We would advise that you wait here. A family liaison officer will be with you shortly. They will keep you informed.'

'I'm not sitting around waiting.'

'You're going to leave me?' Jenna asked.

'You could get out there yourself,' Gareth snapped.

Jenna wrapped her arms around her body and sobbed.

The door opened and a woman entered the room. She was petite, with long auburn hair that cascaded down her back in soft curls. Beside her was a girl of around ten, and a younger boy. The woman glanced at Meadows, and her eyes flickered to Edris before she turned her attention to Gareth.

'Sorry to disturb you,' she said. 'I'm going to take the children to my mother's house and settle them down.'

'Thanks, Laura,' Gareth said.

'I want to stay here,' the girl said. 'It's Daddy's turn.'

Jenna turned on the girl. 'Cora is missing. You are old enough to understand that.'

Gareth shot Jenna a look. 'I'm sorry, Maisie. I'm sure Cora will be back soon, but for now, be a good girl and go with your mother.'

Maisie smiled sweetly at Gareth and nodded.

'I'll be back as soon as I can,' Laura said.

Jenna scowled. 'There's no need for you to be here.'

'You've got work early in the morning,' Gareth said. 'I'll call as soon as there's news.'

Laura nodded. 'I can take Jamie with me if you like. I sure Mum won't mind him staying the night.'

'That will be–'

'No!' Jenna cut Gareth off. 'He needs to be here with his family.'

Laura moved to the sofa. 'OK. If you need anything, call and I'll come straight away. It doesn't matter what time it is.' She leaned forward to embrace Jenna. 'I'm sure she will be found soon.'

Jenna stiffened at Laura's touch. Laura moved away and hugged Gareth. He squeezed her tight and Jenna glared. Laura pulled away from Gareth, and the two children hugged him. The three left the room.

'We'll take a look upstairs now,' Meadows said.

'Whatever,' Gareth said. 'The nursery is the last door on the left.'

Edris closed his notebook, and Meadows followed him out of the room. It wasn't until they were upstairs that either of them spoke.

'What do you think?' Meadows asked.

'There's something not quite right between them.'

'Could have something to do with the ex-partner hanging around.'

Edris shrugged. 'She seemed all right to me.'

Meadows nodded. 'Although I don't think Jenna is particularly comfortable with the arrangement. It looks like Gareth and Laura are the parents of the boy and girl. A new baby comes along, and it changes the dynamics. We can't assume that it was Olwen who took the baby.'

'Then you've got the older boy; Jamie,' Edris said. 'Hanes said he's a teenager. I'm guessing he's Jenna's son from a previous relationship, given that she didn't want him to go with the other children. Complicated family set-up.'

The door to the nursery was open, so Meadows stepped inside and looked around. It was decorated in pale pink with white furnishings. Near the window was a changing unit with a set of drawers. Mobiles were hanging from the ceiling. In the centre of the room stood the crib. It had a mechanism to keep it rocking as the baby slept. On top of another set of drawers, a monitor was placed to watch over the crib. There was no standby light on.

Meadows stepped over to the monitor and trailed the cable down. 'The plug has been pulled from the socket.'

'Gareth did say the monitors had been turned off,' Edris said.

'Why completely unplug it? You'd have to reach down behind the drawers. It's awkward. If you crawled to the plug, you could switch off the monitor without the risk of being seen on one of the screens downstairs.'

'You think that's what happened? Someone came in and took the baby. They would have to have known that the baby was sleeping upstairs while everyone was partying downstairs. Risky with the mother sleeping in the next room.'

'Not if you were part of the party. Easy to sneak up.'

'Maybe the granny pulled the plug,' Edris said.

'It's an odd thing to do. Taking the baby might not have been a deliberate act. It could be the case of something coming into her mind and she just picked the baby up and left.'

'Who knows what she was thinking,' Edris said. 'It seems the most plausible explanation. What are the chances of Olwen going missing at the same time as the baby? The two have to be connected.'

'Unless Olwen was a distraction,' Meadows said. He stepped out of the room and opened the next door. 'This looks like the master bedroom.'

The room was a mess. There were clothes on the floor and an unmade bed. Meadows moved to the large window and looked at the view over the garden. Some of the window was taken up by a dressing table.

'Doesn't look like the cleaner has been in this room,' Edris said. 'How are you supposed to find anything?'

Meadows smiled at Edris' disapproving look as he surveyed the items on the tabletop. Make-up, various creams, perfume bottles, used tissues, and tangled beads and necklaces were jumbled together.

'Cleaning is not a priority when you have a baby,' Meadows said.

'The sitting room was spotless,' Edris said.

Meadows moved to the bedside table where two packets of tablets drew his attention. He read the labels. 'Antidepressants and codeine. It's no wonder she didn't hear anything if she mixed these with alcohol.'

They left the bedroom and checked out the other rooms. One was a young girl's bedroom. It was decorated in lilac with a large mural of a unicorn. Next to it was another child's room. Meadows guessed it belonged to the young boy. There was a darker room that smelled of sweaty socks, and finally, the spare room set opposite the nursery. This room had a double bed with a navy-blue cover. It looked to Meadows as if someone had sat on the edge and left an imprint. The room had two large windows. One overlooking the garden, and the other, the view from the side of the house.

'This must be the room where they found Olwen's shoes and cardigan,' Edris said. 'Clear view of the nursery if both doors were open. If the baby cried, she could have gone to take a look then picked her up and was just confused.'

Meadows nodded. 'It's a good theory. She comes in, sits on the bed, and takes off her shoes. Maybe she was going to have a nap and got disturbed.'

He moved to the window and looked out. Trees stood tall against the twilight sky, and part of the cycle path was visible alongside. He could just make out the river through the trees. It looked ominous in the fading light. An uneasy feeling crept over him. Then the shouting began.

Chapter Two

Meadows rushed down the stairs with Edris close behind. He followed the direction of the commotion until he reached the conservatory. Inside, Beth Hendon was standing in between Jenna, and her mother-in-law, Olwen.

'What have you done with her? You stupid old bitch!' Jenna screamed.

She lunged towards Olwen. Beth struggled to keep her back.

Meadows stepped in and restrained Jenna. 'Calm down. This isn't doing any good.'

Olwen was cowering. Her bottom lip trembled, and tears filled her eyes.

'Edris, take Jenna back to the sitting room,' Meadows said.

Edris guided Jenna out of the room. She looked over her shoulder and shouted a string of obscenities at Olwen and Beth.

Meadows surveyed the two women. Beth Hendon had a full figure. Her grey hair was cut into a pixie style, and she had a no-nonsense look about her. Olwen was thin. Her hair was sparse, and her face a map of wrinkles.

'You're Gareth's mother,' Meadows said.

Beth nodded and looked at Olwen. 'It's not her fault. Come and sit down, Mum.'

Olwen shook her head. 'Why is that woman screaming?'

'She's upset,' Beth said. 'Her baby is missing.'

'Oh dear,' Olwen said. 'I want to go home.'

'Where is home?' Meadows asked.

'Betws,' Olwen said.

'Not anymore, Mum. You live with me and Joe now. Remember?' She looked at Meadows. 'We live just up the road.'

'Come and sit down, Olwen,' Meadows said. 'I'd like to ask you a couple of questions.'

Beth raised her eyebrows. 'I'm not sure she'll be able to help you.'

'I understand the situation,' Meadows said. 'I'll try my best not to cause any more distress.'

'Come and sit with me,' Beth said. She led Olwen to the sofa and they both sat down.

Meadows sat down in a chair. 'Did you have a nice day celebrating Cora's christening, Olwen?'

'Erm...' Olwen looked at Beth.

'Gareth's baby, Cora. Remember?' Beth said. 'It was her christening today.'

'What day is it?' Olwen asked.

'Sunday,' Beth said.

'I go to church on Sundays.'

Beth nodded. 'Cora's christening was after the service this morning.'

Meadows leaned forward. 'There were a lot of people. Did you go upstairs for a bit of peace?'

'I was tired,' Olwen said.

'Do you know what time that was?'

Olwen shook her head. 'Bill will be home soon.'

'Bill was her husband,' Beth explained.

'Did you take Olwen upstairs for a lie-down?' Meadows asked.

'No. She had her meds at quarter past four. She usually has a nap afterwards. Gareth had given me the baby monitor, as Jenna had gone upstairs to sleep. I went back out into the garden. It was such a lovely afternoon, and it had been a busy day. I'm ashamed to say I fell asleep in the summer house.'

'Does Olwen often go missing?'

'Not really. If she leaves the house, she usually ends up at Janet's house. She's Olwen's friend. It's the first place we looked. Janet wasn't home. She sometimes goes to stay with her daughter for a few days.'

'What time did you notice that Olwen was missing?'

'Just after six,' Beth said. 'I was ready to go home by then.'

'Olwen, do you often come to Gareth's house?' Meadows asked.

'Who's Gareth?' Olwen asked.

'We come down a few times a week,' Beth said. 'It's nice to get out of the house, and I can give Jenna a hand. I usually spend a few hours cleaning. Olwen goes to see Janet up the road, or she stays here.'

'So she would be familiar with the layout of the house. I'm just wondering what drew her to the room upstairs,' Meadows said. 'It looked like she was going to rest on the bed.'

'You like that room, don't you, Mum? She spends a lot of time in there looking at the river.'

'Olwen, did you go for a walk by the river after the party?' Meadows asked.

'All the baby boys were thrown into the River Nile,' Olwen said.

Meadows saw Beth's eyes widen, and he felt his stomach turn. 'Is that where the baby is? Did you take her to the river?'

Olwen chuckled. 'You are a funny lad. That was a long time ago.' She looked at Beth. 'Miriam took the baby.'

'Who is Miriam?' Meadows asked.

Beth shook her head. 'I've no idea. It could be someone from way back in her past.'

'Olwen, who is Miriam?' Meadows asked.

Olwen frowned in confusion.

'Was Miriam at the party?'

Worry creased Olwen's face. 'I don't know. Can I go home now? I have to get Bill's tea ready.'

'Can we go?' Beth asked. 'I think it would be better if we were out of Jenna's way.'

Meadows nodded. 'I think that may be for the best. If Olwen remembers anything about this afternoon, please let us know.'

He left the conservatory and met Edris in the hall. 'Has Jenna calmed down?' he asked.

'Yeah, just about. She chucked down a couple of pills. It seemed to do the trick. Family liaison is on their way.'

'Good. She's going to need a lot of support,' Meadows said. He repeated the conversation he'd had with Olwen.

The horror on Edris' face reflected Meadows' feelings. 'You think she threw the baby in the river?'

'It's possible. We need to find Blackwell. Members of the public are searching, including Gareth. We need to get them away from the river.'

Chapter Three

Blackwell was in the community centre organising a group of volunteers. The centre had been opened as a base and was already set up with tables, maps, torches, and refreshments.

Meadows pulled Blackwell away from the group and updated him on his conversation with Olwen.

Blackwell shook his head. 'If she was put in the river, the poor little mite wouldn't stand a chance. It's flowing fast after the recent rain and she'd be carried miles down. She may never be recovered.'

'There is still the chance that she was put on the bank. Maybe hidden in the long grass or bushes. It may also be the case that Olwen is just confused and didn't go anywhere near the river,' Meadows said. 'While there is still hope, we have to keep on searching.'

Blackwell nodded. 'We have lots of volunteers. Not just from this village, but from the neighbouring villages. Information is coming through from people who were walking on the cycle path this evening. It's split in two by the road. Olwen was seen walking the path, heading towards Brynamman, at half past six. No sightings before that. She wasn't carrying anything.'

'What about the other direction?'

'No. She wasn't seen on that side. The baby's sister, Maisie, was playing in the park with friends. It's right on the path. She didn't see Olwen. We've been concentrating the search in the other direction.'

'Olwen was given her medication at quarter past four and she was found at around quarter to seven. If she left the house straight away, then that's over two hours.'

'Average walking speed is three miles per hour,' Edris said. 'That's a lot of area to cover.'

Meadows nodded. 'Even if we allow for her age and say she covered two miles.'

'All gardens and outbuildings in the area have been checked,' Blackwell said. 'It's not like she can move anywhere. She will be cold and hungry by now. Someone should have heard her crying.'

'What about other avenues?' Meadows asked.

'Child Rescue has been activated and the baby's photo circulated through all media channels. Honestly, I can't see that someone just walked in the house during a party and took her,' Blackwell said.

'Maybe someone that attended the party,' Meadows suggested.

'Say goodbye to the hosts, then grab the baby and leave?' Edris shook his head. 'Can't see it.'

'I've spoken to quite a few people that attended the party and have come to help,' Blackwell said. 'Some looked like they had a good few drinks this afternoon, but none of them were acting suspiciously. I've got uniform checking out all the attendees and searching their houses. So far, everyone has cooperated.'

Meadows thought of the family waiting for news. The fear and pain mingling with hope. He tried not to think about the baby going into the cold water. 'OK. Get search and rescue to concentrate their efforts on the river. Start a couple of miles up and work back down. It's not going to be an easy search in the dark. Get the volunteers to concentrate their efforts near the path. We need to keep them away from the river. If Cora is in the water, I don't want members of the public to witness that, particularly Gareth and Jamie.'

'I'll do my best to keep them away, but it's not going to be easy,' Blackwell said, then moved away and called for everyone's attention.

Meadows stepped outside and looked at the helicopter circling overhead. He knew it would be using thermal imaging to locate Cora. Dog handlers were on the scene and the cycle path was lit up with torches. He went to his car, changed into boots, grabbed a torch, and joined the search.

* * *

The search party moved silently and slowly along the cycle path. They had been searching for over an hour and Meadows had expected to hear a shout out by now.

'Blackwell didn't exaggerate the amount of people that have come to help,' Edris said.

Meadows moved the branches of a bush and shone his torch around. 'No, and I don't think any of them are giving up until we find her. Even if that means being out all night.'

They moved in a line that stretched from the path to the riverbank. Torches illuminated the water as eyes scanned for anything that could be snagged in the low branches. It was cold, dark, and muddy, but no one complained. Meadows' hands were scratched from searching among brambles and he'd been caught in the face a few times by low-hanging branches. As the time slipped by, there was an air of desperation among the search party, and Meadows could feel their hope dwindling. Then the call came.

Meadows rushed to the car with Edris. He could see the crowds of volunteers watching him pull away. The news would spread fast, but no one had the full details. Whispers would pass along, and it was only a matter of time before Jenna and Gareth would hear. He wasn't sure if Gareth was still out searching. He hoped that he was back at the house with Jenna.

'This is miles down,' Edris said as they sped along. 'Poor little thing.'

'Blackwell is closer, so he'll be on the scene before us. I had hoped it wouldn't be a member of the public that found her.'

'I think the next turning should bring us as close as we can get,' Edris said. 'After that, it doesn't look like there are any entry points to the path. It veers away from the houses and follows the river. Or we could go to the end of the path. It comes out on the main road.'

'It will be quicker if we turn off now.' Meadows took the turning and parked next to a playground.

They ran down the cycle path with their torches swinging back and forth. There was no one searching the area so all they could see was darkness ahead. Their breathing mixed with the sound of the rushing river and the whirring of the helicopter blades. It felt like the path was never-ending.

'Air ambulance,' Meadows said. 'Looks like it's trying to land. Maybe…'

Edris shook his head. 'Don't go there. We tried our best. There is no way she could have survived.'

Meadows knew Edris was right and tried to quash any false hope.

They were both breathless by the time they reached the point in the path where they could see torches. Valentine was standing with two young men.

'Paramedics have just taken her,' Valentine said. 'She's still alive. They'll fly her to Cardiff.'

'We thought she was dead when we pulled her out of the water,' one of the young men said.

'Blackwell is down by the bank,' Valentine said. 'I'm just taking a statement from these two heroes, and they can be on their way.'

Meadows looked at the two men that were smiling at Valentine. 'Thank you both,' he said.

He moved through the trees and headed for the river.

'How the hell?' Edris said. 'An adult wouldn't survive this amount of time in the river.'

Blackwell was standing near the riverbank talking to Hanes. 'Unbelievable,' he said.

Hanes nodded.

'Where was she?' Meadows asked.

Blackwell trailed a beam of light across the water. 'Caught up in the overhanging branches. She had been put into a storage container. You know, one of those plastic boxes that everyone has in their home to store bits. This one was red. The two men had seen a post on Facebook about the search. They started from where the cycle path ends. They saw the box and thought they heard a noise. One of them waded in, saw the baby, and lifted her out. Once the weight was lifted from the box, it floated away.'

'We better go and tell the parents,' Meadows said. 'I doubt it will be long before the news spreads over social media. Finish up here, then you can all go home and get some rest.'

'I won't argue with that,' Blackwell said.

'It's great to be delivering good news,' Edris said as they walked up the bank.

'The baby is not out of the woods yet,' Meadows said.

'No, but there is hope.'

Meadows knew he should be elated that the baby had been found, but he had a nagging feeling that something wasn't right.

Chapter Four

Jenna looked down at Cora sleeping in the hospital cot. It reminded her of when she was born. She'd been premature, and Jenna had spent weeks in the hospital. It was torturous then, and it felt worse now. Cora had monitors attached to her tiny body, and a drip secured to her hand.

Jenna could feel the panic threatening to overwhelm her. The lights were too bright, the noise seemed to echo through her head, and she couldn't keep still. She wanted to run from this place and keep running.

The nurses had kept a careful watch over Cora all night. They came in and out of the room but never left her completely alone. Jenna knew why. She saw the look of judgement in their eyes. Bad mother. Useless mother. That's what they were thinking. It's what everyone thought. All of them judging her and watching.

She was certain that was why Gareth's mother, Beth, came to the house most days. It was under the guise of being helpful and cleaning the house. Jenna knew differently. She was spying on her. Then she'd gossip behind her back, probably with Laura. She hated Laura. She shifted from foot to foot. The thought of Laura made her want to scream.

A doctor entered the room, talked to the nurse, and looked at Cora's chart. He spoke to Jenna, but she couldn't take in the words. They were muffled. She tried to concentrate. This was important. Her breathing became faster, and she felt light-headed.

'Would you like to sit down?'

Jenna felt the doctor's hand on her arm. She jumped back and lost her balance. The nurse came rushing over and helped her to the chair.

'I'll fetch you a glass of water,' the nurse said.

'You've had a nasty shock and must be exhausted,' the doctor said. 'Perhaps it would be a good idea for you to go home and get some rest. We will call you if there is any change.'

The doctor being kind just made Jenna feel worse. Tears stung her eyes, and she couldn't hold back her emotions. Sobs wracked her body, and her chest tightened as she struggled to breathe. A glass of water was placed in her hand. She tried sipping it, but the water was warm. It made her feel nauseous.

'Maybe some fresh air,' the nurse suggested. 'I can get someone to go with you.'

At that moment, Gareth walked in. Jenna looked at him and her anguish turned to anger. Her body tensed and she balled her hands into fists.

'Where have you been?' she shouted.

Gareth looked mortified. She was glad. Why should she be the only one to suffer?

'Jenna has had a bit of a dizzy spell,' the nurse said. 'I think some fresh air will help.'

'Come on,' Gareth said. 'I'll take you out.'

'Don't you want to stay with your daughter?' Jenna's tone was accusing.

Gareth grabbed her hand and squeezed it tightly. 'Come on. I think you need a break.'

Jenna snatched her hand away and stormed out of the room. She wanted to run away from him, but she didn't know the way out. The labyrinth of corridors brought on a fresh wave of panic. Gareth caught up with her and led the way. He was stony-faced and silent.

'Where have you been?' she demanded.

'I just had a quick shower and then I had to make some work calls.'

'Work!' she shrieked. 'How can you even think about work?'

Gareth put his hands to his head. 'Will you stop it? Everyone is looking at you.'

'I don't give a fuck,' Jenna said. 'I've been stuck in that room all night. I'm going out of my mind. Did you bring my tablets?'

'Yeah.'

'Well give them to me.'

'Can't you wait until we are outside?'

'No. I need them now.'

Gareth put his hand in his pocket and pulled out a packet of tablets. 'Here.' He thrust them at her and stormed off.

'Where's the rest? I told you to bring them all. These are no good on their own.' Jenna chased him down the corridor and out the exit.

Gareth had stopped by a bench. It was getting busy as people queued for a parking space, and ran to make their early morning appointments. Jenna popped a tablet into her mouth and sat down on the bench.

'Better now?' Gareth asked.

'No. I need to go home and get the rest of my pills.'

'So you can get off your face?'

'You know I've been in pain since I had Cora. I can't function without them.'

'Listen to yourself. It's not just painkillers. You're stuffing all sorts of tablets down your throat.'

'They're herbal tablets. They make me feel better.'

Gareth laughed. 'Herbal? I'm not stupid. You're taking something else.'

'I'm not. How can you even think that?'

'You're asleep half the time. If you're not asleep, then you're angry, depressed, or fucked off your face. I can't do this anymore. Do you realise how much you embarrassed me yesterday? You made a fool of yourself. Worse than that, you were bloody irresponsible.'

Jenna jumped to her feet. 'How dare you! The only one being irresponsible was your mother. She should have been keeping an eye on Olwen.'

'Maybe we should have all been keeping an eye on you. It wouldn't be the first time you've put the children's lives in danger. I'm not covering for you this time. If I find out that you had anything to do with what happened to Cora, I'll have you locked up.'

His words sent a chill through Jenna. She already felt like she was losing her mind. She couldn't remember half of what happened at the party. She didn't even remember going to bed.

'No. I would never.'

'Are you sure about that? Maisie told me you forgot to pick up Ieuan from nursery. They had to call you. He was left waiting when all the other children had gone home.'

'That little bitch,' Jenna said. 'Can't you see how she wraps you around her finger? She doesn't like me. She just wants to cause trouble.'

'Don't you dare blame Maisie. You're the adult.'

'I shouldn't be looking after Laura's children.'

Gareth's nostrils flared. 'They are my children. Maybe you should look at your own son.'

'My son! You are unbelievable. You've never given him a chance. You treat him differently from the others. Why should he have to compete for attention? You know what? I'm done. The only children I'm looking after from now on are my own.'

'I have joint custody,' Gareth said.

'That's your problem.'

'You knew what you were taking on when you moved in. We agreed that you stay at home and look after the children while I work.'

'That was before I had Cora. You can't expect me to keep looking after them now.'

'They're in school all day, and you only have them on alternative weeks. Laura manages to work and take care of the kids. It's only fair – I do my bit.'

'I can't deal with them anymore.'

'Fine. Do you want me to choose between you and the children? Because they'll win.'

Gareth was shouting now. His eyes were smouldering with anger. Jenna noticed the looks people gave them as they walked by, but she was beyond caring.

'You can have them on the weekends,' Jenna said. 'You give Laura enough money, she can get a childminder.'

'Is that what this is about? The money?'

'You paid for half her house and set her up in her own business. She still doesn't leave us alone. She comes and goes as she pleases and treats our home like her own. I think she wants you back. She's trying to come between us.'

'Yeah, well maybe I would be better off.'

Jenna drew her hand back and slapped Gareth hard across the face. The crack of her hand hitting his face made a couple of people stop and stare.

'You bitch,' Gareth said.

Jenna held out her hand. 'Give me the car keys.'

Gareth threw them at her and stormed off.

Jenna had to go up and down the car park rows to find the car. She got inside, slammed her hands against the steering wheel, and screamed. At that moment she wished Laura was dead.

Chapter Five

Meadows hadn't slept well, and the first thing he did after getting dressed was phone the hospital for an update on the baby. After that, he made a few more calls and headed into the office. Edris and Blackwell were already in and were soon joined by DS Rowena Paskin. Valentine came in behind him carrying a tray of coffees.

'I made you a lemon balm tea,' she said and handed Meadows a cup. 'Thought you might need waking up.'

'You're getting good at picking the right tea,' Meadows said.

Valentine handed the rest of the team a coffee.

'How come you look so perky this morning?' Edris asked.

Valentine shrugged. 'Carefully applied make-up, a run, and lots of coffee.'

Edris ran his hand through his honey-coloured hair. 'Maybe I should try that?'

Valentine laughed. 'Yeah, a bit of foundation and blush will look good on you.'

'I meant the run,' Edris said.

'What's the news from the hospital?' Blackwell asked.

Meadows blew on his tea. 'She's stable for now but there is a risk of brain damage and kidney failure.'

'The family must be feeling awful,' Blackwell said. 'I doubt there will be any gatherings for a long time.'

'The press has been asking for comments,' Paskin said. 'The last update I gave was that the baby had been found and taken to hospital. There is speculation online.'

'Isn't there always,' Blackwell said. 'Just tell them it was an unfortunate incident and the investigation is closed. The last thing the family needs is Olwen's name all over the news.'

Meadows nodded. 'I think something along those lines, but nothing about closing the investigation. There are still a few loose ends to tie up.'

'What loose ends?' Edris asked. 'Olwen got confused and thought she was floating the baby down the River Nile.'

'Where did she get the plastic container? According to the two men who pulled her out of the water, it was red. I spoke to Beth, Gareth's mother, this morning. She told me she had never seen a container like that at Gareth's house. She visits most days and does the cleaning for Jenna,' Meadows said.

'Maybe it was lying around near the riverbank. People dump all sorts of things,' Valentine said.

'She'd been to church that morning,' Blackwell said. 'Maybe she took Cora, then saw the plastic container by the riverbank. Her mind got confused, and she thought she was putting Moses in the basket.'

'That's possible,' Meadows said. He pulled a map from his desk and pinned it to the wall. 'Olwen was found here.' He pointed. 'There were several people that saw her walking in that direction, but she wasn't carrying a baby.'

'That was after 6 p.m. She'd probably already put Cora in the river by then,' Edris said.

'Let's say for argument's sake that Olwen left the house at around twenty past four. She walks the path upriver and finds a place to put the baby in the water. Then she walks back to the bench. There is no way the box would have gone downriver from any point along this section of the path. There is a weir just before the path ends and crosses the road. The box would have tipped or got caught up in the pool. There is another drop after that.'

'Then obviously she went in the other direction first,' Edris said.

'She would have had to walk past the park,' Valentine said. 'Cora's sister, Maisie, was playing in the park with her friends.'

'Yeah, but you know what kids are like,' Paskin said. 'They get so involved in playing that they take no notice of what's going on around them.'

'Then there's the unplugged monitor,' Meadows said.

'I think you're overthinking this,' Blackwell said. 'There isn't another explanation. No one in their right mind would take a baby from her cot, put her in a box, and float her down the river.'

Meadows thought Blackwell had a point. There was no other explanation for what happened. 'Does everyone agree that Olwen took the baby to the river?' He looked at each member of his team.

Edris was the first to answer. 'Yeah.'

Blackwell and Paskin nodded.

'Valentine?'

'Erm... yeah. It makes sense. Olwen went missing at the same time as Cora.'

'OK,' Meadows said. 'We just need to make sure we have statements from the family, and everyone at the party, to complete the incident report. I want to make sure we haven't missed something on this. Paskin, can you put out a post on social media? Ask for anyone walking the cycle path between four and six-thirty to get in touch.'

Paskin nodded.

'I've got the list of those that were at the party from Hanes,' Edris said and handed it to Meadows.

Meadows took the sheet and was reading the names and addresses when Sergeant Dyfan Folland came in.

'I've got something that might interest you,' Folland said. 'Given you've got a quiet spell.'

Edris raised his eyebrows. 'Quiet? We've been up half the night.'

'Yeah,' Valentine said. 'We're far from bored.'

Folland perched on the edge of Meadows' desk. 'This one is a real puzzle.'

'I think they are all hoping to clock off early today, but you've got my interest,' Meadows said.

Folland smiled. 'So this farmer is clearing one of his fields. It had been left to go wild. He's cutting away and he comes across a car.'

'Yeah, that sounds really exciting,' Blackwell scoffed.

'It wasn't his. Thinking it might be a stolen vehicle that's been dumped, he asked us to check it out. Turns out it belongs to a Mr Alex Morris who has been missing for five years.

'I've asked Missing Persons to send over all they've got. This is the information that was put out in the press and is on their website.' Folland handed a sheet of paper to Meadows.

Alex Morris. Age 30.
Dark brown curly hair.
Blue eyes.
5'10".
Last seen on the 12th of October 2019 in the Amman Valley area.

Edris took a look. 'Not a lot to go on.'

'I've got the parents' address for you,' Folland said. 'It was his mother that reported him missing.'

Meadows took another look at the poster. There was a photograph of Alex. He was dressed in shorts, a blue T-shirt, and hiking boots. He was smiling at the camera. Below was a contact number.

'OK, I'll take a look,' Meadows said.

'I'll come along and get some fresh air,' Edris said. 'It might wake me up.'

'Blackwell, Valentine, can I leave you with the statements and report?' Meadows asked.

Blackwell grunted something and went back to his desk.

'No problem,' Valentine said. 'I guess social services will get involved now.'

Meadows nodded. 'Olwen can't be held responsible for her actions, but recommendations will need to be made. Let's hope baby Cora makes a full recovery.'

* * *

It was another sunny day with only a few clouds hovering over the Black Mountain. It rose to rocky peaks, and rivulets cut deep scars that ran down to meet with the river below. Meadows loved driving this road with its twists and turns that left the valley far behind. On the side of the road, sheep and wild horses grazed, taking no notice as the car went by. They reached the top where the old limestone quarry cut into the mountainside.

'No ice cream van today,' Meadows commented.

'Maybe they're having a day off,' Edris said. He yawned and stretched his arms behind his head. 'Nice day for sitting in the garden with a beer. We haven't had many of those.'

'We can't complain. Even with the rain, I wouldn't want to be anywhere else.' He looked at the valleys opening up below them.

The road twisted downwards and they crossed an old stone bridge at the bottom. It levelled out and here Meadows could pick up speed. There were a few houses, but it was mostly farmland. Fields, and trees with golden, red, and brown leaves whizzed by.

'Should be the next turning,' Edris said.

'Yeah, I can see on the sat nav.'

'Don't trust that thing,' Edris said. 'I prefer my phone.'

They arrived at the farm and Edris jumped out to open the gate. Meadows drove through and waited for him to jump back in.

'Why is it always me that has to open the gates?' Edris asked as he checked his shoes.

Meadows laughed. 'I'm slowly desensitising you to dirt.'

'Well, it's not working.'

The farmer, Ethan, was waiting in the yard when they pulled up. Meadows introduced himself and Edris.

'The car is in the bottom field,' Ethan said. 'It's a bit of a trek.'

Meadows heard Edris sigh behind him. 'That's not a problem,' he said.

They stepped through a gate and walked across the first field. The fresh mountain air ruffled their hair, and Meadows inhaled the smell of the countryside. Being outdoors was where he felt at home.

'You haven't got cows loose in these fields, have you?' Edris asked.

Ethan stopped and looked at him curiously. 'It's a farm. We have cows, sheep, and pigs. You're not afraid of them, are you?' He chuckled. 'Don't worry, they won't hurt you. Just shoo them away.'

They continued walking through the fields until the land started to slope downwards.

'It's just down here,' Ethan said.

Edris kept a watchful eye as they passed a herd of cows. They reached the bottom field, and Meadows could see that trees and brambles had been cleared. The area was muddy.

'When did you start the work here?' Meadows asked.

'Last week, but we had to stop because the rain had saturated the ground. Didn't want the tractor to get stuck. I've just taken over the farm from Dad. He had a stroke. He hadn't used this land for years as it tends to get flooded.'

'Do you know if this area was accessible from the road?' Meadows asked.

Ethan nodded. 'There's an old track. Probably a bridle path back in the day, and a back entrance to the farm. It's mainly stone. We uncovered some of it.' He pointed it out.

'So, we could have parked the car by the roadside instead of walking through the fields,' Edris said.

'Yeah, there is a gate, but you would've had to walk through brambles. The car is over here,' Ethan said.

They walked through the clearing and the car came into view. It was an old green estate car parked between the trees. Ferns and brambles covered the wheels. The windscreen was covered in leaves and moss. Meadows could see where some of the overgrowth had been trampled.

'It's unlocked,' Ethan said.

'Have you looked inside?' Meadows asked.

'I just opened the door and had a quick peek. I didn't touch anything.'

'OK, thanks.'

'I'll leave you to it then,' Ethan said.

Meadows snapped on a pair of latex gloves and opened the door. The first thing he noticed was the position of the driver's seat. He sat inside, put his feet on the pedals, and then got back out again.

'You try it.'

Edris got into the car. 'What am I looking for?'

'Would you be comfortable driving in that position?'

Edris stretched his foot towards the accelerator. 'No. The seat is too far back.'

'That's what I thought.'

'So, he was a big fella,' Edris said.

'Alex Morris is five foot ten according to the information that Folland gave us. That's one inch shorter than you.'

Meadows walked around the other side of the car. Brambles and ferns crunched under his feet. He opened the door and looked in the glove compartment. There was a car manual, CDs, and a packet of mints which had turned into a gooey blob.

'Let's see what's in the back,' Meadows said.

The boot was stiff but with a couple of pulls, it opened. The back seat had been pulled down and the area was filled with various equipment. A lightweight rolled-up ladder, ropes, a harness, torches, hiking boots, and overalls were among the items.

'Looks like he was into outdoor activities,' Meadows said. 'Rock climbing?'

'Looks like the car has been parked here since he went missing,' Edris commented.

'The question is, who parked it here?'

'He could have put the seat back for a rest,' Edris said.

Meadows shook his head. 'He would have reclined the back of the seat if that was the case. If he was sleeping in

37

the car, it would have been more comfortable to shift the equipment to one side and sleep in the back. There is no sleeping bag or blanket. Even if he did move the seat, why park here? It's private land.'

'Yeah, that is odd,' Edris said.

'The next question is, where did he go?'

Edris looked around. 'If he was climbing then he would have walked up the mountain. There's nothing here but farmland.'

Meadows nodded. 'He also would have parked in the quarry car park if that was his intention.'

'Maybe he parked here because he didn't want to be found.'

'Suicide?' Meadows thought about it for a moment. 'If he was in that state of mind, he would have parked near to where he wanted to end his life.'

'OK, an accident then. He parks here for whatever reason, goes off on a long hike, and has a fall.'

'It's possible. If his family thought he was hiking or climbing in the area, then mountain rescue would have been called out. Without the location of the car, they wouldn't have had a starting point. Why hide the car if you are just going for a walk?'

Edris shrugged. 'I guess we better chase up the files from missing persons. We need to know his state of mind when he went missing.'

'First, we need to go and see Alex's parents and tell them about the car. I'd rather talk to the people who knew Alex than read it in a report. We'll get a better picture of who he was.'

'You think he's dead then?' Edris asked.

'Five years missing, and his car dumped in a field. It doesn't look good.'

Chapter Six

Meadows felt a flutter in his stomach as he pulled up outside Alex's parents' house. He hated causing distress to people, and although it was part of his job, he'd never got used to it. They were in Manordeilo, which was a fifteen-minute drive from where they found Alex's car. He knew that being so close to their son's last known location would make the news all the more difficult to bear.

'I bet they're going to get a shock after all this time,' Edris said.

Meadows nodded. 'Five years of not knowing and expecting a knock on the door. It would be better if we had something more to tell them. Even bad news would be better than limbo.'

They got out of the car and Meadows looked at the detached house. It was well kept with rows of pots filled with various coloured heathers. The paintwork looked fresh and the pathway was clear of weeds.

Meadows knocked on the door and stood back. It was opened by a woman in her early sixties. She was slim with a mop of dark curly hair, which had threads of grey.

'Mrs Emma Morris?' Meadows asked.

'Yes.'

Meadows made the introductions.

Emma paled. 'Is it Lloyd?'

'No. There is nothing to worry about. We'd like to ask you a few questions about Alex.'

'Oh. Have you found him?' She put her hand out to the door frame for support.

'No, we haven't found him but there has been a development. May we come in?'

'Erm… Yes, I suppose you better had.' Emma led them into a sitting room. 'Do you mind if I call my husband? The thing is, when Alex went missing, I gave up work. We both did for a while. Lloyd had to go back, but I couldn't. I promised Lloyd I would call him if ever there was a knock on the door so we could hear the news together.'

'That's not a problem. We can wait,' Meadows said.

'I'll make some tea,' Emma said.

She left the room, and Meadows could hear her on the phone. He looked around the sitting room. There were lots of photos of Alex; some with his parents, others with what looked like a younger brother.

Emma came back into the room and set down a tray with three mugs. 'Help yourself to milk and sugar,' she said.

Meadows put a splash of milk in the tea and took a seat on the sofa. Edris sat down next to him.

'Is that Alex's brother?' Meadows pointed at the photograph.

'Yes. Shaun. He moved to Australia. He comes back for a visit now and again. He keeps asking us to go but it's difficult to leave with things as they are. Lloyd is on his way. He won't be long.'

Meadows sensed that she didn't want to talk about Alex just yet, so they made small talk while they waited. It wasn't long before Lloyd rushed through the door. He was a portly man with a bald head and soft blue eyes. He hugged Emma before sitting down and taking her hand.

'Thank you for waiting,' he said. 'What new information do you have?'

'We found Alex's car,' Meadows said.

'Where?' Lloyd asked.

'Hidden among trees and brambles in a field near Pont Aber.'

'I don't understand,' Emma said. 'What is his car doing there?'

'That's what we are trying to find out,' Meadows said. 'It looks as if it's been there for some years. The farmer was clearing the field and came across the car. We haven't had a chance to review the case notes, so we only have the basic information. Sometimes it's better to start afresh. People can sometimes recall information years later that they forgot at the time. If it's all right with you, I'd like to ask you some questions.'

'To be honest, the police didn't take that much interest when he first went missing,' Lloyd said. 'He wasn't considered high risk.'

Meadows nodded. 'I'm sorry if you felt let down. I can't promise we will find him, but I will conduct a thorough investigation.'

'Thank you,' Emma said.

'Alex was last seen on the 12th of October 2019. Is that correct?' Meadows asked.

Both Lloyd and Emma nodded. 'He said he was going to meet a friend,' Emma said.

'What was the friend's name?' Edris asked.

'Henry,' Emma said. 'I can't remember his surname.' She looked at Lloyd who shook his head. 'We'd never met him. We only heard about the meeting later.'

'When did you realise something was wrong?' Meadows asked.

'We didn't at first. It was when his girlfriend, Laura, asked if we had heard anything from him a few days later.'

'He wasn't living at home at the time?'

'No. They had their own place. Laura said he hadn't come home on that Saturday. He sent her a text saying he needed some space. I tried calling and leaving messages, but he never got back to me. He sent another text to Laura, then nothing. The days went by. That's when we got worried. I knew he wouldn't leave Maisie.'

'Maisie?' Meadows asked.

'His daughter. She's ten now.'

'What's Laura's surname?' Edris asked.

'Gibson,' Emma said.

Meadows saw the look of surprise on Edris' face and knew he had made the connection.

'Had Laura and Alex argued?'

'She said not,' Lloyd said. 'She seemed as confused about his leaving as we did.'

'Had Alex been depressed?' Meadows asked.

'No nothing like that,' Lloyd said. 'He'd been upset when his cousin died. We all were, but that was six months before and he was getting on with life.'

'What about financial worries or problems at work?'

'He worked in IT,' Lloyd said. 'I know things were a little tight with the rent, and raising a child isn't cheap, but they were both working.'

Emma nodded. 'I don't think they were in any debt that they couldn't cope with. He would have asked us for help if that was the case. We did help Laura out with the rent when Alex went missing. It was hard for her on her own.'

'It wasn't for long,' Lloyd said. 'I don't think she liked to take the money from us, but we wanted to make sure that she and Maisie were taken care of.'

'Are you still in contact with Laura?'

'Oh yes,' Emma said. 'Maisie comes to stay every other weekend and spends time here in the school holidays. Laura has always been good about letting us have contact with our granddaughter. I think that's what kept us going.'

Lloyd nodded. 'Laura has never forgotten one of our birthdays. She's a lovely girl. That's what makes it so strange. Laura and Maisie meant the world to Alex. He'd never gone off on his own before. We told the police, at the time, that it was out of character. I think because of the texts and the fact there had been money withdrawn from his account over a two-week period, they didn't take it seriously.'

'Can I ask why it was you, and not Laura, who reported him missing?'

'Laura was as worried as we were,' Emma said, 'but I guess she was also a little angry. She thought he'd come back in a couple of days. She couldn't understand why he wouldn't talk to her. The text message she received was just one line. I suggested we ask the police to help but she was concerned it would make things worse. She thought Alex would be upset with her.'

'She also thought the police would think they had broken up and he had gone off,' Lloyd added. 'It was November by this time and there had been nothing since that last text. In the end we all decided that it would be better coming from us.'

'We had no idea where to start looking,' Emma said.

'There was a lot of equipment in Alex's car,' Meadows said. 'Ropes and harnesses. Did Alex climb?'

'Yes,' Emma said. 'He climbed, and hiked, but mostly he enjoyed caving. He'd been exploring caves since he was a teenager. He volunteered with mountain and cave rescue.'

Meadows could hear the pride in Emma's voice.

'He was also a qualified diver. He loved cave diving. It was something he and Laura did together.'

'Did you consider the possibility, at the time, that he may have gone caving or diving and got into trouble?'

Lloyd nodded. 'It is something we thought about. He didn't have his diving equipment with him, but he could have gone caving. I know Laura and her friends travelled around to see if Alex's car was parked within hiking distance of any caves. There are so many. We drove around ourselves but without a starting point, it was difficult. If his car had been found, we would have organised a search of the area. Alex had friends in mountain rescue. They had already offered to help. Then the pandemic hit, and we went into lockdown. It was difficult to do anything then, and I guess he wasn't a high priority for the police.'

Meadows looked across at Edris to see if he had any more questions, but his eyes were down as he scribbled in his notebook.

'Was there anyone, other than yourselves and Laura, that Alex was close to?' Meadows asked.

'Gareth Hendon,' Lloyd said. 'They were best mates.'

'We heard about his baby,' Emma said. 'It's hard enough when your grown-up child goes missing. They must have been to hell and back. I hope the baby is going to be OK.'

'I'm sure we'll get an update from Laura,' Lloyd said. 'We'll have to call her and give her the news.'

'Best wait until she finishes work,' Emma said.

'We can inform Laura,' Meadows said. 'We will need to speak to her.'

'Maybe that's for the best,' Lloyd said. 'I don't think I've got the heart to tell her and bring it back up again. She's made a good life for herself and Maisie.'

'We will need someone to look at the equipment found in Alex's car, to see if anything is missing,' Meadows said.

'Laura is the best person to do that,' Emma said. 'She'll know what was in the car.'

'Is there anything else you feel we should know? Even if it's a theory or a feeling you had at the time?'

'All sorts of things went through our minds,' Lloyd said. 'A nervous breakdown, or an accident. Over the years, we've thought the worst. Even the possibility that he got into something bad and was killed. All I know is that he loved his little girl. I know deep down that the reason he hasn't come back is because…' Lloyd's voice broke.

Emma took his hand. 'We've prepared for the worse and hoped for a miracle. It's the not knowing that keeps you awake at night. There is no closure and moving on for us.'

Meadows nodded. 'It must be very difficult for you both. We'll do our very best to get you some answers.' He stood up. 'We'll keep you informed of any further developments.'

'Thank you,' Lloyd said. 'I'll see you out.'

* * *

Meadows got into the car and was aware that Lloyd was watching from the doorstep. He waited until he had pulled away before speaking.

'What are the chances that a missing man's car turns up at the same time as his best friend's baby ends up in a river?'

'Just a coincidence,' Edris said. 'We know that Olwen put the baby in the river. It can't be connected.'

'Maybe not, but it's an odd set-up. Alex goes missing and his best friend and girlfriend get together. Gareth takes on the child as his own, then they have a child. They split up, but he keeps Laura around. They appeared to be close yesterday. There were definitely vibes between Jenna and Laura.'

Edris huffed. 'Families are complicated. They probably stay friendly for the children's sake. Alex wanted some space. Maybe he parked the car so no one would know where he was, then got lost or trapped in some cave. We don't have a case here.'

'What's wrong with you?' Meadows asked.

'It's just… well… I'm tired, that's all.'

Meadows glanced across at Edris. It's more than tiredness, he thought. Edris was fun, quirky, and good-natured. Even on a bad day, he didn't make snappy remarks. Meadows didn't want to push and figured Edris would tell him at some stage.

'OK, we'll see Laura and then I'll drop you off.'

'Why not Gareth Hendon? He was Alex's best friend. Alex would more likely have confided in him.'

'You're right, but Gareth will be at the hospital. I think we should leave him and Jenna in peace for today. Meanwhile, we need to keep asking questions. If Alex did park his car in the field, then where was he for two weeks previously? He sent texts and withdrew cash. Something made him take off and leave his five-year-old daughter and girlfriend. Then what? He decides to take a walk, climb, or go down a cave.' Meadows shook his head. 'It doesn't make sense. We need to find out what happened five years ago.'

Chapter Seven

Meadows was sitting in the car, in the All Creatures veterinary practice car park, reading from his phone. 'Laura is a qualified vet and co-owner of the practice,' he said.

Edris looked out of the window. 'Looks like she did well for herself after he left her.'

Meadows nodded. 'I wonder where she got the money. Alex's parents were helping her with the rent.'

Edris shrugged. 'She could have borrowed it. Right, let's get this over with.'

'You are in a hurry for your bed,' Meadows said.

Edris didn't crack a smile.

'OK then let's go.'

The reception area was busy with barking dogs, meowing cats, and a rabbit. Meadows sat while Edris hovered at the far end facing the wall. Meadows doubted he was reading the notices. It was more likely that he didn't want a dog to jump up and put paw marks on his trousers.

The door to one of the rooms opened and a man came out carrying a cat in a basket. Laura looked around the reception until she spotted Meadows and beckoned him inside.

'I'm sorry to have kept you waiting,' Laura said as she closed the door behind them.

She went to stand behind the examination table. Her long auburn hair was pulled back into a high ponytail, and she wore green scrubs. She was a petite woman, who Meadows guessed was no more than five feet tall. She had an oval face with delicate features and large brown eyes.

'We're sorry to bother you at work,' Meadows said and introduced himself and Edris.

'We met briefly last night,' Laura said. 'It's so awful what happened to Cora. I'm going to the hospital when I finish up here. Jenna must be exhausted. I'm not sure if I can be of any help. I didn't see Olwen leave the house yesterday. Poor thing. I doubt she realises what she did. It's just as well as it would break her heart. She's such a gentle soul.'

'We not here about what happened yesterday,' Meadows said. 'A car was found hidden in a field this morning. It belongs to Alex Morris.'

'Alex?' Laura paled. She put her hand on the table to steady herself. 'Did you... Is he...?'

'We haven't found him. Is there somewhere you can sit down?' Meadows asked.

'Erm... yes. We can go to the staff room. Sorry, it's just I didn't expect... Well, I suppose I did one day but... The staff room is this way.'

'Take your time,' Meadows said. 'I expect this has come as a bit of a shock for you.'

Laura nodded and led them into the staff room. She sank into a chair.

'Are you OK?' Edris asked.

'Yes. After what happened yesterday, and now this, I guess I'm feeling a little wobbly. I'll be OK in a moment.'

'Would you like a cup of tea?' Edris asked.

'Please,' Laura said.

'We'd like to ask you a few questions if that's OK,' Meadows said.

'That's fine,' Laura said. 'Oh. I have to call Lloyd and Emma. Alex's parents.'

'We've already informed them.'

Laura nodded. 'This must be awful for them. Where did you find the car?'

Meadows gave the location. 'Did Alex know anyone in that area?'

Laura shook her head. 'I don't understand why his car would be there. Does that mean he's been this close all the time?'

'Can you tell us about the last time you saw Alex?'

'It was the Saturday morning. Not a day I will forget.'

Edris placed a cup of tea in Laura's hand and then took a seat.

Laura took a sip of the tea. 'Alex was meeting up with Henry. They were going to go on a hike.'

'Do you know Henry's surname?' Edris asked.

'Tay,' Laura said and gave Edris Henry's address.

'Was the hike a long-standing plan or spur of the moment?' Meadows asked.

'Alex told me the day before.'

'What time did he leave that morning?'

'About seven. I was asleep. He woke me to say he was off and said something like "See you later."'

'Did he tell you where they planned to hike?'

Laura shook her head.

'What did you do that day?' Meadows asked.

Laura appeared surprised at the question. 'Oh… erm. I picked Maisie up from my mum's house that morning. Alex and I had been out on Friday night. It was my work colleague's birthday. We didn't stay late but Maisie would have already been asleep. I took Maisie to the hairdressers on Saturday morning then we did some shopping.'

'When did you realise something was wrong?'

'Not until the evening. Alex sent a text to say he wasn't coming home. He said he needed some space. I texted back but he didn't reply.'

'Had you been having problems?' Meadows asked.

'No, nothing like that. We had arguments the same as any couple, but nothing serious. As far as I was aware, everything was all right between us.' Laura took another sip of tea and set the mug down.

'At the time, what did you think he meant by needing space?'

'I had no idea. It came out of the blue. I thought perhaps that he was seeing someone else, but there had been no signs. He was either working or with me and Maisie. Most of the time we did things together. Occasionally he would spend time with Gareth or Henry. He wasn't secretive. To be honest, I was a bit pissed off at the time. I thought he would just be gone for the night and then we could talk.'

'Did you try to call him?'

'Not that night. It was a few days later I tried to call him, but he didn't answer. I sent a text asking if he was coming back. He said he needed more time. I asked Henry if Alex had said anything to him on their hike. He said that they hadn't met that Saturday, and there had been no plans to do so.'

'Had Alex been depressed or troubled by anything leading up to this point?'

'No. Nothing like that.'

'His parents told us that he'd been upset by his cousin's death.'

Laura nodded. 'We were all shocked and sad after Ceri's death. Ceri was my best friend. Jenna, Ceri, and I grew up together and Ceri was Gareth's girlfriend. We all went caving and hiking together. It was hard on all of us, but worse for Gareth. That was six months before Alex left and, like the rest of us, he was getting on with life.'

'What happened to Ceri?'

'Hiking accident.'

'Did Alex witness the accident?'

Laura shook her head. 'She was alone at the time.'

'Did Alex take any clothes with him when he left?'

'I don't think so. He was wearing his hiking clothes and took his rucksack. He usually carried water and snacks with him.'

'How many times did Alex contact you after he left?'

'Twice.' Laura nodded. 'Yeah, the second text just said he needed more time. After that, there was no contact.'

'Were you concerned about him?'

'Of course.'

'Given that it was so out of character, why didn't you go to the police? I understand that it was his parents that reported him missing,' Meadows said.

Laura folded her arms across her chest. 'I didn't think there was anything the police could do. He had sent text messages. Made it clear that he wasn't ready to come home.'

'So you didn't think any harm had come to him?'

'I had no reason to at the time. After he'd been gone over a month, I agreed with his parents that we should involve the police. Even if, for some reason, he didn't want to be with me anymore, I didn't believe he would leave Maisie. I even drove around various locations looking for his car. Then we went into lockdown. Time moved on.'

'You and Gareth got together not long after that, I understand.'

Laura raised her eyebrows and Meadows could see she was offended by the question. There was something else. Guilt, maybe? She shifted in her chair before answering.

'Gareth was very supportive. He'd lost Ceri, and Alex had left me and Maisie alone. We grew close. I struggled to work, pay the bills, and look after Maisie. Alex's parents helped but it wasn't fair on them. Gareth asked me to move in. Things just grew from there. Then we had Ieuan.'

'Did you have any theories about what may have happened to Alex?'

Laura shrugged. 'Not really. It was a difficult and painful time. I couldn't understand why he would want to hurt us by leaving. I tried not to think the worst, but the thoughts crept in. I had to move on for Maisie's sake.'

'Does Maisie remember Alex?' Meadows asked.

'I don't think so. She knows she has another father, and Emma and Lloyd talk about Alex. Gareth treated Maisie as his own and he became her father. That's why, although we split up, we keep things friendly for the children's sake.'

Meadows nodded. 'There was a lot of equipment in Alex's car. I would like you to take a look to see if anything is missing.'

'OK. What happens now?'

'That will depend on the outcome of our enquiries, but we will likely search the area where the car was found.'

Laura nodded. 'If there is nothing else, I should get back to work.'

'Of course. Thank you for your time.'

Laura led them back to the reception and was calling for her next appointment when they left.

'I'll drop you home so you can get some sleep,' Meadows said to Edris.

'Are you not going home?'

'Not yet. I want to check out the statements taken at the time. I don't think we are being given the whole picture.'

Edris shook his head. 'You still think there's something suspicious about Alex's disappearance? It's not like we've turned up a body. All we've got is a car in a field and a guy saying he needs space. We should just give it back to Missing Persons and let them deal with it.'

Meadows' phone rang and he glanced at the car screen. The name displayed was Mike Fielding from forensics.

'Hey, Mike,' Meadows said.

Mike's voice came through the car speakers. 'That car you asked us to look at. I thought you might be interested to know that initial examination shows traces of blood.'

Meadows looked at Edris. 'Still think there's no case here?'

Chapter Eight

Henry Tay padded barefoot into the kitchen. His head was fuzzy, and his mouth parched. After drinking a pint of water, he made a coffee and carried it into the sitting room.

'Shouldn't have gone to that christening party,' he said. 'Seeing them all together having fun, and watching the children running around, reminded me of what we lost.'

There was no one else in the house but that didn't stop Henry having conversations. Quite often, he heard a reply in his mind. It was enough for him.

'You saw what happened when I came back. I haven't drunk that much since… well, you know when. And what the bloody hell did I take? I was off my tits. I've been clean. You know I have. Maybe someone spiked my drink. I just kept on drinking. I think all night. I can't remember. What day is it?'

Henry looked at his phone. 'Oh shit. It's Tuesday. I've lost a day. I'm sure the police came around last night, or was it the night before? Maybe I imagined it?'

He closed his eyes and waited. The answer came like a movie playing in his mind. The police had explained about the missing baby and asked if he minded if they searched the house. He'd let them in and continued his party.

'I behaved myself,' he said. 'I feel bad about the baby. She shouldn't have been caught up in this, but after what I heard yesterday. Hang on, yeah. Yesterday. The phone call. I knew all along I was right. You tried to tell me. First Ceri, now Gareth is being made to suffer, and then there's Alex. I should shower, they'll be here soon.'

He sniffed his baggy T-shirt but didn't move from his chair. Instead, he took an elastic band from his lounge pants' pocket, tied back his long chestnut hair, and ran his hand over his goatee. 'It could do with a trim,' he said.

There was no work today so he could afford to sit and let his mind wander. There were two large freestanding mirrors in the room. They were positioned so that Henry could see in them without seeing his reflection.

He stared in the mirror until his eyes went out of focus and the mirror appeared to cloud over. He sat in a trance-like state waiting for the shadows to appear. There were no shapes today and no voices came to him. After a while, he sat back to meditate. He'd found this was the best way because the visions came naturally. He needed to hear something.

A loud knocking at the door brought him back to the room. He got up and ambled to the door. Two men were on his doorstep. One with dark curly hair, green eyes, and a friendly face. He introduced himself as Detective Inspector Meadows. The other man, Detective Sergeant Edris, was younger, with honey-coloured hair, blue eyes, and perfect teeth. Both wore suits, and held up identification cards.

'Come in. I've been expecting you.'

He led them into the sitting room and offered them a seat. 'Can I get you a tea or coffee?'

'No. We're good, thanks,' Meadows said as he sat down.

Henry plonked himself down in the armchair and studied the detectives. He got a good vibe from Meadows. He had an open face, and a relaxed manner. He wasn't sure about Edris, who was looking around the room. His eyes travelled from the mirrors to the pack of tarot cards Henry had left on the table.

'You said you were expecting us,' Meadows said. 'Did Laura tell you about the discovery of Alex's car?'

'Arthur told me to expect you,' Henry said.

'Who is Arthur?' Edris asked. He had his pen poised on his notebook.

'My spirit guide,' Henry said.

Edris' eyebrows shot up. 'Your what?'

'Spirit guide. Arthur helps me navigate the spirit world.'

'Is Arthur a person?' Edris asked.

'Of course he's a person. He's just on the other side of the veil. Doesn't make him any less than you or I.'

Henry could see the look of bemusement on Edris' face. Meadows was listening to the exchange with interest. Edris wrote something in his notebook and then scribbled it out. He opened his mouth to speak again but Meadows cut in.

'Are you a practising medium?'

Henry turned his attention to Meadows. 'Depends on what you mean by practising. I don't charge people when I pass on a message, but I am receptive if someone wants to speak to me. I've been trying to contact Alex.'

'Let me guess. He didn't answer you,' Edris said.

Henry could see Edris' lips twitching. He closed his eyes for a moment and opened his mind. The message was clear. There was no point in telling the detectives what he knew. They were not going to take him seriously.

'Are you still with us?' Edris asked.

'Yes, sorry.'

'How does this work then? Do you have an Ouija board and ask it questions?' Edris asked.

He's taking the piss, Henry thought. 'It doesn't work like that. I doubt you would understand, even if I tried to explain. Let's not waste each other's time.'

'I don't think Sergeant Edris means to be disrespectful,' Meadows said.

'It's fine,' Henry said. 'He's a little troubled at the moment. I'm sure he's usually amicable.'

'I'm not troubled,' Edris said.

Henry sat forward and looked intently at Edris. 'I'm good at reading people. Your aura is muddy. Yes, a sort of muddy red-purple – moody and secretive. I can also see danger.'

Colour rose in Edris' cheeks. 'I better not walk under any ladders then.'

Henry looked at Meadows. 'You have a bright aura. Yellow and green.'

Meadows smiled. 'I've been told that on a few occasions.'

Henry detected no mocking in Meadows' comment. He thought it possible that this detective could be open-minded and listen, but he wasn't sure. The voice in his head told him it was best to keep his mouth shut about things he heard from the spirit world.

'OK, so you heard that we found Alex's car,' Meadows said.

'Yeah, Gareth called.'

'When was the last time you saw Alex?'

Henry thought for a moment. 'It was about a week before he went missing. We met up one evening for a drink with Gareth.'

'Did he seem troubled?' Meadows asked.

Henry took his time to answer. He was thinking back to that evening. From what he remembered, it was Gareth who was troubled. His aura had been all wrong. At the time, he thought he knew the reason for it, but now he wasn't so sure. 'Alex was chilled. Yeah. There was nothing in his aur– erm, behaviour that was unusual.'

'Can you recall what you talked about that evening?' Meadows asked.

'Not really. We were thinking of taking a caving trip. I remember that much because we were trying to persuade Gareth to go. He'd been struggling since he lost Ceri. We thought it would do him good to get away for a couple of days.'

'Was Alex up for this trip?' Edris asked.

'Yeah.'

'Where had you planned to go?'

'Wookey Hole. It had been years since we'd been there.'

Henry watched Edris scribble some notes.

'Alex had arranged to meet up with you the day he went missing,' Meadows said.

Henry knew this was coming. 'Laura said that, but we hadn't made any arrangements.'

'Did you see or talk to him at all that day?' Edris asked.

'No.'

Meadows sat forward in his chair. 'Do you have any idea why Alex would lie and say he was meeting you?'

Henry started to feel uncomfortable. 'No, and if you think it was because he was seeing someone else, then you'd be wrong. Alex was loyal.'

'What makes you so sure?' Meadows asked.

'I told you. I am good at reading people, especially those I've known for years. I took him on his first cave dive. You have to trust your dive partner and I trusted Alex. We did a lot of exploring together. I watched the romance bloom between him and Laura. You've met her, and I expect you've seen photos of Alex. They made a striking couple. He was devoted to her and Maisie.'

'Why do you think he left? You must have had some theories at the time.'

'Honestly? I've no idea but I never thought he'd stayed away deliberately. Something stopped him from coming back. If he needed someone to talk to, he could have come to me or Gareth. He knew we would help him if he was in trouble.'

'Was he taking drugs or gambling?' Meadows asked.

Henry laughed. 'Nah. Alex used to say his body was a temple. He took good care of himself. Even when we went out he'd only have two pints. That was his limit. I wasn't aware of any gambling. I meant trouble up here.' Henry tapped the side of his head.

'A breakdown?'

'You'd have thought we'd see some signs of that. Especially Laura, but she said he was fine.'

'What did you make of the text he sent her?'

'The one saying he needed space? Odd, but I did travel around to various caving sites. If he needed space, I was sure that's where he would go to gather his thoughts. You are deep underground, alone. The deeper you go, the further away you are from people, and all the shit going on in the world. There is no other feeling like it. Now you've found his car, we know where to look. There are plenty of caves in the area.'

'You think he had an accident?' Meadows asked.

No accident, Henry thought. 'Alex was a good caver but there is a reason we go in pairs. Even the best can get into trouble. I'll start looking. At the very least, we can bring him back to Laura and his parents.'

'We will likely be searching the area and asking professionals to assist,' Meadows said. 'I'd advise you not to go searching independently.'

'Professionals?' Henry laughed. 'I've been caving for years. I've even assisted rescues in flooded caves. Don't worry. I won't interfere with your search.'

'OK,' Meadows said.

Henry thought Meadows didn't look too happy about him going out searching, but he needed to be there. He didn't want the team stumbling upon that place. He would make sure it wasn't disturbed. He closed his eyes. I won't let them go there. I promise, he thought.

He opened his eyes and looked at Meadows. 'Is there anything else?'

'I think we've covered everything for now.' Meadows stood up. 'Thank you for your time.'

Henry was glad to see them out. He shut the door and walked back into the sitting room. 'So now we know. Alex was part of it.' He moved to the bedroom and ran his fingers across a photo on his bedside table. 'What did you do, my love?'

Chapter Nine

Meadows grabbed a cup of blackberry tea and then gathered the team.

'Where are we at with the Cora Hendon incident?'

'Just about done,' Blackwell said. 'We've been working on a timeline, taken from the statements of those who attended the party. No one saw Olwen after 4.15 p.m. One reported sighting of her on the main road at 6.15 p.m. It would have taken her twenty to twenty-five minutes to get to the bench she was found on, from there.'

'She must have followed the path downstream first,' Edris said, pointing to the map. 'Circled back by going onto the main road. There is an exit from the path here.' He pointed. 'Then she walked up the road before picking up the path upriver.'

'We had a good response to the social media appeal,' Paskin said. 'People who were walking the path between 4 and 6.30 p.m. have come forward. No one saw Olwen, but there were enough gaps in the time for her to have got to the river.'

Blackwell handed a sheet of paper to Meadows. 'Timeline with all the information.'

Meadows looked at the times and information. 'Great work.'

'I think we've covered everything,' Blackwell said. 'It's not like we can hand it over to the CPS. They're not going to bring charges against Olwen.'

Meadows nodded. 'Is everyone agreed that this concludes our enquiries?'

'Yeah,' Edris said.

The others nodded.

'We'll just give it a day or so to make sure no more information comes to light on the social media appeal.'

'I'll keep a watch on it,' Paskin said.

'OK.' Meadows nodded. 'Alex Morris.'

Edris filled the team in on the interviews. 'Henry Tay is barking.'

'I think we might have got more out of him if you hadn't been so dismissive,' Meadows said.

'You don't believe in all that crap, do you?' Blackwell asked.

'It doesn't matter what I believe,' Meadows said. 'It matters what Henry believes. Whatever information he gives us, even if he claims it came from the other side, we have to take it seriously. It may be his subconscious speaking to him. His way of processing information. It could be something he's seen or heard. He may not remember but it's stored in his memory. Could even be a feeling that something wasn't right.'

'I never thought of it like that,' Edris said.

'Maybe you should open your mind,' Valentine said. 'There have been mediums that have helped solve cases.'

'I don't think Henry will be solving this puzzle anytime soon,' Meadows said. 'There was only a small amount of blood found in Alex's car. It's not enough to suggest that he was seriously injured.'

'Maybe he just cut himself,' Edris said.

'The blood was found along with mud in the footwell of the driver's seat. More likely it came off footwear. Forensics are testing the rest of the car, and the items found in the boot.'

'He could have taken off somewhere,' Blackwell said. 'Met someone else and is living off the grid. He dumps the car because he doesn't want to be found.'

'Yeah, I'm with Blackwell,' Edris said.

'That's a first,' Blackwell said.

Meadows smiled. If there were arguments in the team, it was usually between Blackwell and Edris. 'Any other theories?'

'Drugs or gambling debt,' Paskin said. 'Maybe someone caught up with him.'

Valentine nodded. 'I can't see that it's a domestic. I know Edris' idea of ending a relationship is by text but–'

'Hey,' Edris said. 'I don't dump by text.'

Valentine raised her eyebrows.

Edris frowned. 'Well maybe on the odd occasion. It's easier.'

'In this case a child was involved,' Meadows said. 'Then there is the fact that he didn't contact his mother. Would you do that?'

Edris shook his head. 'My mother would have the army out looking for me if I went two days without checking in.'

Valentine nodded. 'Same here.'

'Maybe he only meant to stay away for a few days,' Paskin said.

'The texts are odd,' Meadows said. 'The first one, "I won't be home tonight I need some space." No kisses or mention of Maisie. Most men would at least say something like "Give her a hug from me" or "Tell her I'll be home soon." By all accounts, Alex was a good and devoted father.'

'If he wasn't in the right headspace, maybe that's all he could say,' Blackwell said.

'There's a transcript of the messages, both text and voicemail, sent by Laura and Alex's parents,' Paskin said. 'Laura asking when he's coming home. Laura getting angry. Laura pleading. Same sort of thing from Emma and Lloyd Morris. There's a couple from Henry and Gareth.'

'The last text sent from his phone was the 19th of October. A week after he left. He would have been able to pick up the messages and see how worried everyone was. He just texted saying he needed more time. No reassurance that he was OK, and nothing sent to his parents,' Meadows said.

'Are you thinking someone else sent those texts from his phone?' Blackwell asked.

'But his bank card was used,' Edris said.

'Five times,' Paskin added. 'ATMs at small outlets. All in the early hours of the morning. Cleared out his account and put it in overdraft.'

'Goes with the theory that he just wanted to disappear for a while,' Blackwell said.

'Yeah,' Edris said.

Blackwell turned his beady eyes on Edris. 'Is something wrong with you?'

Edris frowned. 'No.'

'That's the second time you've agreed with me. Are you trying to suck up to me or something?'

'Why would I suck up to you?' Edris said. 'You're the last person I'd ask a favour from.'

'Good,' Blackwell said.

Paskin looked between the two of them. 'I reckon you're both wrong. One thousand pounds wouldn't get him far. He'd need a lot more than that to disappear completely.'

'Any footage from the ATMs?' Meadows asked.

Paskin shook her head. 'Most small outlet recordings automatically delete and re-record after thirty days. By the time the records were requested, it was too late.'

'I think the only way forward now is to search around the area where the car was found,' Meadows said. 'Given that his main hobby was exploring caves, there is the possibility that he had an accident.'

'Laura has looked through the items found in Alex's car,' Valentine said. 'She gave a list of items she thinks are missing. A hard hat with a torch, wellies, harness, bib pants – that's like waterproof dungarees – and a red, heavy-duty waterproof jacket.'

Meadows nodded. 'Does sound like he planned on caving. At the very least Laura, Maisie, and his parents deserve closure.'

'I'll get on to mountain and cave rescue,' Paskin said.

Folland walked into the office. 'Are you organising a search for Alex Morris?'

Meadows nodded.

'Let's hope you turn up something. Missing people always get to me. It's the families. They never give up hope. It's cruel. Anyway, I've got a lady downstairs. Her name is Janet Matthews. She wants to talk to you about Olwen Hendon. I've put her in interview room one and given her a cup of tea.'

'OK, thanks,' Meadows said. He followed Folland down the stairs with Edris in tow.

* * *

In interview room one, they found an elderly lady sitting at the desk. She held herself upright and had a red handbag placed on her lap.

'Sorry to have kept you,' Meadows said and introduced himself and Edris.

'Oh don't worry about it, *bach*. I know how busy you must be.'

Meadows took a seat opposite Janet. 'I understand you want to talk to me about Olwen.'

'Yes. I've been away for a couple of days with my daughter. I sometimes stay with her if I have an early hospital appointment, so I've been away since Sunday evening. When I got back, I heard about the baby. Well, I heard what was being said about Olwen. I had to come and see you. Olwen would never do something like that. I've known her nearly all my life.'

'I appreciate how difficult it must be for you to hear those things. We can't stop rumours circulating,' Meadows said.

'I heard it from Beth Hendon. She was very upset.'

Meadows nodded. 'It does appear that Olwen got confused. We know she suffers from Alzheimer's and I'm sure she would never have deliberately harmed the baby.'

'It's not that I think she wouldn't throw the baby in the river. I know she couldn't have. I saw her.'

Meadows leaned forward. 'Where?'

'I took Bertie for a walk on Sunday along the river path. I was on my way back, passing Gareth's house, when Olwen came out. She wasn't wearing any shoes, and she was a bit flustered. I could hear everyone in the garden. I knew it was Cora's christening that morning because I'd seen them in church. I asked her if she was coming to see me, and she said yes. I suggested we go and get her shoes because her feet would get dirty, but she didn't want to go back into the house. She became upset.'

'What time was this?' Edris asked.

'About half past four. Maybe a little later. I'd checked my watch when I left the bench. So I guess maybe around twenty to five. No later than that.'

Edris wrote down the time. 'Which direction were you walking?'

'Upriver.'

'Did Olwen say what was upsetting her?' Meadows asked.

'Something about the window. Should be looking out, or they shouldn't be looking out. I'm not sure now. I took her home with me. I knew Beth would know where to find her as she often sends her up the road from Gareth's house.'

'Did Olwen say anything about the baby?' Meadows asked.

'No. I don't think so. Like I said, she was upset. Maybe a little agitated. I commented that it was a lovely christening and then she became flustered. She said something like "No one saw." I told her all the family were there. Then she said she had something to do or somewhere to go, but she couldn't remember. It happens often now. I told her we were both getting old and forgetful so not to worry. That seemed to do the trick. We walked up the road together and I gave her some slippers to put on.'

'How long did she stay with you?' Meadows asked.

'Until my daughter came to pick me up at six o'clock. Olwen was fine. She was walking down the road when we pulled off. So you see now why Olwen couldn't have done it. I came on the bus as soon as I heard.'

Meadows nodded. 'You've been very helpful. Thank you. I'll arrange for someone to take you home.'

'There's no need to go to any trouble,' Janet said.

'No trouble at all.'

Meadows walked with Janet back to the reception and arranged a car to take her home. By the time he returned to the office, Edris had filled the team in on the latest development.

'Olwen could have taken the baby to the river and was going back to the house when Janet saw her,' Blackwell said. 'Maybe that's why she was upset and didn't want to go inside the house. She couldn't remember what she'd done with the baby.'

Meadows shook his head. 'Where's the timeline?'

Valentine handed him a copy.

Meadows scanned the entries. 'Jenna put Cora in the crib at 4 p.m. Beth gave Olwen her medication at 4.15 p.m. A Mr Rob Evans exited the path from downriver at 4.30 p.m. He'd been running, so he checked the time. He didn't see Olwen. Janet came from the upriver direction. There is no time for Olwen to have gone in either direction, put the baby in the river, and get back to the house in time to meet with Janet. Then Olwen stayed at Janet's house until 6 p.m.'

'It's around that time that Beth noticed Olwen was missing so she would have been searching around the house and grounds,' Valentine said. 'The first place Beth checked was Janet's house. She must have just missed Olwen going onto the cycle path.'

Meadows looked at the team. 'We got it wrong. Someone else put the baby in the river.'

Chapter Ten

Edris could feel his shirt sticking to his back. He opened the car windows and let the cold air blow in. It didn't help much. Stress was quickening his heart rate and causing his body to overheat. He'd struggled to conceal it in the office. He hoped no one had noticed his discomfort. What he needed now was someone to talk to. He was torn between going home for a shower and heading to his girlfriend's house. The shower won him over. No matter how bad things were, feeling clean was his priority.

His hair was still damp when he pulled up outside his girlfriend's house. He checked his reflection in the mirror and then took a deep breath. Everyone makes bad decisions, he thought.

He knocked at the door and felt his troubles melt away when it opened. Laura stretched up to kiss him. He moved forward with his lips still on hers and shoved the door closed behind him.

'The kids are with my mum for the night,' Laura said as she snaked her hands around him.

He felt heat ignite his body as she led him upstairs. All his problems were banished from his mind as he peeled off her clothes. The kisses became hard and urgent as his hands explored her body. She moaned and pushed him onto the bed. In this moment, nothing else mattered.

Afterwards, Edris lay in the bed. Laura was next to him with her hand draped over his bare chest. He could still feel his heart thumping as his breathing returned to normal.

'I'm sorry about yesterday,' she said. 'I didn't know how to react when you turned up with your boss. I thought it best not to show I knew you. Then by the time I went to the hospital, and got the kids to bed, it was late. I didn't want to call you then.'

Reality came crashing back. Edris sighed. 'About that—'

'It's fine, Tristan,' Laura cut in. 'I know you have your professional standards or whatever you call them. You shouldn't be seeing me at the moment.' She lifted her head to look at him and smiled. 'I just thought I'd have you one more time. We'll just break it off until this thing with Alex is sorted. If you want to see me after, we can pick up where we left off.'

'No. I don't want to do that,' Edris said. 'There's no point now. I've really fucked up.'

'I'm sorry.'

'It's not your fault. I should have said something the moment I saw you at Gareth's house. Then the baby was found so it didn't seem to matter. I got a bit of a surprise when I learned that Alex Morris was your ex and nearly said something then, but it's not like I was compromising an investigation. No crime had been committed. I thought the whole thing would blow over. When we turned up at your work I thought you might say something, and I would have to deal with it. I don't know why I didn't just tell Meadows. He's easy-going. I'm bloody stupid.'

Laura sat up. 'I should have told you about Alex, but that was in the past. It's the reason why I haven't introduced you to the children or my family. Maisie has already lost one father and then I separated from Gareth. It wouldn't be fair to complicate her life further unless I was really sure.'

'Don't worry about it,' Edris said. 'There is no reason we should bring up our past love life.'

'Well, you already know everything about Alex. What I said to you at work was the truth. I don't know why he left, and I don't expect a happy ending. Even if he turned up now, there would be no going back. Too much time has passed.'

Edris was tempted to tell her about the blood found in the car, but he held back. 'That's good to know.'

'I don't think you have anything to worry about. I know there is a search for Alex. We'll just wait it out and see what turns up. It will go away one way or another and then we can get back to normal. You'll only have to see me in an official capacity if he is found. That won't be too difficult for you, will it?'

'I wish it was as simple as that,' Edris said. 'If it were just Alex then it likely wouldn't be a problem unless…'

'Something bad happened to him,' Laura finished.

Edris nodded. 'The thing is, it's much worse than a missing person. I shouldn't be telling you this but you're going to find out soon. It wasn't Olwen that took Cora.'

'What! No, it had to be.'

'I can't go into details, but we have evidence that she couldn't have taken Cora to the river. Now there's going to be a full investigation.'

Laura shook her head. 'I can't get my head around it. Who would do such a thing?' Tears filled her eyes.

'My guess would be someone who attended the party,' Edris said. 'Everyone will fall under suspicion.'

'Including me,' Laura said.

'I'm probably going to get suspended when this comes out.'

'It's not going to,' Laura said. 'I really think we should stop seeing each other. I don't want you to get into trouble.'

'The best thing I can do now is find out who put Cora in the river. Once that person is caught, it won't matter anymore. I can always say I started dating you after that. In the meantime, you can help me.'

'How?'

'You know everyone that attended the party. Spill the dirt.'

'You can't expect me to do that.' Laura threw back the covers and jumped out of the bed. 'They are my family and friends.'

Edris watched as she put her clothes on. He hadn't meant to upset her. He tried to put himself in her shoes. Could he give all his family secrets away? Repeat things that had been told to him in confidence? He doubted it. Then again, if he thought one of them had committed a crime, he wasn't sure he could keep quiet.

Edris got out of bed and pulled her to him. 'I understand this is difficult for you. Maybe you could just tell me a bit about them.'

'And where would you say you got that information from?'

Edris kissed her. 'Don't worry about that. I can ask the right questions.'

Laura sighed. 'I need a drink.'

Edris got dressed and followed her downstairs. She opened a bottle of wine and poured two glasses. She handed one to Edris, grabbed the bottle and walked into the sitting room.

Edris followed her in and plonked himself down on the sofa next to her. The sitting room was brightly decorated with a feature wallpapered wall and complementary colours on the other three. It wasn't a room he felt comfortable in. There was too much stuff for his liking. A wall-mounted TV screen, and what looked like every game console ever made filled shelves underneath. There was a pile of chargers in an open basket. Miniature figures, from films and games, dotted everywhere, and all sorts of stuffed toys. He guessed they belonged to the children. It still didn't explain the huge teddy bear he'd seen in her bedroom, along with a porcelain doll which creeped him out.

He could overlook this. Everything else about her was perfect. She shared his quirky sense of humour and was kind and intelligent. He never imagined that he would settle for a ready-made family. He hoped, when the time came, the introduction to the children would go smoothly.

He looked at Laura. She was sitting with her legs tucked beneath her and her glass of wine cradled in her hands. She appeared to be deep in thought.

'What are you thinking about?' Edris asked.

'Cora, and who would do such a thing. Poor Jenna and Gareth. They must be going through hell as it is, but to find out someone intentionally put Cora in the river.' She shook her head.

'They haven't been informed yet. We've only just had this information. Some facts had to be checked. You must keep this to yourself.'

Laura nodded. 'Do you think Cora could still be in danger?'

'We'll be putting security in place. What we need is a lead.'

'I wish I could help you. Honestly, I can't think of a reason that anyone would do that. It's just sick.'

Edris nodded.

'Then there's Alex. I was so angry that he left me. What if he didn't mean to… what if he meant to come back? I worked hard to put him out of my mind and my life. I thought if he didn't want me, why waste my energy crying. Now I don't know how I feel.'

Edris took hold of her hand. 'It's understandable. Why don't you tell me about him?'

'I thought we weren't going to do the past lovers thing.'

'I'm just curious,' Edris said. 'You never know what information might help. If we find him, it will be one less thing to worry about.'

Laura took a sip of her wine. 'We met when I was still at university. I saw him during the holidays, and he'd come for visits. Once I graduated, we moved in together.'

'What was he like?'

'He was a nice guy. Not perfect, but we were happy, and he was a good father to Maisie. He liked his outdoor adventures, didn't drink much, and rarely got angry.'

'I heard he liked caving.'

Laura nodded. 'We were all part of the caving club. Me, Alex, Ceri, Gareth, and Jenna.'

'I can't imagine you crawling through caves,' Edris said.

Laura laughed. 'Believe it or not, I'm very good at it. Being small has its advantages. I can squeeze myself through gaps that most can't.'

'Do you dive as well?'

'Yes, though I haven't in a while. I could take you to some of the easier caves.'

'I think I'll pass on that.' Edris topped up Laura's glass and refilled his own. 'What about Henry? Was he part of your group?'

'Yeah.'

'I met him. He's a strange one. All that afterlife stuff.'

Laura smiled. 'Henry's OK, once you get to know him. He's a nice guy. Kind and thoughtful. He's always been there for me.'

'Henry told us that if Alex was to go anywhere to get some headspace, it would be a cave.'

Laura nodded. 'That's why Henry is going out searching. I'm going to try and get some time off work to join him. One way or another, I would rather know.'

'Gareth, Henry, and Alex were good friends?'

'Yeah.'

'So they would be likely to share each other's secrets.'

Laura raised her eyebrows. 'Are you interrogating me, Detective Edris?'

'No. I wouldn't dream of it. I'm just Tristan when we're together, but it wouldn't hurt to know a little background. I don't expect you to point a finger at anyone. Just a bit of help in finding out what happened to Alex and Cora. If I know where to look then there's a better chance of solving this case before I lose my job.'

Laura's face creased with concern. 'It won't come to that, will it?'

'I don't know.'

Laura sighed. 'I really don't know anything.'

'You'd be surprised at what information can make a difference. How long have Gareth and Jenna been together?'

'She moved in with him about eighteen months ago.'

'I got the feeling that something wasn't right about her. She was all over the place when Cora went missing. One minute she was like a zombie, the next she had to be restrained from attacking Olwen.'

'Jenna has had a rough time since Cora was born. Postnatal depression. What happened to Cora could send her spiralling down. I'm really worried about her.'

'She has an older son.'

'Yeah, Jamie. He's going through that teenage stage at the moment. It hasn't helped moving home and school. It doesn't help having younger siblings. He doesn't always get on with Maisie. To be fair, she winds him up. He's always polite to me. He's a good kid; not been in any trouble that I'm aware of.'

'What about his father?'

'His father?' Laura looked surprised. 'That isn't my story to tell.'

'But something happened?'

'Yes. A long time ago.'

Chapter Eleven

Edris was out the door as soon as Meadows pulled up outside his house. He got into the car with a waft of aftershave and appeared far more relaxed than the previous day.

'Morning,' Meadows said. 'You look refreshed.'

'Yeah. I had a good night's sleep and I'm ready to solve this case.'

Meadows laughed. 'Both of them?'

'Search and rescue will find Alex if he got himself trapped. That just leaves us with Cora. I think we should start with Jenna. You saw the way she acted the night Cora went missing. One extreme to the other. If we hadn't been there, she probably would have hurt Olwen. She could have just snapped. Couldn't cope anymore.'

'Why put Cora in a plastic box, if she intended to kill her?' Meadows asked.

Edris shrugged. 'Well, she's obviously got issues so wouldn't have been thinking straight. Maybe she thought the container would carry her so far that she would never be found.'

Meadows mulled it over. 'She had the opportunity. Everyone thought she was in bed.'

'It makes sense,' Edris said. 'What possible motive is there for anyone else putting Cora in the river?'

'Ransom,' Meadows suggested. 'Judging by the house and the cars, it doesn't look like Gareth is short of money. Two people could be involved. One takes the baby and floats her down the river for a second person to catch. Then they return to the party unnoticed. Only the container gets caught up before it reaches the second person.'

Edris twisted in his seat, so he was facing Meadows. 'That would make more sense. Someone on the inside. What about if Jenna was working with someone? Maybe her ex-partner, the older boy's father. She gets together with Gareth, has the baby, and then sets up the kidnap and ransom. Gareth pays up, maybe some offshore transfer, and she plans on disappearing with the kids and the ex.'

'That's a bit far-fetched,' Meadows said. 'But keep the theories coming. You've given it a lot of thought. If Jenna was involved then she would have to be a very good actress. Besides, it would be a huge risk to put her baby in the river for someone else to catch. She'd have to be cold-hearted.'

'OK, so if the motive isn't money, it could be revenge. Maybe Gareth or Jenna did something.'

'Or it could be jealousy. One of the siblings is not happy to share the attention. Then there's Laura. She seemed comfortable in Gareth's house. Maybe she wasn't too happy about a baby taking the attention away from her children.'

Edris laughed. 'And you call my theories extreme. She spends her days caring for sick animals. I can't see her putting a baby in the river.'

'Some people prefer animals over people,' Meadows said.

Edris looked out of the window. 'Where are we going?'

'To see Gareth and Jenna. I called ahead and asked them to wait at home. We have to break the news that Olwen did not put Cora in the river. So far no one knows. It will be interesting to see what reaction we get from them. Also, whoever took Cora, thinks they are safe. When news gets out, they are going to be rattled.'

It wasn't a long drive to Gareth and Jenna's house. Meadows parked in the drive and got out of the car. The air was crisp and leaves from a nearby tree crackled under his feet as he walked to the door. He inhaled deeply. He loved the smell of autumn.

Gareth opened the door and invited them inside. He was wearing a pair of jeans and a tight-fitting black T-shirt. It showed off the contours of his chest, and his thick biceps. They followed him into the kitchen where the aroma of coffee mingled with the lingering smell of hot buttered toast. Jenna was standing by the breakfast bar staring at a piece of untouched toast on a plate. Her grey jumper swamped her body, and her hair looked unwashed. In her hands, she cradled a mug.

'Thank you both for meeting with us,' Meadows said. 'How is Cora?'

'She's doing well,' Gareth said.

Jenna shook her head. 'She's all wired up and I can't hold her.'

'But she's doing better,' Gareth said.

Meadows noticed the tremor in Jenna's hands and the dark circles under her eyes. Gareth was hovering close to her and appeared to be having difficulty staying still.

'We need to be at the hospital,' Jenna said.

'We won't keep you long,' Meadows said. 'Some new information has come to light which throws doubt on Olwen's involvement.'

'Are you saying someone else put Cora in the river?' Gareth asked.

'I'm afraid that appears to be the case.'

The mug slipped from Jenna's hand and hit the tiles with a crack. She jumped back as coffee and bits of ceramic hit her legs. Her eyes were wide, and her nostrils flared as she stared at the floor. Then she fled from the kitchen.

Gareth looked at Meadows. 'I, erm... hold on a minute.' He chased after Jenna.

Edris raised his eyebrows.

They waited until Gareth returned to the kitchen. 'She's just changing her trousers. He took a wad of kitchen towel and started cleaning up the mess.

'Take your time,' Meadows said. 'This must have come as a shock for you both.'

Gareth nodded. 'Jenna's hardly slept since it happened. Well, neither of us has. Perhaps it would be better if I dealt with this and let Jenna go to the hospital.'

'I would prefer to speak to the two of you,' Meadows said. 'It's important that we get as much information as we can from both of you.'

'I'll go and get her.'

Gareth left the kitchen and could be heard calling to Jenna. She came down the stairs and they remained in the hall. There appeared to be a heated exchange, but they spoke too low for Meadows to make out any words. He looked around the kitchen while he waited. It looked new, with country-green kitchen cupboards and sparkling stainless-steel appliances.

Edris leaned toward the doorway. 'She looks like she's about to lose her shit,' he whispered.

Gareth came back in first with Jenna behind him. She walked straight to the kitchen cupboard, opened it, and took out a small tub. She pulled the lid off, shook out some tablets, and popped them in her mouth.

Gareth looked mortified. 'Herbal tablets,' he said. 'They help you. Don't they, love?'

'Valerian?' Meadows asked.

Jenna nodded.

'Are you OK to answer a few questions?' Meadows asked.

'Yeah.' She grabbed a mug, poured another coffee, and leaned against the breakfast bar.

'I understand how distressing this must be for you to hear,' Meadows said, 'but it's unlikely that this was a random incident. We're looking at someone close to the family who possibly attended the party. Likely they used the opportunity to take Cora.'

Anger flashed across Gareth's face. 'Are you saying someone planned this?'

'I'm saying that's the line of enquiry we are taking,' Meadows said. 'A stranger passing by and coming into the house is highly unlikely. Is there anyone you can think of who might wish harm on your family?'

Gareth took Jenna's hand. 'No.'

'Any arguments? Threats?'

'What about the fire?' Jenna asked. 'I told you that—'

'That was an accident,' Gareth cut in.

Meadows noticed Gareth squeeze Jenna's hand and she pulled it away. 'What fire?' he asked.

'It was nothing,' Gareth said. 'A fire started in the conservatory and spread to the kitchen. The fire brigade was called, and it was put out.'

'When was the fire?' Edris asked.

'About six months ago,' Gareth said.

Meadows looked at Jenna. 'Was there something about the fire that concerned you?'

Jenna looked at Gareth. 'Erm… no… it's just–'

'Bad shit happens to me,' Gareth said. 'It always has. I guess I'm just unlucky. None of it has anything to do with what happened to Cora. It's old stuff.'

'What sort of things have happened?' Meadows asked.

'People spreading rumours, Granddad dies, and I have to take on the family business, my girlfriend dies, my best friend goes missing, and now this. I'm a shit magnet, that's all.'

'What rumours?' Meadows asked.

Gareth's eyes narrowed. 'Just people stirring things up to wreck my relationships. Screwing with my head, so you don't know who to believe.'

Meadows didn't miss the hurt expression on Jenna's face. 'Your girlfriend had a hiking accident, is that correct?'

'Yeah.'

'She was hiking alone?'

Gareth nodded.

'Laura was with her,' Jenna said.

'She wasn't with her when she fell,' Gareth snapped. 'The two of them were hiking the Four Falls Trail. Laura slipped and broke her ankle. She thought she had just twisted it at the time. She told Ceri to go on without her and take photos. Ceri never came back. She fell from the top of Sgwd Clun-Gwyn.'

'That must have been a very difficult time for you,' Meadows said.

Gareth nodded. 'I had good friends and family around me. I don't know how I would have got through it without them. Now Alex. Laura told me about you finding his car. It doesn't look good, does it?'

'Did Alex talk to you about any concerns he had, or did you get the sense that something wasn't right?'

'Nothing like that,' Gareth said.

'Why are we talking about Alex?' Jenna asked. 'You should be trying to find out what happened to my baby.'

She's got a point, Meadows thought. He wondered if Gareth was deliberately leading him off track. The series of incidences did bother him though. 'It's important to look at every angle to determine if anything in the past has a bearing on what happened to Cora.'

'Alex left five years ago,' Jenna snapped.

'It doesn't make it any less painful for Laura,' Gareth said. 'I've heard there is a search and I'm happy to help.'

'Help!' Jenna shrieked. 'Your daughter is in hospital, and you want to go running to Laura.'

Gareth's nostrils flared. 'Don't start on Laura.'

'Why is it always about her?'

'Fine. I won't help if that makes you feel better.'

Edris cleared his throat.

Gareth looked at Edris and colour rose in his cheeks. 'Sorry. It's just…'

'It's fine,' Meadows said. 'I understand the last few days have been stressful for you both. What's important now, is that we concentrate on finding the person responsible for taking Cora.' He looked at Jenna. 'Has there been any animosity between Laura and yourself?'

'She doesn't give us space as a family,' Jenna said.

'Do you think Laura is jealous of your relationship with Gareth?' Meadows asked.

'I don't think she was happy when I got pregnant.'

'For fuck's sake,' Gareth said. He pushed his hands through his hair. 'Laura has been nothing but helpful. She picks up your shopping, your prescriptions, and anything else you want. She even helped decorate the nursery.'

'I didn't ask her to do that,' Jenna said.

'Has Laura said or done anything that makes you think she would want to harm Cora?'

Jenna scowled. 'No.'

'I'm sorry to have to ask this, but how did Cora's brothers and sister react to her arrival?' Meadows asked.

'As you would expect,' Gareth said. 'Ieuan can't wait for her to be old enough to play with him. Maisie is delighted. She helps feed and bathe her, and Jamie, well, he's a teenager. No interest at all.'

'That's not fair,' Jenna said.

'Oh come on, he was embarrassed when we told him you were pregnant.'

'That doesn't mean that he would hurt Cora. Why would you even think that?'

Gareth sighed. 'I don't. He's a good kid. He'd never do anything like that.'

'No he wouldn't,' Jenna said. 'If anyone is jealous of Cora, it's Maisie.'

'Maisie is good with Cora and Ieuan,' Gareth said. 'She even helps you around the house.'

'Only when you are around,' Jenna said.

Meadows listened with interest while Edris scribbled in his notebook. 'It sounds like you've all had to make some adjustments,' he said. 'What about your extended family? Have there been any arguments?'

'No,' Gareth said. 'Everyone gets along OK.'

'What about ex-partners?' Edris asked.

They both shook their heads.

'What about Jamie's father?' Edris asked. 'Is he in the picture?'

Jenna's eyes narrowed. 'Gareth is Jamie's father.'

'Oh. I'm sorry,' Edris said.

'This is the second time around for us,' Gareth explained.

'What about work?' Meadows asked. 'You mentioned that you had to take on the family business when your grandfather died.'

'Yeah. Granddad and Dad were in business together. Hendon Haulage. Granddad left his share of the company to me.'

'Was that expected?'

'Yeah, he'd already discussed it with me. It wasn't my plan to get involved so soon, but it's been OK.'

'Any problems with employees?'

Gareth shook his head. 'A few of them were here for the christening. Most have been with the company for years. I haven't had to sack anyone, if that's what you mean.'

'Jenna?'

'I gave up work when I got pregnant with Cora,' she said.

'Where did you work?' Edris asked.

'Care home.' She gave him the name and address.

'What about anyone hanging about the house or someone taking an unusual interest in Cora?' Meadows asked.

Jenna shook her head.

'There isn't anyone I know who would do something like this,' Gareth said. 'We're just an ordinary family.'

Meadows gave Edris a slight nod.

'We'd like you to talk us through your movements on Sunday afternoon. Who you sat by and talked to. Anyone's absence you noticed.'

'We've already been through this when Cora was taken,' Gareth complained.

'There may be some details you left out at the time,' Edris said.

'Well, I never left the house,' Jenna said. 'I talked to everyone at the party then went to bed.'

'I only left around five to go to the shops,' Gareth said.

It took some more questions and some coaxing to get a detailed statement from them both, by which time Jenna had become silent. She stared down at her cold coffee with her shoulders slumped.

'We'll leave it there for today and let you get off to the hospital,' Meadows said.

Jenna didn't raise her head.

'We'll see ourselves out.'

They left the house and Meadows walked past the car and to the cycle path.

'That one is a handful,' Edris commented. 'They split up before. You think he would have learned his lesson.'

'She has good cause to be angry. Her baby was taken.'

'Yeah, but she appears to be unreasonable and she's paranoid about Laura.'

'Is she though? Would you like your girlfriend's ex-partner hanging around? I know I'd feel uncomfortable. She's just had a baby, and it sounds like Laura spends a lot of time at the house.'

'Maybe she's just a nice person.'

'You could be right. Then again, Laura didn't tell us about being with Ceri the day she had her accident.'

Edris stopped and pulled out his notebook.

'What are you doing?'

'Just checking something.' Edris flicked through the pages. 'You asked Laura if Alex had witnessed Ceri's accident. She said no and that Ceri was alone. It's what Gareth said.'

'I think we should request the accident report.'

'Do you think there could be more to it?' Edris asked.

'I don't know, but it's not just one accident. There's the fire, Alex missing, the rumours, and now the baby.' Meadows looked around. 'You can't see the house from here. Come on, let's walk a bit further.'

'Whoever took Cora wouldn't have to go far to be out of view,' Edris said. 'Minutes and they could be in among the trees.'

Meadows nodded and kept walking. Now and again he would look back to check the view through the trees. He stopped when they passed the weir.

'They could have set the container down at any point from here,' Edris said.

'There must have been some planning involved. There wasn't a container at the house, so they must have put it somewhere before the party.'

Meadows walked down to the riverbank and then moved backwards slowly until he could see the house.

'From the upstairs window, you'd have a clear view. I think Olwen saw who put Cora in the water. That's why she was outside without shoes. She was in a hurry and by the time she got outside, Janet was there and she got distracted.'

'Somewhere in her memory is the answer,' Edris said.

'The problem is, if she saw who put Cora in the river, then that person could have also seen her in the window.'

Chapter Twelve

As soon as the police left, Gareth turned on Jenna. 'What the fuck?'

She looked at him and sighed. 'Don't start.'

'You're chugging down pills in front of the police and acting like a crazy person. Will you take a look at yourself?'

'Me? You're the one accusing Jamie.'

'I didn't accuse him, but you have to admit he's out of control. You know he's drinking and smoking weed. He stinks of the stuff.'

'It sounds like you are trying to shift the blame.'

Her words sliced through him, and he knew, at that moment, he couldn't trust her. 'Me? You're the one pointing the finger at Laura. Are you afraid the police will look too closely at you? You're off your face half the time.'

Jenna picked up the mug of coffee and threw it at him. Gareth managed to duck in time. The mug hit the wall with a crash. He watched rivulets of coffee track down the paintwork and guilt turned his stomach. What am I doing?

he thought. He knew the blame lay with him. It was payback.

Jenna was crying now. 'How could you think I would hurt my baby? You're the one who didn't want her in the first place.'

'Is that how you remember it?'

'I don't know what I remember. I feel like I'm losing my mind.'

Jenna's body shook with sobs. Gareth went to her and wrapped his arms around her. 'I'm sorry. All of this is screwing with my head. I'll try to help out a bit more and spend some time with Jamie. I know this hasn't been easy on him.'

'He only wants you to give him some attention. He sees you with the other two and feels he missed out. Maybe if it was just the four of us for a little while when Cora gets out of the hospital.'

Gareth pulled away. 'You can't expect me not to spend time with my other children.'

'Child,' Jenna corrected.

'I've been a father to Maisie since she was five years old.'

'Yeah, you had no problem bringing up someone else's child but–'

'Don't you dare,' Gareth snapped. He felt guilty enough about Jamie, and what he did to Jenna, without her throwing it in his face.

'I said I would try harder with Jamie. I'll take some time off work, and we can all go on holiday. Get away from here. I'll check with Laura. I'm sure she won't mind the kids coming with us.'

'Of course she won't mind. She barely looks after them as it is.'

'That's not fair.'

'You only see what you want to. If they're not with us, they're with your mother or Laura's mother. Alex's mum has Maisie every other weekend. I don't know why she bothered having children.'

'Will you listen to yourself? This jealousy has to stop.'

'I'm not jealous of Laura, but she's got you wrapped around her finger like everyone else. Ceri told me–'

Gareth slammed his hand down on the breakfast bar. 'Shut up!' He felt his whole body tense and was suddenly afraid of what he would do. 'I've got to get out of here.' He stormed out of the kitchen.

'You're supposed to go to the hospital with me,' Jenna shouted.

'I'll come later.'

He stepped out of the front door and slammed it. He saw the two detectives pulling out of the driveway and wondered what they had been doing all this time. Had they been listening at the door? Fuck them, he thought.

He was about to get into his car when a battered Land Rover pulled into the drive. 'That's all I need,' he hissed.

Henry jumped out of the vehicle, walked over to Gareth, and pulled him into a hug. 'I'm so sorry, mate.' He thumped him on the back and released him. 'Shit thing to happen. Hope the kiddie is going to be all right. How's Jenna?'

Gareth didn't know how to answer that. 'She's stressed out.'

'Yeah, I can imagine,' Henry said. 'Have the police been round to talk to you about Alex?'

'Yeah. They've just left.'

'What did they ask you?'

'Just about the last time I saw him, and you?'

'Yeah, I talked to them. Gave them some background.'

Gareth's insides squirmed. It was clear that Henry wasn't going to elaborate. He couldn't have told the police, or they would have asked about it. The question was, why would Henry stay quiet?

'I've been trying to talk to him,' Henry said.

'Who?'

'Alex. Nothing is coming through, so there's still a chance that he's not dead.'

Gareth wasn't in the mood to indulge Henry. 'Maybe he's crossed over.'

'Doesn't work like that,' Henry said. 'Perhaps he's not ready to talk. Do you think he knew something?'

'About what?'

'About what happened. I knew something wasn't right. No one would listen to me. First Ceri and then Alex. They were both there. Now this is happening to you.'

'Don't start that again.'

'There's only three of us left. Alex was right there. Perhaps he saw something or maybe...'

Gareth could feel his heart thudding in his chest. A cold sweat broke out over his body. He was never going to be free. He felt like Henry could see right through him, or maybe he really could talk to the spirits. What would they tell him? The thought made him feel sick. Henry was looking at him expectantly and Gareth wasn't sure if he was toying with him.

'I've got to get to the hospital.'

'Right. Yeah,' Henry said. 'Are you planning on joining the search for Alex?'

'I don't know. Jenna needs my support.'

'I understand,' Henry said.

The words were loaded. Gareth knew it would look a lot worse for him if he didn't go, but if he did, he would have to contend with Henry.

'I'll see if Laura will come,' Henry said.

'I'm sure she will, but it's going to be hard on her.'

'It depends,' Henry said. 'Like I said, I haven't been able to contact Alex. Perhaps he's hiding because he's afraid or guilty.'

'Why would he be afraid or guilty?' Gareth asked.

'It wasn't long after Ceri–'

'That was an accident.'

'Yeah, forget it. It's just that Alex's car being found brought everything back. I can't stop thinking about it. If I'd–'

'Henry, stop! Don't go there. You were in a bad place.'

Henry nodded. 'The ravings of a lunatic.'

'You know I don't mean that. I understand better than anyone else.'

'Do you ever wonder why all this bad shit keeps happening to you?'

Gareth felt his chest tightening. Did Henry know and want him to break? Want him to say the words. He'd been OK at the party but there were a lot of people around. This was the first time they had been alone together since… 'What game are you playing?'

'Chill, man,' Henry said. 'I'm just laying things off on you. Sorry, you've got enough on your plate. I'll let you get to the hospital.'

Gareth exhaled. 'We'll catch up soon. Let me know how the search goes. If I can, I'll come and help.'

'Sweet. Give my love to Jenna.'

Gareth watched Henry drive off. Maybe it will be OK, he thought. He just had to make sure that Laura kept her mouth shut.

Chapter Thirteen

Meadows read through the fire investigation report, then called the team around for the morning briefing. The previous day had been spent gathering statements and cross-referencing them. They'd worked late into the evening with Edris being the one pushing them all to stay and finish the task. Meadows wondered if things were cooling between him and his latest girlfriend. Until now, Edris hadn't been able to wait to leave the office. He looked at him now. He seemed happy enough, but Meadows could still detect a little tension.

'The fire that Gareth Hendon mentioned does look on the surface to have been an accident,' Meadows said. 'A cigarette was left unattended in an ashtray, and it tipped onto the sofa in the conservatory. With a breeze coming from the open back door, the fire quickly spread to the kitchen. Only Jenna was in the house at the time. It was the school holidays, and she had asked Maisie to watch Ieuan in the garden when she went for a lie-down.

'Maisie took Ieuan to the park and Jenna fell asleep. Jenna was woken by the fire alarm and got out of the house and called for help. In her statement, Jenna said she did not smoke before going upstairs. She claimed she only smokes a few cigarettes a day and does so outside.'

'It's a bit irresponsible to leave a four-year-old in the care of a ten-year-old,' Valentine said. 'I'm surprised social services didn't get involved.'

'Gareth stated that he was due home to take over the care of the children but was running late. Jenna thought he'd be home in a matter of minutes,' Meadows said.

'You'd think she'd phone to check. It sounds like he's covering for her,' Edris said.

Meadows nodded. 'I had the feeling that Jenna wanted to say more about the fire, but Gareth interrupted. He appeared to be worried about what she would say. Like he was on edge the whole time. We'll need to talk to her alone and see if she will open up.'

'Are you thinking that the fire wasn't accidental?' Paskin asked.

'I think we need to look into it. Put in a request for Jenna's medical records. Then there's a teenage son, Jamie. I guess he could have been the one smoking, but according to the statement, he was out with his mates in Swansea for the day. There is the possibility that someone else deliberately started the fire.'

'They would have had to been watching the house, and how would they know Jenna was sleeping?' Edris asked.

'Maybe they happened to turn up and took the opportunity,' Meadows said.

'Like Sunday,' Valentine added. 'Everyone was occupied and had a few to drink.'

'I've also requested the inquest report into Ceri Rees's accident. According to Gareth, she died at Clun-Gwyn waterfall and was alone at the time.'

'Are you thinking these two things are related and not accidents?' Blackwell asked. 'I don't see it.'

'The accident was over five years ago,' Paskin added.

'Yes, and six months later, Alex goes missing,' Meadows said. 'Ceri's accident, Alex goes missing, the house fire, and now the baby is taken. It's a lot of coincidences involving the same group of people: Gareth, Jenna, Ceri, Laura, Alex, and Henry.'

'Gareth has had relationships with all three women,' Valentine said. 'Could be some jealousy is involved.'

'We know that Gareth was with Jenna first and had a son,' Edris said. 'Then he gets with Ceri, she dies, and he gets with Laura. Then back to Jenna. Maybe he gets bored.'

'Bit like you,' Blackwell said.

'So he breaks up with Jenna to get with Ceri, then gets rid of Alex so he can get with Laura, and now he's trying to get rid of Jenna,' Edris said.

'If that was the case, why didn't he get rid of Laura? She's still around,' Valentine said.

'Just a thought,' Edris said.

'Maybe Gareth is the target,' Meadows suggested. 'The question is, what's the motive?'

'Love, money, revenge,' Blackwell said. 'It's usually one of them, or maybe the accidents were just that.'

'There's still the baby,' Meadows said. 'That was no accident. Forensics haven't turned up anything interesting from the nursery or Cora's blanket. Everyone at the party held Cora at some stage. Anything on the plastic container?'

Blackwell shook his head. 'It could have been washed out to sea by now. Even if we did have it, I doubt it would help. It's been tossed around in the water for days.'

Meadows nodded. 'OK, we've got our timeline pinned down, as much as we can. Some accounts were vague, but we've managed to eliminate quite a few that were at the party. Particularly the ones that left before Cora was put in her crib. I've put them on a separate list. We'll call that list B. It could be that one of them came back for some reason and took the opportunity. We can't rule them out completely. We need to check for witnesses who saw them arrive home, activity on their phones, or anything else that can completely rule them out. That leaves us with list A.' He pointed to the board. 'First up is Jenna.'

'She claims she wasn't drinking but several people mention that she was drunk,' Valentine said. 'No one saw her from the time she went to bed until she discovered Cora was missing.'

'Gareth claims he went to the shops at around 5 p.m. CCTV shows him in the shop at 5.30 p.m,' Meadows said.

'It's only a ten-minute walk to the shops,' Blackwell said.

'Twenty minutes is enough time to get to the river,' Edris added.

Blackwell read from his notes. 'Yeah, he claims he came back via the cycle path. He said he wanted to check on Jamie and his friends. They usually hang out further down, but he didn't see them. Henry left just after Gareth. He could have easily slipped upstairs and grabbed the baby before leaving, as no one saw him out.'

'Laura claims she was in and out of the kitchen,' Paskin said. 'She could easily have sneaked out.'

'Jamie was in and out of the house all afternoon,' Edris said. 'He came back with some friends, ate some food and then left again. The same with Maisie. It's unclear if she left before Cora was taken upstairs or after. Beth Hendon says after, whereas Deryn Gibson, Laura's mother, says before. Deryn says she went into the sitting room for a while to get some peace. She claims she dozed off. Same sort of story with Beth Hendon. She says she fell asleep in the summer house.'

'Can't see one of the grannies doing it,' Blackwell said.

'Why not?' Valentine asked. 'Because they are older women? It doesn't rule them out. Deryn is only Maisie and Ieuan's grandmother. No relationship to Cora.'

'That leaves us with Gareth's father Joe, his work colleague Scott Davies, and his wife Eleri,' Meadows said. 'Background checks?'

'Nothing on any of them,' Paskin said. 'I'm going through social media accounts.'

'Blackwell and Valentine, I'd like you to check out Hendon Haulage. I don't buy that everyone who works there is one happy family. Edris and I will talk to the grandmothers. If anyone is going to spill the dirt on the family, particularly Jenna and Gareth's relationship, it will be one of those two.'

* * *

Beth Hendon opened the door. She was dressed in a cream woollen dress and brown leather boots. Despite her styled hair and flawless make-up, she looked tired.

'Is this a bad time?' Meadows asked. 'We can come and talk to you another time.'

'No. Olwen is asleep upstairs, so I have a bit of time to myself.'

They stepped through the door. Beth locked it and put the key in her pocket.

'How is Olwen?'

'Completely oblivious.' Beth smiled. 'I've tried talking to her about Sunday to see if she remembers anything, but I've had no luck. Some parts seem clear. She talked about the christening service, but even with prompting, there's not much about the afternoon. It was such a relief when you phoned to say it wasn't Olwen, but now I'm so worried. What if she did see something?'

Meadows didn't want to add to Beth's worry, but he couldn't take a risk with Olwen's safety. 'As I explained, it's not certain that she was at the window. Even if she was, she may have not been seen. Whoever took Cora will possibly assume that Olwen won't remember or even be believed. It's important not to ask her about this. Better that she remembers things herself. Meanwhile, you are doing the right thing. Locking the door and keeping an eye on her.'

'It's not been easy. I feel like I'm keeping her prisoner. Usually, she goes to the day centre a couple of times a week, but I didn't want to take any risks. I had thought about taking her to Gareth's house and maybe up to the bedroom. If she looked out of that window again, maybe it would jog her memory.'

'That's a good idea.'

'Yeah, but Jenna won't let me near the house or hospital. We're Cora's grandparents and she is treating us like it's our fault.'

'I'm sure she will come around. I'll ask an officer to visit them and arrange for you to take Olwen to the bedroom. I'm sure Jenna will want to help get some answers. Maybe that will break the ice.'

'Thank you,' Beth said. 'Come and sit down.'

They walked into the sitting room and Meadows sat down on the sofa. Edris sat next to him and took out his notebook. The sofa faced a patio door which gave a view over the garden. He could see birds flitting back and forth from the feeders.

'Gareth told us that this was a second-time-around relationship with Jenna,' Edris said. 'We got the impression that there was more to the story.'

Beth smiled. 'I suppose it is a bit unusual, but maybe they were meant to be together. They were very young the first time. Both of them were barely out of school. They seemed well matched though. They were always off on some adventure together, either caving or climbing. They even learned to dive together. Gareth was happy and seemed settled.'

'What happened?' Edris asked.

'Jenna got pregnant and there was some unpleasantness. Something about the baby not being Gareth's.'

'Was Jenna seeing someone else?'

'I don't know,' Beth said. 'I never heard a name mentioned, and I didn't like to ask. Gareth was upset. I suppose you couldn't blame him for... well, leaving her.'

Meadows got the impression Beth wasn't telling them everything but figured he'd have to ask Jenna for her side of the story. Beth would only be able to give Gareth's version and would naturally take his side.

'So, after the break-up, Gareth got together with Ceri?' Edris asked.

Beth bristled. 'Not straight away. Jenna moved away so Gareth didn't get the chance to be part of Jamie's life when he was growing up. I know that upsets him. He was down for a while but managed to put it behind him and move on. Ceri was a lovely girl. A little timid at times but always happy. Even when Gareth came into money she didn't change. She would have been happy in a flat, but Gareth wanted to build that big house, and they were talking about starting a family.' Beth smiled sadly. 'They were really happy. When she died, I thought Gareth would never get over it.'

'Alex and Laura spent a lot of time with him,' she continued. 'I was so worried about him. He sunk into a deep depression. I'm not sure he would have pulled out of it without those two. Then Alex disappeared. I suppose it was inevitable that Laura and Gareth would get together. It's such a shame they didn't stay together. Laura was good for him. Even now they are good friends. Maybe that's better.'

'Do you get on with Jenna?' Meadows asked.

'I try my best to help out but she's not the easiest of people to get on with. She used to be such a sweet thing. When she came back into Gareth's life, I was happy for him. Then she changed.'

'In what way?' Meadows asked.

'She got ill. She'd been dieting and exercising. I think she wanted to get back into hiking and caving so she went running with Laura and they would go to the gym. Then she started losing too much weight and became… I suppose anxious. It turns out she had a problem with her thyroid, and it took a long time to level out with the medication. Then after Cora, she seemed to spiral into a depression. I know she isn't well, but she can be so nasty.'

'Physically?' Meadows asked.

Beth shook her head. 'Not that I know of. She just seems unreasonable sometimes. Like Sunday, you'd think she'd make an effort when they had a house full of people.'

'What happened?'

'She got drunk and aggressive towards Laura. She was having a go at Maisie and shouting at Ieuan for no reason. Laura suggested nicely that Jenna go and have a lie-down, and she would look after the baby. Jenna kicked off. She accused Laura of wanting her out of the way so she could be alone with Gareth. She was right up in her face. Poor Laura was so embarrassed. We all were. Laura tried to reassure Jenna that she was only trying to help. In the end, Gareth took Jenna into the kitchen. They came out a few moments later, Jenna grabbed Cora and went upstairs.'

'What did Laura do after that?' Meadows asked.

'She started clearing up. She said that Jenna must be exhausted, and she didn't need to get up to a mess.' Beth leaned forward. 'Honestly, sometimes I think it would have been better if Jenna hadn't come back and he stayed with Laura.'

'When did Jenna return?' Meadows asked.

'Erm… about five years ago. Yes, that's right because it was just before Ceri's accident.'

Chapter Fourteen

Deryn Gibson was standing by the window, waiting for a car to pull up. She felt sick. She pulled at the collar of her lilac jumper and wondered if there was time to get changed. She had thought of wearing a dress, but she didn't want to appear like she was making too much effort. The less attention she drew to herself, the better. She'd settled on a pair of grey trousers and a jumper. Now she was too warm.

'I'm hungry,' Maisie said.

Deryn turned around. 'Go and get a biscuit or something. The police will be here any minute and they'll want to talk to you.'

Maisie scowled. 'I don't want to talk to them.'

Deryn turned back to the window. She felt the same way. Keeping up the pretence that everything was OK was bad enough around family, but the police would be harder to fool. A pain stabbed at her chest, and she rubbed the heel of her hand down her breastbone. She heard Maisie leave the room and let out a long breath. She didn't want the child to see her fear. She wished now that she had never accepted the invitation to the christening party. She knew Gareth had only invited her because she was Laura's mother. Jenna had made it obvious that she didn't want her there.

A car pulled up and she watched two men get out.

You can do this, she told herself. Just answer their questions and don't volunteer any information. She moved to the mirror and smoothed her short auburn hair. She could see grey roots on her scalp. She had meant to pick up a box of hair dye but kept forgetting. It's all right for Beth Hendon, she thought. She can afford to go to the hairdresser every week. Beth always made Deryn feel dowdy.

There was a knock on the door and she turned away from the mirror. She knew what she had to do. Keep it together. Protect Laura and Maisie. Ieuan was OK as he had Gareth. It was at times like this that she missed Alex. None of this would be happening if he was still around.

She moved slowly to open the door and forced a smile for the two detectives. She led them inside, offered them a seat, and then settled down close to Maisie on the sofa. The detectives smiled. They both looked friendly enough, but they couldn't help her.

'Laura wanted to be here, but she couldn't get cover at work,' Deryn said.

'That's fine,' Meadows said. 'I know you've already given a statement. We wanted to go over some details, as well as talk to Maisie.'

Deryn felt Maisie move closer. 'Yeah, that's OK.' Her voice came out a little higher than she wanted.

'You said in your statement that Maisie went out to play before Jenna went to bed. That doesn't tally with the other statements we've been given,' Edris said.

'Oh right. Well, I guess it could have been later. She went out a few times.'

'Maisie, can you remember what time you left the party?' Edris asked.

Maisie leaned in close and whispered in Deryn's ear. 'I don't want to talk to them.'

Deryn smiled. 'She's a little shy. Come on, Maisie, you can tell them.'

Maisie shrugged her shoulders.

'You're not in any trouble,' Meadows said. 'We just need some help to find out what happened to Cora.' He sat forward. 'How old are you?'

'Ten.'

'I bet you are a big help to Jenna. Do you look after Cora?'

Maisie nodded. 'I feed her sometimes.'

'You must have been very upset when she went missing.'

'Yeah, but she's okay now.'

Meadows nodded. 'Was Cora in her cot when you left the party?'

Maisie shook her head. 'Jenna was being mean to me, so I left.'

'It's been a little difficult with the new baby,' Deryn said.

'She was mean before that,' Maisie said.

'How is she mean?' Meadows asked.

'She doesn't want me around,' Maisie said. 'She's always shouting at me and Ieuan.'

'She's just busy,' Deryn said. She could feel her anxiety threatening to overwhelm her as she worried about what Maisie would say.

'Where did you go when you left the party?' Meadows asked.

'To Emily's house,' Maisie said.

'That's her friend,' Deryn said.

'Then we went to the park.'

'Did you see anyone when you were at the park?' Meadows asked.

Deryn held her breath as Maisie fidgeted beside her.

'There was a man, running.'

'Do you know the man?' Edris asked.

Maisie shook her head. 'I've seen him running on the path before.'

'Anyone else?'

'Erm... I... saw...' She looked at Deryn. 'No.'

'Are you sure you didn't see anyone else?' Meadows asked.

Maisie nodded.

'Do you remember the fire in your father's house?' Meadows asked.

Maisie nodded.

'Can you tell me what happened that day?'

'Mum and Dad were working so we had to stay with Jenna. I wanted to go to the park, but she made me stay to look after Ieuan in the garden. Ieuan wanted to go inside and play on the PS5. Dad bought it for us, and Jenna won't let us on it when he's not around. She says it's for Jamie.' Maisie looked at Deryn. 'It's for all of us.'

Please don't go off on a rant about Jenna, Deryn thought. It will lead to more questions. 'I don't think the detective is interested in the games you want to play,' Deryn said. 'Just tell them what happened the day of the fire. Like you did before. Remember?'

Maisie nodded. 'Jenna was smoking in the conservatory. She always does that when Dad is not home. Then she said she was going to bed, and I had to look after Ieuan. I was bored so I took him to the park.'

'Did you expect your dad to be home soon?' Edris asked.

'No. He was at work. He doesn't come home until teatime.'

'Did you go into the house before you went to the park?' Meadows asked.

'No. Jenna would have been pis– er, angry if we went inside and woke her up. We played in the park for a while and then we heard the fire engines. When we got home everyone was looking for us.'

'Do you look after Ieuan a lot?' Meadows asked.

'Yes, and Cora. Jenna lets me feed her. Can I go now?'

'Yes. You've been very helpful, thank you,' Meadows said.

Maisie grabbed an iPad from the table before leaving the room.

'She likes playing on that thing,' Deryn said. 'If I let her, she'd be on it all day. I much prefer her to be outside in the fresh air. She'll go out once her friends come home from school.' Deryn became aware that she was rattling on instead of convincing the detectives that everything was OK. 'Things haven't been easy for the children, but they have adjusted. I don't think Jenna is as bad as Maisie makes out. You know what kids are like.'

'Does Laura get on with Jenna?' Meadows asked.

'Yes, they've been friends a long time. They went to school together. Jenna moved away for a while, but they stayed in contact.'

'We've been made aware of an argument between Jenna and Laura at the party,' Meadows said.

Deryn felt the heat rise in her cheeks. 'I wouldn't say it was an argument as such. Jenna just had a bit too much to drink. I think they all had. Mind you, I think Beth put enough brandy in the christening cake to get us all drunk. I even nodded off for a while.'

'Do you think the argument was just because Jenna had been drinking?' Meadows asked.

How much do I tell them? Deryn thought. 'I think perhaps Jenna is a bit jealous of Laura?'

'Why do you think that?' Edris asked.

'Laura has a good degree and she worked hard to get it. She co-owns the vet practice with Gareth. He put up most of the money but Laura does all the work. Gareth just does the books. I don't think Jenna likes that they have the business together, and shared custody of the children.'

'Do you think money is the problem?' Edris asked.

'No. I mean, Gareth has always been good to Laura and the children, but Laura earns her own money. Jenna is the one living in the big house.'

'Why did Laura and Gareth split up?' Edris asked. His phone rang and he took it from his pocket. 'Excuse me a moment.'

Deryn watched him leave the room and then turned back to Meadows. She hoped whatever the call was would take them off.

'You were telling us about Laura and Gareth,' Meadows said.

'Erm... I think they got together too soon after Alex. Both of them were on the rebound. I think they were a great support to each other at the time. The split was amicable. They are still good friends.'

Edris came back into the room and Deryn saw a look pass between the two detectives.

Meadows stood up. 'I think that's all for now. Thank you for your time.'

Deryn felt the tension leave her body. 'I'll see you out.'

She opened the door, and they stepped outside. She didn't close the door tightly but left a tiny gap and pressed her ear against it.

'Search and rescue have found remains,' she heard Edris say, and the ground shifted beneath her feet.

Chapter Fifteen

Edris drove up the winding mountain road and Meadows looked out of the window. The light was fading, so there wasn't much time before darkness would prevent them from viewing the discovery.

'Doesn't sound like he was too far away,' Edris said.

'Still a fair walk from where we found his car. It would make more sense for him to have parked in the quarry car park.'

Edris shrugged. 'Henry thought he wanted some headspace. Maybe he thought if he left the car in view, someone would find him and persuade him to go home before he was ready.'

Meadows wasn't convinced but he didn't say anything. They reached the car park where two mountain rescue Land Rovers were parked. Two men were standing beside one. Meadows got out of the car and grabbed his coat from the back seat.

'Detective Meadows?' one of them asked.

'Yes, and this is DS Edris.'

'I'm Eddy, and this is Rob.'

'Is the cave far from here?'

'No,' Eddy said. 'It's just across the road. I've called back the rest of the team. They were searching further afield. We were just about to pack it up for the day when I remembered this cave. It's not often used but I thought it best to check it out.' He shook his head. 'Rumour is, it's Alex Morris we've been looking for. I heard his car had been found.'

Meadows nodded. 'Did you know Alex?'

'From years back,' Eddy said. 'He used to be a volunteer.'

'He was part of the Beacons Caving Club, for a while,' Rob said.

Meadows looked around at the landscape. 'I'm guessing Alex would have good knowledge of the cave systems in the area. Is this cave known to be dangerous?'

Eddy shook his head. 'You can see for yourselves. We've got a couple of spare harnesses and helmets for you both. It's a bit of a drop down.'

'Erm… I'll think I'll pass,' Edris said.

'Oh it's not far in,' Rob said. He handed Edris a harness. 'You won't have to crawl.'

Meadows stepped into the harness and secured the helmet on his head. He tried not to smile at the look of apprehension on Edris' face.

'OK, let's go before we lose the light,' Rob said.

They crossed the road and walked onto the rough grass. They hadn't walked far when they came to a sinkhole around twenty-five feet deep.

'You've got to be kidding me,' Edris said.

Eddy laughed. 'Go sideways down, it's easier.'

Meadows made his way down without any problems and watched as Edris slipped and cursed. Rob helped Edrid until they were all standing at the bottom. At the far edge of the sinkhole, Meadows saw a corrugated-steel sheet. Next to it, a hole opened up between rocks.

'The sheet was covering the entrance,' Eddy said. 'As the cave goes all the way through the mountain, we thought perhaps some amateurs had explored and not gone too far down, or maybe someone covered it up for safety. We checked it out just in case Alex had gone deep and got stuck.'

'Is that what you think happened here?' Meadows asked.

'No,' Eddy said. 'I'll show you why. We've rigged up a flexi ladder, but it will be better to lower yourself down on the rope and use the ladder to get back up. I'll go down first.'

Eddy demonstrated how to secure the rope to the harness and position the hands to slide it through. Then he lowered himself into the hole.

Rob turned to Edris. 'There is a switch on the side of the light on your helmet. It will give off plenty of light until you get down. Eddy has a torch.'

Edris switched on his light, stepped up to the hole, peered down, and froze.

'Do you want some help to secure the rope?' Rob asked.

'I can't.' Edris stepped back. 'I can't go down there.'

Meadows could see the terror on Edris' face as he backed away. 'Don't worry about it. You can wait up here.' He tried to give him a reassuring smile. 'Loads of people have claustrophobia.'

Rob nodded. 'It's not for everyone. You can help me keep the tension on the rope when they climb back out.'

Meadows stepped up to the hole, fixed the rope, and Rob double-checked it. He placed his feet on the rock, tilted backwards, and started his descent.

The light on his helmet illuminated the rock as he went down. He felt a thrill as the light from above dimmed and he got further below the surface. The temperature dropped and dampness permeated the air.

'About another six feet,' Eddy said.

Meadows let out more rope and sailed easily to the bottom.

'You look like you've done that before,' Eddy said.

'Not for a long time.' Meadows unhooked the rope and looked around. The floor sloped downwards and was muddy and uneven. 'Does this cave flood?'

'No. The water sinks from the mountain and then drains below. We won't be going anywhere near water.'

Meadows followed Eddy a few metres along the cave then around a bend. He had to stoop to avoid hitting his head on the rock. Eddy stopped and trained his flashlight on the ground.

'We didn't touch anything,' he said.

Meadows looked down at the remains which were lying face up. It was mainly bones. Around the bones, the clothes were mostly intact. Waterproof jacket, trousers, wellington boots, and a harness. The helmet had rolled off to the side but still had the rusty remains of the fixed torch. Meadows rooted around in his pocket for latex gloves and snapped them on before crouching down.

'Do you think it's Alex?' Eddy asked.

'Right size,' Meadows said. 'His red waterproof jacket was missing from his car but it's difficult to make out a colour with all this mud. Hopefully, there will be some identification.'

He started examining the jacket, feeling gently around the pocket areas for any items. He did the same with the trouser pockets. There was nothing to be found. He then searched the area with the help of Eddy's powerful torch.

'Nothing?' Eddy asked.

Meadows shook his head. 'OK, let's go back up.'

This time they used the ladder. Meadows could feel the tension in the rope as Rob pulled from above. He got to the top and heaved himself over the ledge. Edris looked relieved to see him.

'Do you think you'd be able to get down without ropes or a ladder?' Meadows asked.

Rob shook his head. 'Too risky. There are not enough places to get a foothold.'

Eddy came up out of the hole and unlinked the rope. 'Would you like us to take a board down to move him?'

'We're going to need to get a photographer down there first,' Meadows said. 'You can probably get off home now and we'll start at first light.'

'No problem,' Eddy said. 'Give us a call when you're ready.'

Meadows helped them replace the cover, then they walked back to the vehicles. He handed the harness back. 'Thanks for your help. I'd appreciate it if you kept this to yourselves for now. We need to inform Alex's family of the development and get an identification.'

'Of course,' Eddy said. 'We'll wait to hear from you.'

As Meadows watched the two men remove their harnesses, a thought struck him. 'Is it unusual for someone to go caving alone?'

Eddy shrugged. 'There are some people that like the solitude, but it's a bit risky, especially if you're going down an unknown cave. It's always a good idea to have someone to call for help if a problem arises.'

'If you're asking if there's something odd about this, then yeah,' Rob said. 'Alex was experienced. He wouldn't have gone down without a rope, even if he was alone. You saw for yourself that there is a harness with the remains.'

'You mentioned you knew Alex from the caving club. Was there anyone in particular that Alex went caving with?' Meadows asked.

'It's a long time ago,' Eddy said. 'From what I remember, Alex and Gareth were tight. They'd go off on weekends together.'

'Gareth Hendon?'

Rob nodded. 'Gareth and Alex took up diving along with a couple of the women. They didn't have much to do with the club after that.'

'Didn't one of the group die?' Eddy asked.

Rob thought for a moment. 'Yeah, that's right. A few years back. Gareth's girlfriend, Jenna.'

'No,' Eddy said. 'She was the red-haired one. He split up with her.'

'Oh yeah,' Rob said. 'Jenna disappeared after they broke up, and then Laura and Ceri joined us. I think it was Ceri that died.'

'Was there a reason why they left the caving club? Any disagreements?' Meadows asked.

'No, nothing like that. We're a friendly bunch,' Eddy said.

'What about any accidents? Or a cave rescue gone wrong?'

'There are plenty of accidents,' Rob said. 'Some fatal.'

'Can you send any records you have of accidents? From when Alex joined the club and volunteered, until his disappearance five years ago?'

Eddy nodded. 'Just in the local area? I know Alex travelled around a lot.'

'Local area to start with.'

'OK.'

'Thank you. I appreciate your help.'

They drove off and Meadows got into his car where Edris was waiting.

'I feel like a right idiot,' Edris said.

'Don't worry about it. I won't tell a soul.'

'I was right about one thing,' Edris said. 'Search and rescue did find him. Confirm ID and we can tick that off our list. Just need to charge someone with putting the baby in the river.'

Meadows shook his head. 'Finding him is just the start of it.'

'You don't think it's an accident?'

'No, and neither do those two. Alex didn't pull the cover back over the hole, did he? There were no ropes or ladders.'

'No, but someone could have come upon the cave, taken the ropes, and put the cover back for safety.'

'That doesn't answer the question of no mobile phone, and more importantly, no car keys. If that is Alex Morris down there, he didn't go down alone.'

Chapter Sixteen

After the photographer and forensics had been down the cave at first light, the remains had been brought to the surface. A thorough search had been carried out for the car keys, phone, and other belongings. Not one item was recovered.

Meadows felt sad as he pulled up outside Alex's parents' house. Lloyd opened the door before he had a chance to knock.

'It's not good news, is it?' Lloyd asked.

'I'm afraid not,' Meadows said.

'It's OK, lad. We were expecting as much. Come in.'

Meadows and Edris followed Lloyd into the sitting room where he sat down next to Emma and took her hand.

Meadows sat down in the armchair and leaned forward. 'We found remains in a cave near Herbert's Quarry. While we can't be certain that it is Alex, given the location of the car and the time that he has been missing, it seems more likely than not.'

Meadows watched all the hope drain from Emma. Her face crumpled and a sob escaped her mouth. Lloyd wrapped his arms around her, and tears ran down his face. Edris had bowed his head and Meadows did the same, allowing the couple a few moments.

'I'm sorry,' Emma sobbed.

'You've nothing to be sorry for,' Meadows said. 'Take your time. If you like, we can leave and give you some space to process the news.'

Emma shook her head. 'What happens now?'

'There will need to be a formal identification. This will be done from dental records. It shouldn't take too long.'

'Did he get trapped?' Lloyd asked.

'The remains will be examined to determine the cause of death, but I have to inform you, at this stage, we are treating the death as suspicious.'

'Are you saying this wasn't an accident?' Emma asked.

'I'm afraid we have to look at that possibility,' Meadows said. 'I can't give you any more details now, but I assure you there will be a full investigation.'

'You've done more than anyone else has so far,' Lloyd said. 'You found him, and I trust you to find out what happened to my boy.'

'When will we be able to… to lay him to rest?' Emma asked.

'Once the identification and examination are complete. We'll do our best to make sure the process is as quick as possible.'

'Can we have his St Christopher necklace?' Emma asked.

'I'm sorry, we didn't find one with him,' Meadows said.

A flicker of hope sparked in Emma's eyes. 'He never took it off.' Emma stood up and walked to the mantle and took down a photograph. She handed it to Meadows.

Meadows looked at the two smiling young men on a beach. They were dressed in swim shorts.

'They were given them on their eighteenth birthdays,' Emma said. 'My father was a devoted Catholic. Alex's name is engraved on the back with the words "May our Lord keep you safe".'

'It may have been washed away in the cave, isn't that right?' Lloyd looked at Meadows.

'It's possible,' he said. Even though he knew there had been a thorough search of the cave and the bones had been intact. If Alex had been wearing the neckless, it would have been anchored. 'May I take the photograph to make copies?'

Emma nodded and slid the photo from the frame. She touched Alex's face before handing the picture to Meadows.

'What happened to Alex's belongings?' Edris asked.

'We boxed them up and put them in his old room. It wasn't fair for Laura to keep hold of them.'

'Did he have a laptop?'

'Yes,' Emma said. 'Would you like to take a look at it?'

'Please,' Edris said.

Emma left the room and Meadows turned to Lloyd. 'I have to ask, is there anyone you can think of that would have wanted to harm Alex?'

'No. Absolutely not,' Lloyd said. 'He wasn't the type to get into fights and he didn't have any drug problems. He was just an ordinary boy. He loved his family and was happy at work.'

'You said he worked in IT,' Edris said. 'What was the name of the company?'

'Tech SM. It had something to do with implementing new systems into various businesses. He did coding.'

'Did he talk about his work with you?'

Lloyd smiled. 'It was over my head, but I'm sure if he had a problem, he would have told us.'

Emma returned with the laptop and handed it to Edris.

'We'll get it back to you as soon as possible,' Edris said.

'We'll be in touch as soon as we have an identification,' Meadows said.

'What do we say to Laura?' Emma turned to Lloyd. 'I don't think I can... Poor Maisie. We have to tell her that her father is never coming home.'

'Don't worry, we'll inform Laura of the developments,' Meadows said.

'Thank you,' Emma said.

Meadows took a card from his pocket and handed it to Emma. 'That's my direct number. If you think of anything, or just need to ask a question, give me a call.'

Lloyd and Emma saw them to the door and watched them pull away.

* * *

Laura sat quietly as Meadows repeated what he had told Alex's parents. Her eyes misted and she rubbed at her knees. Edris was making her a cup of tea and Meadows got the impression she was struggling to hold her composure. He was sitting in an armchair and Laura was on the sofa. All around, he could see shelves and cabinets full of knick-knacks. The room had a childlike quality. He guessed she indulged the children.

Laura shook her head. 'He never left me and Maisie.'

'No,' Meadows said. 'We will be looking at everything Alex did, and who he spoke to, leading up to his disappearance. Particularly the last Saturday he was seen. It's possible that Alex went into the cave on that day.'

'But he sent me text messages after that.'

'Did you find anything about those text messages unusual?' Meadows asked.

'You mean other than the fact that he told me he needed space?'

Meadows nodded.

'Erm... I can't remember exactly what they said but they were a bit impersonal. No emojis. He always used the one with hearts for eyes or blowing a kiss. I thought perhaps he was angry with me but we hadn't argued.'

'Emma mentioned a necklace Alex wore.'

Laura nodded. 'His St Christopher.'

'Did he have it that morning?'

'I guess so. He never took it off, and he didn't say anything about losing it.'

Edris came back into the room and handed Laura a cup of tea. He sat on the opposite side of the sofa and took out his notebook. 'Is there anyone you can think of who may have held a grudge against Alex?' he asked.

Laura shook her head.

'What about someone from his past?' Edris asked.

'What do you mean?'

'Someone he'd known from years ago that came back into his life.'

Meadows wondered where Edris was going with this, but it seemed to make Laura uncomfortable. She shifted in her seat and tucked a lock of hair behind her ear.

'Maybe an old friend from school. Something like that. Someone who could have known something from Alex's past and had a hold on him.'

Laura started twisting her hair around her finger. 'Erm… not really.' She looked down, avoiding eye contact with Edris.

Meadows saw Edris raise his eyebrows and took it as his cue to take over. He leaned forward in the chair. 'Laura, even if you think it's unimportant, you need to tell us.'

Laura looked at him. 'I just feel uncomfortable bringing it up. Especially given what happened.' Laura sighed. 'Jenna came back a few months before Alex left, but I'm sure that has nothing to do with it.'

'Was Alex unhappy about Jenna coming back?' Meadows asked.

'They argued. She blamed Alex for the break-up with Gareth. You'll have to ask her about that.'

'Did Jenna and Alex ever go caving together?'

'She was part of the caving club, so yes, they did for a–' Laura stopped, and a look of concern creased her face. 'If you're thinking... no... Jenna wouldn't hurt Alex. No way.'

'Gareth was with Ceri when Jenna came back, is that correct?'

'Yes.'

'How did Ceri and Jenna get along?' Meadows asked.

'I think Jenna has enough to deal with at the moment. She doesn't need anyone gossiping about her.'

'I appreciate your loyalty to Jenna, and your other friends, but if we are to find out what happened to Alex, and to Cora, then it's important that we know everything that happened at the time. We will handle anything you tell us with discretion and sensitivity,' Meadows said.

Laura nodded. 'Things were a little awkward between Jenna and Ceri to begin with. I think all Jenna wanted at the time was for Gareth to have a relationship with Jamie. We all used to be friends, and we were working it out. Ceri was a very generous and kind person. She was happy for Gareth to spend time with Jamie and even tried to include Jenna in any family gatherings. I'm sure things would have settled.'

'We have requested the details of Ceri's accident, but I'd like you to tell me what you remember of that day.'

Laura's eyes widened. 'What's this got to do with Alex? Do you think that what happened to Ceri wasn't an accident?'

'We have to look at all related incidences,' Edris said. 'Just to check if they have any bearing on the case.'

Laura didn't look reassured. 'It was just a stupid accident.'

'If you could just talk us through that day,' Meadows said.

'We were walking the Four Falls Trail. We'd been taking a few days here and there to get out hiking. We were taking our time to explore the area around the waterfalls, as there are a lot of caves.'

'What was the weather like that day?' Edris asked.

'Cold and wet,' Laura said. 'It had been raining heavily for a few days before, but it was only a few showers that day. We set off early as we were going to see the waterfall and then go to Porth yr Ogof. It had been years since we'd been down that cave and we filled the car with equipment.'

'Was it usual for just the two of you to go off together?' Meadows asked.

'Yes. We did a lot of hiking and exploring together when we had time off work. Maisie was in school and Alex was picking her up that day, so we had plenty of time. We left the equipment in the car and started on the path to the waterfall. We were about halfway there when the path got a little tricky. It goes up and down and there are a lot of tree roots. I fell. I don't know how. One minute we were talking, and the next I was on the ground. Ceri helped me up but I couldn't put any weight on my foot. I told her to go ahead without me so she could take photos. I thought if I soaked my ankle in the river, and rested for a bit, I'd be OK.'

'And she was happy to leave you injured and alone?' Meadows asked.

Laura shook her head. 'You make it sound bad, but it wasn't like that. We weren't that far from the waterfall, and I didn't want to waste the day. I persuaded her to go. She even gave me her coat to keep me warm. I only had a light raincoat over my fleece, but Ceri's coat was insulated. I gave her my raincoat and I put on hers. That's what I mean about her being kind and generous. She would have been cold in my coat but she insisted I stay warm.'

'Did you see any other walkers?'

'No. There were some cars in the car park.'

'So you waited for Ceri to come back?' Meadows asked.

'Yes. She helped me down to the river and then went off. I took off my boot and put my ankle in the water. It was already swollen. I thought I'd just twisted it, but it was broken. I waited on the riverbank for a long time. I couldn't phone Ceri because I had no signal. I tried to hobble but it was impossible. Some walkers came along. I told them I was worried about Ceri. One stayed with me.' Laura wrapped her arms around her body.

'I never imagined that…' Her voice broke. 'They found her at the bottom of the waterfall. She must have slipped and gone over the edge.'

'Who knew where you were going that day?'

'Erm… Alex, Gareth, and…'

'And?'

Laura bit her lip. 'Jenna. We invited her to come but she said she couldn't make it.'

Chapter Seventeen

Heavy grey clouds darkened the sky and threatened rain, reflecting the vibe Meadows felt coming from Edris. The hospital car park was quieter than usual, so Meadows managed to find a parking space.

'All these hours we're putting in, and still we've got no lead on who put Cora in the river,' Edris said.

'We have made some progress,' Meadows said. 'We've eliminated quite a few people that were at the party.'

Edris sighed. 'It's not enough though. I spent all day yesterday looking at caving accidents, and now we're going to talk to these two again and probably come away with nothing.'

Meadows smiled. 'Get out of bed the wrong side, did you?'

'I shouldn't have been getting out of bed at all. It's the weekend.'

'Come on then, let's go. If the two of them are in with Cora, we need to separate them. You can take Gareth off for a coffee and a chat while I speak to Jenna alone. See if you can get his version of the break-up.'

Edris huffed. 'I'll try but he seems to be the one in control.'

'I'm not so sure. Jenna is the one refusing to let Olwen back in the house. Apparently, she kicked off when asked.'

'You'd think she'd want to find out if Olwen saw someone out of the window.'

Meadows nodded. 'Perhaps she is afraid of what Olwen will remember.'

They found Jenna alone in the room with Cora who was sleeping in her arms.

'She looks much better,' Meadows said.

'Yeah,' Jenna said. 'Her chest infection is clearing up, so she can breathe easier now.'

'Hopefully, it won't be long before you can take her home,' Meadows said.

'That's what I worry about. She is safe here. There's CCTV and codes to open the doors. What happens when I take her home? What if someone tries to take her again?'

'We are working hard to find the person responsible,' Meadows said.

'It's been a week, and you still don't have a clue, do you?'

'If we are going to catch this person, then you need to be honest with us. Last time we spoke, I had the feeling you wanted to say more about the fire.'

'No one believes me,' Jenna said.

'Try me.'

Jenna stood up, kissed Cora's forehead, placed her in the cot, and then sat back down. Edris quickly grabbed two chairs from the other side of the room and placed them to form a small triangle.

Meadows waited until they were all seated and Edris had taken out his notebook.

'Tell us what happened the day of the fire,' he said.

'I didn't smoke before I went to bed,' Jenna said. 'Even if I had, I would have done so out the garden. I always do.'

'Who knew you would be alone in the house with the children that day?' Meadows asked.

'Obviously Gareth, probably his mother, and erm… Laura. She was working so she knew I had the kids.'

'If someone did deliberately start the fire, why do you think they would target you?' Meadows asked.

'I don't know!' Jenna clenched her fists. 'You think I'm mad like everyone else, don't you? They are always watching me.'

Meadows could see the tension in Jenna's body and the wildness in her eyes. It would be easy to put it down to paranoia. He'd witnessed her mood swings and knew she was struggling with her mental health. That would make her an easy target. Who would believe her?

'Who is always watching you?' he asked.

'All of them. Gareth, and when he's not around, Beth or Laura. That's why they are always at the house. They don't trust me. They all think I'm losing it. Even I think that sometimes. Things are never where I leave them in the house, or they go missing.' Tears leaked from her eyes, and she wiped them away. 'I'm just so bloody tired. Someone has got it in for me. I didn't see it before, but the fire, and now Cora.'

'When did this all start?' Meadows asked.

Jenna thought about it. 'When I moved in with Gareth. No… I think it was before that, that things started to go wrong. I think someone doesn't want Gareth and me to be together.'

'Is that what you think all this is about?' Meadows asked.

Jenna nodded.

'Who do you think wants to split you up?'

'Laura.'

'But it wasn't Laura who was with Gareth when you moved back,' Edris said.

Jenna looked at Edris and scowled. 'No, it was Ceri. She always liked him. He was in the year above us in school. I was the first to join the caving club. Laura and Ceri had no interest in coming with me at the time. Then Gareth joined. Alex was already part of the club. He and Gareth became good mates. Laura didn't know Alex then, because he went to a different school. The three of us spent a lot of time together exploring caves and learning to dive. To be honest, I was glad to be doing something different from Ceri and Laura. For the first time, I didn't feel like the odd one out. I never felt good enough around them. Gareth and I were happy together.'

'Tell us about the break-up?' Meadows said.

Jenna's eyebrows rose. 'Break-up? Is that what you are calling it?'

'What happened?'

'I got pregnant with Jamie. Gareth was really good about it when I told him. He said he would look after me and the baby. He asked me to marry him. We were both young at the time, but I wanted that security for me and the baby. We planned the wedding. It wasn't meant to be a big affair but Gareth's family wanted a church wedding and it kind of grew. It was rushed so I wouldn't be showing too much in my dress.

'On the morning of the wedding, Alex told Gareth that the baby wasn't his. Gareth didn't turn up at the church.' Jenna visibly cringed. 'Can you imagine how humiliating that was? I was waiting in the church in my wedding dress! Just standing on the porch with my bridesmaids as the guests became restless. All our family and friends were there. Alex turned up to say Gareth wasn't coming. I could hear the whispers going around the church. I remember running out. I couldn't face anyone. A couple of days later, I spoke to Gareth on the phone. I wanted to know why he had left me there. That's when I found out what Alex had told him. Gareth was my first boyfriend. I hadn't been with anyone else.'

'You must have been very angry with Gareth and Alex.'

Jenna nodded. 'I couldn't understand why Gareth would believe Alex over me. That's why I left. If he didn't believe that Jamie was his son, then I thought I was better off without him.'

'What made you come back?' Meadows asked.

'Jamie started asking questions. He wanted to meet his father. I got in contact with Gareth and he asked for Jamie to take a DNA test. Finally, he knew I was telling the truth. I was still angry with Gareth, but he wanted to try and make it up to the two of us. I guess everyone deserves a second chance.'

'Did that cause problems with Ceri?'

'No, not at first. Ceri wasn't a bitch. She was happy for Gareth to spend time with Jamie. Gareth helped us move back. I never got the impression that Ceri was unhappy about that. She was always friendly to me. If anything, I was the one who felt awkward. I got into an argument with Alex. I wanted to know why he had lied about me. He told me that Ceri was the one who told him about me cheating on Gareth. I couldn't look at Ceri after that. I feel bad now for how I treated her, but I thought at the time she had lied so she could have Gareth.'

'What changed?' Meadows asked.

'Laura tried to get us all back together. She kept inviting me to go out walking with her and Ceri. In the end, I agreed to go. I thought it would be best for Jamie if we could all try and get along. They switched the day of the walk and I couldn't get out of work. Ceri came to see me the morning of the accident. She thought I had backed out of the walk because I was avoiding her. She was troubled. She said she didn't like having bad feelings between us. I told her why I was upset. She was shocked. She told me that it was Laura who told her I was cheating. Laura didn't want to tell Gareth herself, so Ceri talked to Alex. She asked him what to do with the information and he said he would tell Gareth. It was Laura all along. She is the one who started all of this.'

Chapter Eighteen

It had been another long day at the hospital and Jenna was glad to get home. She parked in the driveway and got out of the car. Rain lashed down and seeped into her light jacket. She didn't seem to notice. Her eyes were drawn to the double garage. Inside, she could see Gareth hoovering his jeep. Anger welled inside her, and she felt her body stiffen. She marched over to the garage and stood staring at her partner. She was sure he could feel her eyes burning into him, but he appeared to be ignoring her.

'Gareth!'

He carried on, so she grabbed the cord of the hoover and yanked until it came out of the socket.

Gareth looked around, saw her, and smiled. 'Oh, you're back. How is Cora?'

She ignored the question. 'What are you doing?'

'Just cleaning the jeep.'

'Well, it's all right for you. I've been stuck in the hospital all day.'

'I've been working.'

'Working!' Jenna shrieked. 'You just didn't want to come to the hospital. I knew you were lying when you said you were going in today. You never work on a Sunday.'

'I had to catch up with some things. I haven't been in most of the week.'

'You've only been to the hospital twice in the daytime. You come for an hour in the evening and think you've done your bit.'

Gareth huffed. 'Don't start. It's pointless for us both to be there all day. Cora is doing well now, and I'll come with you this evening.'

'Don't bloody bother,' Jenna said. 'I'm going for a shower. I need something to eat before I go back. I suppose you expect me to cook your dinner as well.'

'I said I will go with you. Go and get changed, and I'll cook us something.'

Jenna clenched her fists until she could feel her nails digging into the palms of her hands. She wanted to scream at him. Hit him. Take the cord from the hoover and wrap it around his neck. She fought against these intrusive thoughts and turned away before she said or did something she would regret.

She hurried into the kitchen, downed her tablets with a glass of water, and then ran up the stairs. She kept telling herself to keep moving until the tablets kicked in. The calmness would come. She stripped off, stepped in the shower and turned the jets up high. The water pounded against her body and stung her skin. The sensation felt good. Any physical pain felt good. It helped numb the pain within. She watched the water draining away and her mind wandered. She came out of her trance only when she swayed and bumped against the glass. She had no idea how long she had been under the water, but the room was full of steam.

She got out of the shower and quickly dried herself. She didn't bother with her hair. She pulled on a pair of jeans and opened a drawer to grab her red top, but it wasn't there. She opened all the drawers and pulled out the clothes. Still no red top. She knew she hadn't worn it. There were other tops she could put on, but she was now fixated on the red one. She checked the washing basket and then ran downstairs to check the washing machine.

She was about to go into the kitchen when she heard Gareth's voice. She crept closer to the door and listened.

'She's getting worse,' Gareth said. 'No, I've tried to persuade her to go back to the doctor ... Yeah, yeah, I know. Best not to drop the kids off here for a while. I'll have them at the weekend.'

Jenna's stomach twisted as she realised he was talking to Laura. It took all her self-control not to march into the kitchen, grab the phone, and smash it into his face. She remained still, listening.

'Yeah, he came around here,' Gareth continued. 'He spouted the same bullshit to me ... No ... He knows nothing ... Don't be stupid.'

Jenna pushed her ear against the door.

'Laura, listen to me. You need to keep your mouth shut. You know what will happen if anyone finds out ... Jenna doesn't know ... Of course ... I didn't tell her ... Fine ... I'll see you soon.'

Jenna pushed open the door.

'I thought you'd drowned in the shower. I was about to come and look for you.'

'Who was on the phone?'

'Just work.'

'Don't lie to me! I heard you. You were talking to Laura.'

Colour rose in Gareth's cheeks. 'OK, yeah. She just wanted to talk about the kids. You get so weird when I talk to her.'

'You were talking about me.'

Gareth turned away and checked the food in the oven. 'I'm just worried about you.'

'Then talk to *me*, not Laura.'

Gareth turned around to face her. 'I'm sorry.'

'What is it that you haven't told me? You told Laura on the phone that I don't know. What don't I know?'

'Erm... I... Why are you only half dressed?'

Jenna had forgotten that she'd been looking for her top. 'My red top is missing.'

'Probably in the washing basket,' Gareth said.

'No, I've checked.' Jenna moved to the washing machine and opened the door. It was empty. She moved her hand around the drum to make sure. 'It's not here. Where is it?'

'How the hell would I know?' Gareth snapped. 'You are always losing things.'

'I'm not. She's taken it.'

'Who?'

'Bloody Laura.'

'For fuck's sake. Why would Laura take your top? She hasn't been here since last Sunday. Please, Jenna, you need to get some help.'

'What I need is for you to listen to me and be honest with me. Not go running to Laura with all our problems. I don't want her to know everything that goes on in this house.'

Jenna could feel her anxiety building. It felt like something was clawing at her insides. The tablets didn't seem to be working. She moved to the cupboard and took out the bottle of pills. She'd already upped the dose way past the maximum.

Gareth snatched them from her hand. 'You're not going to take more of them.'

Panic gripped Jenna like a vice. 'Give them back. They make me feel better.'

'How many are you taking?'

'Just a couple. Three times a day.' Jenna hoped he didn't see the lie on her face. The truth was, she needed more and more to feel the effect. 'Please give them to me. They make me feel better.'

'If you promise to go back to the doctor and check you can take these with your antidepressants. Some of these herbal remedies don't mix well.'

'OK, fine.'

Gareth handed her the tablets, and she swallowed two. 'I'll grab a top then we better get going.'

'We haven't eaten yet.'

'I'm not hungry.'

Gareth's phone rang and he checked the screen. 'It's Deryn. I better get this.'

'If it's not Laura, then it's her bloody mother. Why can't they leave us alone?'

Gareth ignored her and answered the call. 'Hi, Deryn. Is everything all right? … Yes, Cora is doing well … No … Jenna is fine. You can speak to her yourself.'

Gareth put the phone on the kitchen table and hit the speaker. Deryn's voice filled the kitchen.

'No. Don't put Jenna on. It's you I need to talk to.'

Gareth went to hit off the speaker, but Jenna slapped his hand away. If Deryn had something to say, she wanted to hear.

'What's wrong?' Gareth asked.

'I… oh… I don't know how to say this,' Deryn said.

'It's OK,' Gareth said. 'Is it something about the kids?'

'I can't talk now. Maisie will be home in a minute.'

Jenna heard Deryn sob. She went to pick up the phone, but Gareth stopped her. He put his finger to his lips.

'Do you want me to come over?' Gareth asked.

'No, not now. It's about… Hold on.' Deryn's voice became distant. 'I'm just talking to your dad. Go upstairs and change. Your clothes are soaking. Dinner will be ready soon.' Deryn's voice became clear again. 'Gareth, I'm going to have to go. I don't want Maisie to hear.'

'I can come over tomorrow about ten. Will you be OK until then?' Gareth asked.

'Yeah. I can't believe this is happening again.'

Chapter Nineteen

Meadows could feel the frustration in the air as he gathered the team around for the morning briefing.

'It's unbelievable that someone can take a baby from her cot, put her in the river, and yet no one saw a thing,' Blackwell said.

'How did you get on with Gareth's work colleagues?' asked Meadows.

'No one had a bad word to say about him. He puts in the hours like everyone else. He even covers sick leave. Driving, loading, and admin. Happy to get his hands dirty.'

'No recent redundancies, accidents, or pay disputes,' Valentine added.

'Given that it's a haulage company, I'm checking with customs to see if there are any red flags. Could be bringing drugs into the country, weapons, or even trafficking.'

Meadows nodded. 'It's worth checking out. That's family, friends, and work. So far, we have turned up nothing. We need to dig deeper into the family. That includes the children. I want school records, financial records, phone records, and even voluntary DNA swabs to see if that rattles anyone. Meanwhile, we have confirmation that the remains found in the cave were that of Alex Morris. The blood found in the footwell of his car is also a match. Paskin, we will need to put out an appeal on social media. "Last seen wearing" type of post. It may turn something up. Edris and I will be visiting the morgue to see if there have been any developments in establishing the cause of death.'

'I've been looking at the list of cave accidents which Eddy sent,' Edris said. 'Mostly, it lists the name of the cave, time, date, duration of rescue, and depth. There is a summary of each rescue detailing how the accident occurred. Stating whether the victim was male or female, and their age. There are no specifics on the rescuers that took part or the name of victim. I have to request further information on each incident, and inquest reports on fatalities. Without knowing which one we need to take a closer look at; it's going to take time.'

'It may be that Alex's death has nothing to do with caving,' Valentine said.

'I think whoever put Alex in that cave would have had some skill and knowledge,' Meadows said. 'Alex was kitted up. Whoever he was with would have been expected to go down the cave with him.'

Edris nodded. 'We've got a few of them on our list.'

'Shouldn't we be concentrating all our efforts on Cora's case,' Blackwell said. 'Alex has been dead for five years.'

'To his parents, it may as well be yesterday,' Meadows said. 'We could well be looking at the same person in both cases. Alex was Laura's partner and Gareth's best friend. Jenna blamed him for the break-up with Gareth, and Alex said he was meeting Henry that day. All these people are on list A of possible suspects in Cora's case. Without anything else to go on, this is our best lead.'

'There are also others on the list who are connected to Alex,' Valentine said.

'If we can find a motive for one, we may be able to solve the other,' Meadows said.

'Alex disappeared five years ago,' Blackwell said. 'If the two cases are connected, why wait until now to act again?'

'The farmer, Ethan, reported Alex's car the day after Cora was taken,' Meadows said. 'He said they had been working to clear the field all week, but had to stop because of the rain. That field can be seen from the road. If we go with the theory that someone killed Alex and then hid his car, then that person could well have known that the car was about to be discovered.'

Valentine nodded. 'Gareth and Alex could have been involved in something dodgy. Someone could be making sure Gareth keeps quiet.'

'We also have the fire,' Meadows said. 'If Jenna is to be believed and didn't accidentally leave a cigarette burning, then she could be the target. Then there's Ceri Rees.'

'Which according to the inquest was a hiking accident,' Paskin said.

'PC Ryan is coming in to talk us through the details of Ceri's accident shortly. Her death was only six months before Alex's disappearance.'

'It is a lot to be happening to one group of people,' Valentine said.

Blackwell huffed. 'OK, I suppose it may not be coincidental.'

'Theories?' Meadows asked. He looked around at the team. 'Let's look at the ones on the list involved in caving. That narrows it down.'

'Gareth and Laura got together after Alex's disappearance,' Paskin said. 'Maybe Gareth wanted Laura, or Laura wanted Gareth.'

Blackwell shrugged. 'If it's not lust, then you're left with money or revenge.'

'Laura doesn't benefit from Alex's death and neither does anyone else,' Valentine said.

'Henry is odd,' Blackwell said.

Meadows shook his head. 'That doesn't make him a killer.'

'We've got a jilted bride,' Edris said. 'Jenna blamed Alex, and then Ceri.'

'What about Cora?' Blackwell asked.

'She didn't want the baby,' Edris said.

'What makes you say that?' Meadows asked.

Colour rose in Edris' cheeks. 'Erm… I think someone implied it, or maybe it's a feeling I had.'

'Well, if Golden Boy has a feeling, then we must be on the right track,' Blackwell said.

'Oh piss off,' Edris muttered.

'Have we had anything back on the request for Jenna's medical records?' Meadows asked.

'Yes,' Paskin said. 'Nothing more than we already knew. She was treated for an overactive thyroid and more recently for depression. Nothing of interest before that. There was a note in her file, from the midwife. She suspected Jenna was taking drugs. Jenna denied the use of any illegal substances.'

Meadows looked at the list of names. 'What about the rest of them? They all had an opportunity to put Cora in the river, and possibly opportunity to kill Alex. We haven't got a time of death for Alex. Checking out alibis is going to be nearly impossible after all this time. The problem is, not one of these people has a decent motive. There's got to be something we are missing. Anything on the background checks?'

Paskin shook her head. 'Everyone is clear, and nothing on Alex's laptop of interest. Henry has an enhanced DBS as he works with children and young adults. He doesn't even have a social media account. There are no convictions, cautions, or anything else that flags up, on any of them. I'm trawling through social media accounts to see if anything stands out.'

'Jenna is very active on social media,' Paskin continued. 'Lots of photos of the baby and Jamie. Laura, the same sort of thing, but add in animal pics. Gareth rarely posts anything. The other family members post periodically. Nothing of interest there. Both Maisie and Jamie have Snapchat accounts. These are more difficult to get information from. Even with a formal request, there is only limited access to content. "Snaps" and "chats" would need to be saved by the user, otherwise they are permanently deleted. I did take a look at Ceri's social media accounts. She had lots of posts on Instagram. Hiking and caving. That sort of thing. There was also a memorial page. These are her last posts.' Paskin pressed a few keys on her tablet and the photos appeared on the whiteboard.

The first photograph showed Ceri in front of a waterfall. 'Sgwd yr Eira,' Paskin said. 'Falls of the snow.'

'She looks a bit sad,' Valentine said.

Meadows studied the photo. 'It does look like she's been crying.'

Paskin clicked her tablet, and another photo appeared. This time it was Laura and Ceri under the waterfall, with water bouncing off their raincoats.

'So who took the photo?' Blackwell asked.

'Looks like a selfie to me,' Valentine said. 'Ceri's arm is extended.'

Paskin clicked through several more photographs. There were different poses and some where they had changed coats and hats.

'They look remarkably alike,' Meadows commented. 'Same build, auburn hair, and brown eyes. Laura is about an inch shorter, and her hair is a little longer.'

Edris nodded. 'They do look like sisters.'

PC Liam Ryan entered the office and put his laptop on a desk.

'Thanks for coming in,' Meadows said.

'No problem,' Ryan said. 'I've brought my notebook with me. I'll just set this up.' He switched on his laptop and connected it to the whiteboard before taking out his notebook.

'OK,' he said. 'A call came in on Wednesday, 17th of April 2019 at 9.45 a.m. Mountain rescue and an air ambulance were dispatched. I arrived on the scene with PC Abbey Taylor. Ceri had been pulled from the water by a member of the public and CPR was attempted.'

Ryan sounded like he was giving evidence at a trial and Meadows imagined he had gone over this many times before presenting it at the inquest.

Ryan clicked on his laptop and a photo appeared on the whiteboard. It showed Ceri lying face up on the stony bank of the pool below the waterfall. She was wearing a pink coat. Her face had a grey tinge and her wet hair trailed behind her head.

'This photograph was taken at the scene before Ceri was taken to the hospital.'

'She's wearing Laura's coat,' Meadows said.

'Laura did say they had switched coats before Ceri went on without her,' Edris added.

PC Ryan tapped his computer. 'This shows the view from the top of the waterfall. The red circle shows the point from which Ceri fell. You can see the prints from her boots and where earth and stones have fallen away from the edge.' He tapped again. 'This one shows the trajectory of her fall, which was consistent with her injuries. Post-mortem results showed an injury to her head which likely resulted in unconsciousness. There were other injuries noted from the fall. The official cause of death was drowning. Toxicology was clear.'

'Did you speak to Laura Gibson that day?' Meadows asked.

'Yes. I took her initial statement.'

'What was your opinion of her?'

Ryan thought for a moment. 'I remember she was in a lot of pain from her injury, and very distressed about her friend. I spoke to her briefly there, and then later at home. She was still very emotional the second time I spoke to her.'

'Do you think she could have walked from the waterfall to the location where she was found, with her injury?'

'No. Her ankle was broken. Mountain rescue moved her from the location where she was found to an ambulance in the car park. I took statements from the two walkers who met with Laura. One stayed with her while the other went to look for Ceri. All three accounts matched.'

'Was there anything that stood out as odd to you at the time?' Meadows asked.

Worry flitted across PC Ryan's face. 'I don't think so, why?'

'It's nothing for you to be concerned about,' Meadows said, 'but given our ongoing investigation, we needed to look into the accident to see if it has any bearing on the case. I can see you've been very thorough, and the coroner ruled it as an accident. Any insight you can give us would be helpful.'

PC Ryan appeared happy with this explanation. 'It had been raining heavily in the days leading up to the accident, which made the ground very slippery. Ceri was wearing good hiking boots. I did talk to her partner and family at the time. Ceri was an experienced hiker, caver, and diver. Not one to take risks. It did strike me as a little odd that she would move that far back on the ledge to take a photo. I guess these things happen. There weren't many people walking the trail that day. Some came forward but no one saw her fall. No reports of attacks on hikers in the area previously, or any time since as far as I am aware. It's a safe area.'

'Laura blamed herself for the accident,' he continued, 'as she hadn't gone with Ceri to the waterfall. Honestly, I didn't come across anything that aroused my suspicion.'

'Were there any photos recovered from Ceri's phone taken that day?' Meadows asked.

PC Ryan nodded. 'I've got a slide show of the last photos taken. It appears she was using the burst function which takes several photos in succession.' He called up the file and hit play.

The whiteboard displayed a series of photos. The first one was of Laura and Ceri in the car park. The next few showed entrances to the cave system at the start of the trail. A few showed the waterfall taken from different angles, then the burst sequences that PC Ryan had mentioned. The first one was of Ceri with the waterfall visible over her left shoulder. The photos were almost identical but for a slight movement of the head. The next series of photos showed she had moved to a crouched position. The waterfall this time was behind her head. The last series of shots was taken with her standing and her arm raised to catch the waterfall falling into the pool. Then there was one with shock registered on her face, followed by a blurry shot which showed her hair flying upwards. That was the last.

A shiver ran up Meadows' spine. 'She captured the last moments before her death. Can you send those to me?'

'Yeah, no problem,' PC Ryan said. 'Is there anything else you need to know?'

'I think you've covered it all. Thank you,' Meadows said.

PC Ryan put away his laptop. 'Good luck with the case,' he said before leaving.

'Looks like it was just an accident,' Blackwell said.

Meadows returned to his desk and opened the file that PC Ryan had sent. He clicked back and forth through the photographs. On each, he checked the position of her feet and the angle of the camera. He looked for any shadows. He did this several times until something caught his attention. He flipped back the photos and put the last two side by side. In one Ceri was smiling, and in the other, she had a shocked expression.

Meadows called Edris over. 'Come and look at this.'

Edris rolled his chair over to Meadows' desk and peered at the screen. 'What am I looking at?'

'Firstly, look at the position of her feet. She is not dangerously close to the edge at this point.'

'So she stepped back before the next photo.'

Meadows shook his head. 'Her left leg is already back. Even if she swung her right leg back, it wouldn't be enough to put her over the edge. Most people would look back before taking another step.'

'She wouldn't be the first to fall taking a selfie.'

'These are continuous shots where she is only moving her head.

She moves position before each set. Going from the previous photos, she wouldn't have pressed the shutter until she changed position again.'

Edris' brow wrinkled in confusion.

Meadows stood up. 'Stand up, get out your phone, and I'll show you.'

Edris took out his phone. 'OK, now what?'

'Take a selfie. First with the door to your left, then to the right, then centre with the phone raised so you can see the bottom of the door. Imagine it's a waterfall. Use the burst function for each shot. Hang on.' Meadows grabbed a pen from his desk and positioned it behind Edris. 'You mustn't go over the pen.'

The rest of the team had stopped working and were all watching.

Edris lifted his phone, checked the position of the door, and then hit the shutter. A snapping noise came from his phone. He moved so the door was to his left and repeated the exercise. For the centre shot, he raised his phone to get in the bottom of the door and checked behind for the pen. He hit the shutter.

Meadows waited until two clicks issued from the phone then he shoved Edris. Edris stumbled back and Meadows caught his arm to stop him falling.

Laughter rang out around the office.

'What did you do that for?' Edris asked.

Valentine walked over. 'You went over the pen.'

'Only because he pushed me.' Realisation dawned on Edris' face.

'Let's take a look at the photos,' Meadows said.

Edris swiped through the photos, with Valentine and Meadows on either side of him. The last one showed a look of surprise on his face.

Valentine laughed. 'Send me a copy of that one.'

'Notice that you can't see my hands pushing you,' Meadows said. 'I kept them just below your ribs to keep them out of shot. Now look at Ceri's photos.'

The three of them peered at the photographs on the screen.

'Look at the coat on the last but one photo. Now look at the last shot.'

Valentine leaned closer. 'It's creased. Sort of puckered.'

Meadows nodded. 'Looks like the coat has been pushed in from below. Ceri didn't do that. One hand has the camera, and you can see the other hand.'

'Why didn't anyone pick up on this before?'

'I guess they had no reason to be looking that closely. Alex hadn't gone missing at that stage. There would be nothing to suggest that it was anything other than an accident.'

'It would have to be someone she knew, and was comfortable with,' Valentine said. 'Look how relaxed she is in the previous photographs.'

'Jenna knew she would be going to that particular waterfall,' Edris said.

'She wouldn't have known that Ceri would be alone,' Valentine said.

'Maybe she had something planned for the both of them. She could have had a weapon with her, then was presented with an opportunity,' Edris said.

Blackwell sauntered over. 'Laura would have seen Jenna walking the trail.'

'It's not the only entrance,' Paskin said. 'There is a car park further up. You come down from a different direction.'

'So now you think we have three victims,' Blackwell said. 'Alex, Ceri, and Cora.'

'All connected to Gareth, Jenna, and Laura,' Valentine said.

'And Henry,' Edris added. 'He's friends with all three.'

Meadows looked at his team. 'The question is, are they all targets or is one of them a killer?'

* * *

The morgue was located in the hospital basement. Meadows always felt uneasy when he walked down the long silent corridor. The only sound came from their footsteps and the buzzing of the flickering strip lights.

'I feel so sorry for Alex's parents,' Edris said. 'They won't be able to see him to say their final goodbyes.'

'They've asked to come anyway. I've arranged for Alex's remains to be placed in a casket this afternoon, so they can come and spend a little time with him before the funeral. I hope it will help a little.'

They reached the end of the corridor and entered through double doors. Daisy looked up from her computer screen and smiled at them. She wore blue scrubs and her long black hair was twisted into a knot at the back of her head. This had been where Meadows had first met his wife. With less than a year since they got married, he still felt a flutter of excitement every time he saw her.

'Have you come to see Alex?' Daisy asked.

'Yes,' Edris said. 'Please tell me you've got something for us. We could do with a breakthrough.'

Daisy laughed. 'You're not expecting much, are you? Come on, I'll take you through.'

Meadows followed Daisy through another set of double doors. The temperature instantly dropped, and the smell of chemicals permeated the air. Alex's remains were laid out on a metal gurney, but it was not this that drew Meadows' eyes. Under the harsh lights, he could see a paleness to Daisy's skin, and under her eyes were dark circles. He thought back to that morning when he kissed her goodbye. She had looked unwell, but when he asked her, she had reassured him that she was fine.

'As you can see, all the bones were recovered,' Daisy said.

Meadows switched his thoughts back to Alex.

Daisy moved to the top of the gurney. 'There is a fracture to the front of the skull. This would be just above the forehead.'

'Would that injury have killed him?' Meadows asked.

'I can't say with any certainty. There is also a fracture to his shoulder.' She pointed. 'As well as to his left humerus and radius.'

'Could he have sustained these injuries from a fall?' Edris asked.

'It's possible, particularly if he fell head first. There is no damage to the leg bones, but if that was the case, I would expect to see some injury to the right arm. You would automatically put out both arms to break your fall.'

Meadows thought about the drop down into the cave where they had found Alex. 'Unless he was unconscious. He could have been hit over the head and then pushed into the cave.'

'Or he could have just fallen,' Edris said. 'The entrance was narrow. Maybe he didn't have enough room to put forward both arms. He would have been injured and possibly disorientated. He could have dragged himself forward, further in the cave, and died.'

Meadows shook his head. 'He would have gone down the cave feet first. Then you've got the fact that the entrance was covered and his phone and car keys are missing.'

'The injuries could also have been caused by a weapon,' Daisy said. 'A lot of it is guesswork. It's not my speciality, but I can make a few calls and get in an expert.'

'Even if it was a weapon, the chance of finding it after all this time is virtually zero,' Meadows said. 'The only way we'll know what happened to Alex is if the killer tells us.'

'We have to catch them first,' Edris said. 'The trail is not only cold, it's evaporated.'

'Alex's clothes are with forensics,' Daisy said. 'Initial tests show blood on the coat and trousers. I imagine a lot of it would have come from the head wound.'

Meadows' phone rang at the same time as Daisy's phone. Meadows moved away to answer it. As he listened to the call, he could hear Daisy talking in the background. He ended the call and turned to Edris.

'Suspicious death. Deryn Gibson.'

Chapter Twenty

Edris was quiet in the passenger seat and Meadows wondered what was troubling him. He'd been working flat out on the case. Staying late and getting in early. It was almost like an obsession to solve the case quickly. On top of that, his usual spark and quirky sense of humour were dimmed.

'OK, enough. What's going on with you?' Meadows asked.

Edris scowled. 'Nothing.'

'Is it girlfriend trouble? I know we all tease you, and the team enforced a ban on talk of your love life, but forget about that. Talk to me. You know I won't judge you.'

'Has it been that obvious?' Edris asked.

'Yes. Anything you tell me will stay in this car. I promise.'

'I know, and I trust you. If there is one person I could talk to, it would be you, but I can't right now. I'll tell you everything as soon as the case is over.'

'You're not ill, are you?'

'No.'

'OK, I'm here for you when you're ready.'

'Thanks.'

Meadows glanced at Edris and saw the mist in his eyes. It gave him an uncomfortable feeling in the pit of his stomach. He was tempted to offer some time off but knew Edris wouldn't take it. At least he could keep an eye on him at work. Up ahead, he could see an ambulance and police car parked by the curb outside a semi-detached house. He forced away his concerns over Edris as he parked the car.

The back of the ambulance was open, and two paramedics sat inside. PC Matt Hanes was talking to a neighbour and a few people gathered on the opposite side of the road.

'They're all out now, but I bet not one of them saw or heard anything,' Edris said.

'You can't blame them. Wouldn't you want to know what was going on if you saw this lot outside your neighbour's house? I imagine they have known Deryn for years. They see an ambulance and police cars, and Deryn hasn't been brought out. They know it's not good.' Meadows saw Daisy pull up behind them. 'OK, let's go.'

Hanes moved away from the neighbour and joined the three of them outside Deryn's house. 'She was found by Gareth Hendon. Looks like she's taken a fall down the stairs,' he said. 'Given her connection to recent events, I thought it best to call it in.'

Meadows nodded. 'You did the right thing. Did Gareth say why he was here?'

'He said Deryn called him last night. She was a bit upset but didn't want to talk to him over the phone, so he arranged to call around.'

'Did he have any idea what she was upset about?' Meadows asked.

'No. She said something like "I can't believe this is happening again" but he had no idea what she meant by that.'

'How did he get in?'

'He said the door was unlocked. He checked for a pulse and then called for an ambulance.'

'Right, let's take a look.' Meadows opened the boot of his car and took out latex gloves and shoe covers. He handed a set to Edris and Daisy, then he moved to the porch before slipping the covers on discreetly.

Meadows pushed open the door and was met with warm air which carried the smell of urine. The room was open plan with a staircase to the right. Deryn lay at the bottom of the stairs. Her eyes were open and her jaw slack. He stepped closer and his eyes moved over her body. There was a gash on her forehead and her hair was awry. Her jumper had risen and there was a dark stain on the crotch of her jeans. Her left leg was twisted at an awkward angle.

'Looks like a fall,' Edris said.

Daisy knelt to start her examination as Meadows looked up and down the stairs and then to the wall behind Deryn's head. There was a white radiator, and on inspection, he saw blood on the corner.

'Take a look at this,' Daisy said.

Meadows crouched down next to Daisy.

'See these small red-purplish spots in her eyes and on her face.' Daisy pointed. 'Petechial haemorrhage. You see this in cases of asphyxiation.'

'Are you saying this wasn't an accident?' Edris asked.

'I'll know more when I do the post-mortem, but from initial examination, it does appear that asphyxiation could be the cause of death.'

'Are there any marks on her neck?' Edris asked.

Daisy moved Deryn's hair to take a closer look. 'No.'

'Better call in forensics,' Meadows said.

Edris nodded and moved away.

'Time of death?' Meadows asked.

'I'll take some readings,' Daisy said.

Meadows moved and looked around the room. It was decorated with pink floral wallpaper, and while not untidy, it looked like a well-used room. There was a large-screen television on a stand with plastic boxes, filled with toys, stacked at the side. He thought about the container that Cora had been found in. These boxes were clear, while the one in the river had been red. On the coffee table, there was a magazine, a half-empty mug of tea, and a mobile phone. He moved into the kitchen.

The small room was cluttered with various jars, containers, and appliances on the worktops. The shelving held a steamer, coffee machine, and three blenders. There was just enough room for a small table and two chairs. The sink was empty and the drainboard was clear. A door led off to a bathroom. He took a quick look and then returned to the sitting room.

'Forensics are on their way,' Edris said.

'If she had breakfast, then she cleared it away. She's dressed and the bathroom is downstairs. If she fell down the stairs, then what was she doing up there?'

'Her leg is broken,' Daisy said. 'There is also swelling to the wrist and a dislocated shoulder. It's consistent with a fall.'

'Or a push,' Edris said. 'That would mean someone went upstairs with her, pushed her down, and when that didn't work, they finished her off.'

'She hasn't been dead long,' Daisy said. 'I'd say she died roughly between eight and nine this morning.'

'She was expecting Gareth,' Edris said. 'Maybe he turned up early and didn't like what she had to tell him. He kills her, then phones for an ambulance. He said he checked for a pulse, so that would account for any of his DNA being found.'

'If that was the case, why push her down the stairs? He could easily overpower her,' Meadows said.

'Because he wanted it to look like an accident.'

'Whoever pushed her persuaded her to go upstairs, or she was showing them something,' Meadows said. 'Let's take a look.'

He carefully moved around Deryn to get up the stairs. At the top was a small landing with a door on each side. Meadows opened one of the doors and stepped inside.

'Looks like this one belongs to the granddaughter,' he said.

'Where does she sleep?' Edris asked.

The room was packed with toys. Two large doll houses, dolls of various sizes, and piles of soft toys covered the floor space. In between were games, art materials, and Lego. Meadows noticed all the teddy bears had necklaces or beads around their necks. Some even had earrings pushed through their ears. The walls were painted purple with unicorn decals. The bed had so many soft toys covering it, you couldn't see the duvet.

'If this is Maisie's room, then she's a little old for all these teddy bears,' Edris said. 'There is nothing here for Ieuan, so where does he sleep?'

'Maybe she only looked after Maisie. It could be it was too much for her to look after both the children.'

'Looks like she spoilt the child,' Edris said.

Meadows nodded. 'Compensating for something? Perhaps the fact that Maisie lost her father, or because of the new baby.'

They moved to the next room which was a little bigger. There was a double bed in the centre with overhead storage. The bed was made, and a set of pyjamas was folded neatly on the pillow. Most of the cupboards contained clothes. There was a drawer filled with various documents, including an out-of-date passport. A second drawer was filled with photographs. Meadows flicked through. They were mainly of Laura during different stages of her life. A few featured Deryn and Maisie.

'There's nothing here,' Meadows said. 'It doesn't look like anything has been disturbed. We'll bag the phone and get it to tech to see who she called in the last few days. We need to go and inform Laura before someone else tells her.'

As Meadows walked down the stairs, he tried to visualise the events that led to Deryn's death. He imagined the poor woman's fear as she fell. The confusion. The thought that the person who should be helping was killing her. Had she realised her mistake in those last few moments?

Daisy stood up when he reached the bottom of the staircase. 'There's nothing more I can do here,' she said. 'I'm happy for her to be photographed and moved.'

'Go and get yourself something to eat,' Meadows said. 'You look exhausted, love.'

Daisy smiled at him. 'I'm fine. I didn't sleep all that well last night. I'll see you later.'

Edris bagged the phone, tagged it, and they stepped outside the house. As Meadows was taking off his shoe covers, he heard a car screech to a stop. He looked up in time to see Laura get out of the car and start running towards the house. He moved quickly to intercept her.

'Where's my mother?' Laura looked past Meadows to the waiting ambulance. 'Gareth called to say there had been an accident.'

'Laura, I'm so very sorry—'

'No, don't say it,' Laura said. She looked from Meadows to Edris. 'She can't be… The ambulance is here. Why are they not doing anything?'

'I'm sorry, Laura,' Edris said. 'It was too late to help her.'

'I want to see her.' Laura tried to move past Meadows.

Meadows put his hand gently on her arm. 'You can't go in there at the moment. I promise you'll have a chance to see her later.'

Laura's eyes were wild, and she was breathing fast. She put her hand to her chest. Meadows could see the panic and shock was about to overwhelm her.

'Come and sit in the car for a moment,' he said. He guided her to the back of the police car and waited for her to calm down. 'Is there someone we can call for you? Family, or a friend?'

'Erm… no. Gareth has enough to deal with at the moment and so do Alex's parents.'

'What about Gareth's mother, Beth?' Edris asked. 'She could sit with you, and help look after the children.'

Laura nodded.

'When was the last time you saw your mother?' Meadows asked.

'This morning, when I picked up Maisie for school. Ieuan stayed with Beth last night. Mum found it difficult to manage the two of them.'

'We are going to have to talk to Maisie. The sooner the better. We can arrange for Beth to go to the school.'

'Why?'

Meadows hated to do this on top of the shock of her mother's death. 'I'm afraid until we know more, we will be treating your mother's death as suspicious.'

'I don't understand.' Laura put her head in her hands. 'This can't be happening again.'

That was the second time Meadows had heard that phrase spoken today. It was the word "again" that troubled him. Deryn knew something that got her killed, and as he looked at Laura, sobbing, he wondered if she was the next target.

Chapter Twenty-one

Meadows watched Beth making tea in Laura's kitchen. Laura was with Maisie in the sitting room, and they were giving them some space for Laura to explain what had happened.

'I don't know what to say to her,' Beth said.

'Just being here for them both is a help. It's all anyone can do at the moment,' Meadows said.

'I can stay for a few hours, but then I have to get back for Olwen. She's gone to the daycare centre. Ieuan is still in school. I thought it best to leave him there for now.'

Meadows nodded.

'Laura was reluctant to ask Gareth, or Alex's parents to help,' Edris said. 'Do you know if she has any other family?'

'A brother, but they don't stay in touch. As far as I know, Laura had very little to do with her father growing up. I don't think there is any other family.'

'What about a boyfriend?' Meadows asked.

'I'm sure she goes out on dates, but there is no one special.'

'Did you know Deryn well?' Meadows asked.

'I wouldn't say very well. I'd see her at family gatherings and sometimes she would pick Ieuan up when I was looking after him.'

'Did she ever share any concerns she had about the family? Or tell you anything about her past?'

Beth shook her head and handed a cup of tea to Edris. 'She wouldn't have confided in me. She never shared any personal information. To be honest, I know very little about her life. She mainly talked about Laura and the children.'

'We know she rang Gareth last night. He said she was upset. Would that be something she would usually do? I mean turn to Gareth for help.'

'Deryn was very fond of Gareth. It was the same with Alex. Before he went missing, he was like a son to her. I guess Gareth took his place and—'

Beth was interrupted by shouts coming from the sitting room.

'Doesn't sound like it's going too well,' Edris said.

'Let's go in,' Meadows said. 'The sooner we get the questions out of the way, the better it will be for the two of them.'

Meadows was first through the door. Maisie was standing in front of Laura. Her face was red, and her fists were balled at her sides.

'I told you. She was OK this morning,' Maisie shouted.

Laura gave Meadows a desperate look. 'Come here.' She held out her arms to Maisie. 'I know this is difficult.'

Maisie turned, saw Beth, and ran into her arms.

Beth wrapped her arms around the child. 'It's OK to be upset,' she said. 'Come and sit with me. You need to be brave now and help your mum.' Beth led Maisie to an armchair and sat. Maisie squeezed next to her.

Meadows took a seat next to Edris. 'Maisie, I need to ask you a few questions. Is that OK?'

Maisie shook her head and tried to whisper in Beth's ear. Beth moved her head away.

'None of that,' Beth said. 'You're old enough to speak for yourself, and you know it's rude to whisper.'

'I hear you are a very good pupil in school,' Meadows said. 'What's your favourite subject?'

'I like writing stories,' Maisie said.

'What's your favourite colour?'

'Purple.'

'What do you like for breakfast?'

'Jam on toast.'

Meadows could see the child relaxing. 'Did you have breakfast with your grandmother this morning?'

Maisie nodded. 'Nanna always makes me jam on toast.'

'Did you eat breakfast in your pyjamas?'

'Yeah. I always have breakfast first, then get dressed.'

'Was Nanna in her pyjamas?'

'No, she was already dressed when I got up.'

'What did you do after you got dressed?'

'I came back downstairs, Nanna did my hair, then Mum beeped the horn. I kissed Nanna goodbye and went to school.'

'Did anyone call at the house to see your Nanna before you left?'

Maisie shook her head.

'Did she speak to anyone on the phone?'

'No.'

Meadows leaned forward. 'Last night, your nanna phoned your dad. She wanted to talk to him about something. Something she was worried about. Do you know what that was?'

Maisie fidgeted in the chair.

'You won't get into any trouble if you tell me.'

Maisie looked at Laura, then at Beth who nodded her encouragement.

'When Gran was making the cake for Cora, Jamie came into the kitchen. He tipped something into the cake mix. I thought it was poison. That's why I didn't eat any.'

'You mean the christening cake I made?' Beth asked.

Maisie nodded. 'Then at the party, he tipped a bottle of stuff into the fishbowl.'

'Fishbowl?' Meadows asked.

'I made a bowl of punch,' Beth said. 'It was non-alcoholic, for those who were driving or didn't want to drink. Jamie made some joke about it being a fishbowl. It's some large bowl of cocktails that are shared at student parties.'

'I told Nanna last night what he had done, and she said she would sort it out.'

'Thank you for telling us, Maisie,' Meadows said.

'You won't tell Jamie that I told you, will you? He'll hit me.'

'No. Don't worry about it. You've done the right thing. I don't need to ask you any more questions. You've been very helpful.'

Maisie smiled.

'Why don't we go upstairs and pack a few things? The detectives need to talk to your mum,' Beth said. 'You can stay with me tonight.' She looked at Laura. 'Is that OK?'

'Thank you,' Laura said.

'But I want to go to Dad's house,' Maisie said.

Beth stood up and took Maisie by the hand. 'Come on, we'll talk about seeing your dad later.'

Meadows heard Beth and Maisie going upstairs. He turned to Edris. 'We're going to need to talk to Jamie.'

'I'll make some calls,' Edris said. He excused himself and left the room.

'I don't think you should read too much into what Maisie says about Jamie,' Laura said. 'She has a very active imagination. I really can't see that he would hurt Mum. He's just a kid.'

'This morning, when we told you about your mother, you said, this can't be happening again. What did you mean by that?'

'It's just Alex, and Ceri, and now Mum. It seems like everyone close to me is taken.'

'Your mother said a similar thing to Gareth last night. What do you think she meant?'

'I don't know. Maybe the same thing.'

'But that wouldn't make sense. She found out about Alex a week ago. I'm just wondering why she would say that to Gareth last night. Perhaps she made some sort of connection or knew something. Is there anything in the past, that you can think of, that is similar to recent events? Something to do with Cora or perhaps Alex being found.'

Laura thought for a moment. 'No. I can't think of anything.'

'Did she call you last night?'

'No.'

'Why do you think she phoned Gareth?'

Laura twisted her hands. 'I don't know. Maybe she didn't want to worry me.'

'Did your mother seem upset or worried when you saw her this morning?'

'I didn't see her this morning.'

'Oh, I thought you said that's the last time you saw her.'

'I didn't go into the house. I just pulled up outside and beeped the horn. Maisie came out, got in the car, and I waved before pulling off.'

'How has your mother been since Cora's party?'

'OK. I mean, she was upset about what happened to Cora, and then Alex was found. She loved Alex. He was always doing odd jobs around the house. It was Alex, Gareth, and Henry who laid her patio for her and redesigned the garden. They'd always be around doing something. She'd bake cakes for them and take them cups of tea. I'm sure she used to invent jobs for them so she could have them around.'

'Did she talk to you about what she thought might have happened to Alex, or who might have put Cora in the river?'

'No.'

'Not even speculation?'

Laura shook her head. 'To be honest, I haven't spent much time with her over the past couple of weeks. With work, and everything that's been going on.' Her eyes filled with tears. 'Do you think she knew something and that's why…' She rubbed her fingers under her eyes. 'I'm sure she would have told me.' Her lips quivered. 'I'm going to miss her so much.'

'We'll leave it there for now,' Meadows said. 'There is just one more thing I need to ask you. We know that when Gareth jilted Jenna, it was because Alex had told Gareth that Jenna was cheating. More specifically, that the baby wasn't his. We've learned since that it was Ceri who told Alex, and she said that information had come from you.'

'Let me guess. You heard that from Jenna.'

Meadows didn't comment.

Laura sighed. 'It's true that the information came from Ceri. She didn't want to be the one to tell Gareth. She hated causing upset to anyone. We thought it best that the information came from Alex. I didn't know him very well at the time, but he was Ceri's cousin. Ceri was relieved when Alex agreed to talk to Gareth. She made him promise to keep her name out of it. She was afraid of Jenna finding out.'

'Afraid in what way?' Meadows asked.

'Jenna has always had a temper. I don't mean she would have hurt Ceri, but she would have been angry. I know Jenna and Alex argued when she came back, but I didn't know that he had thrown Ceri under the bus. Maybe Ceri told Jenna it was me to avoid an argument. She was with Gareth by then. Still, I can't see Ceri doing that. I don't think she would lie.'

'Did Ceri tell you the name of the other man Jenna was supposedly seeing?'

Laura shook her head.

Edris popped his head around the door and beckoned to him. Meadows went through to the kitchen and closed the door behind him.

'I spoke to Gareth and told him we need to talk to Jamie. I asked if he could bring him to the station. Then I arranged for an appropriate adult. I thought it was the best option. Gareth called back to say Jamie didn't turn up at school this morning. No one has seen him all day.'

Chapter Twenty-two

'Where did you find him?' Meadows asked.

'Down the cycle path,' Blackwell said. 'He was by the river with a bunch of mates. Stoned. They all were. Most of them scarpered. He's had something to eat and drink. I've put him in interview room one with the AP, and a solicitor. Think he's sobered up now. Gareth and Jenna are kicking off in reception.'

'OK, you can lead the interview. Valentine, Edris, can you have a chat with Gareth and Jenna? Keep them occupied and see what you can get out of them.'

'Yeah, no problem,' Valentine said.

Jamie was slouched in the chair next to the appropriate adult who introduced herself as Debbie. The solicitor, Callum Daley, sat on the other side. Meadows took a seat and looked at the teenager in front of him. He had red hair, like his mother. It was shaved in at the sides, and the top was grown out so it flopped over his eyes. He had a pale complexion, a smattering of freckles across his nose, and acne on his cheeks.

Jamie looked at Meadows. 'Are you going to read me my rights or what?'

Meadows smiled. 'You're not under arrest, yet, but we would like to ask you a few questions.'

'Yeah, well I'm not gonna answer your questions.' He pushed the chair back. 'I'm going home.'

'Not so fast,' Blackwell said. 'Just because you are not under arrest now, doesn't mean you won't be if you don't cooperate.'

'I think it's best you stay and talk to us,' Meadows said.

Jamie huffed. 'So I bunked off school and had a toke. Big fucking deal.'

'This isn't a game, Jamie,' Blackwell said. 'Deryn Gibson was found dead this morning.'

'Fuck all to do with me.'

'You can cut out the language, and the big-man act,' Blackwell growled.

The solicitor raised his eyebrow and Blackwell sat back in his chair.

'When was the last time you saw Deryn?' Meadows asked.

'Dunno. Probably the christening party.'

'Have you spoken to her since?'

'No.'

'We received some information that you put a substance into the christening cake mix,' Meadows said.

A grin spread across Jamie's face. 'You got any evidence of that?'

'You were seen,' Blackwell said.

'Yeah, well she's lying,' Jamie said.

The solicitor touched Jamie's forearm as a warning.

'Who is lying, Jamie?' Blackwell asked.

The solicitor leaned over and whispered something in Jamie's ear.

'I'm not getting in shit because of that little bitch,' Jamie said.

The solicitor sighed. 'You don't have to answer.'

'That's true,' Meadows said. 'Your solicitor is here to give you advice. You can choose to give a no-comment answer. In that case, we will conclude that you have something to hide. On the other hand, if you think someone is lying about you, it's your opportunity to tell your side of the story.'

Jamie looked at the solicitor.

'Would you like some time alone to take some advice?' Meadows asked.

'I think a few minutes would be a good idea,' the solicitor said.

Meadows nodded and stepped out of the room with Blackwell.

'You're being too soft,' Blackwell complained.

'He's right. We have no evidence. Our best chance is to get him to talk.'

'He's not going to confess.'

'No, but if he clams up, we know we are on the right track.'

They went back into the interview room. Meadows could tell by the solicitor's face that the talk hadn't gone well.

'OK, Jamie. You said someone lied about you putting something in the cake. Who do you think is lying?'

'Probably Maisie. Spiteful little bitch, or it could be Gran. She doesn't like me much.'

'The thing is. If you say Maisie or your grandmother lied, then that implies that you had the opportunity, at a time when you think one of them could have seen you, to put something in the cake,' Meadows said. 'For example, if someone accused me of putting something into the christening cake, my answer would be, I haven't been near the cake. Then I'd ask when the incident was supposed to have happened. Bit of a giveaway that you think it was Maisie or your gran that saw you. You were also seen tipping a bottle into the punch at the party. There were a lot of people at the party.'

Jamie's eyes narrowed.

Blackwell leaned forward. 'The cake was laced and so was the punch. Your baby sister was put in the river, and a woman who was going to confront you about what you did, is dead.'

For the first time since the interview started, Meadows saw fear in Jamie's eyes.

'You didn't turn up for school this morning,' Meadows said. 'It doesn't look good for you.'

'I was with my mates.'

'Really,' Blackwell said. 'I'm sure that's what they'll say when asked, but did they meet you at your house this morning? Or did you arrange to meet them by the river? Were you alone for any length of time before you met up with them?'

Jamie reddened. 'I didn't do anything to the old bat.'

'Then you better be straight with us,' Meadows said.

Jamie glanced at the solicitor and then looked back at Meadows. 'OK, I put some weed in the cake mix.'

'How much?' Meadows asked.

Jamie shrugged. 'I had a half bag. I only had a couple of joints from that. I tipped the rest in.'

Blackwell raised his eyebrows. 'Half an ounce?'

Jamie nodded.

'Why?' Meadows asked.

'For fun, innit. I was pissed at Dad. He caught me smoking and had a right go. I bet he smoked when he was my age, but now he acts like he has a stick up his arse.' Jamie huffed. 'I didn't want to go to the stupid party. I thought if everyone loosened up it would be more fun. It worked. You should have heard them giggling. Then some of them had the munchies and scoffed more cake. Gran was flaked out in the summer house.'

'What about the punch?' Meadows asked.

'It was just a bottle of vodka. It was a laugh, that's all.'

'You think it's funny to spike people's drink and food,' Blackwell said. 'Do you think it would have been funny if one of those guests had an accident when driving home? Killed themselves or somebody else. Or what if someone had a bad reaction to the cannabis and alcohol? Would that have been funny? Look what happened to your sister.'

'That wasn't my fault.'

'Everyone at the party was stoned. Less observant. Is that what you wanted?' Blackwell asked. 'You could sneak off with Cora without anyone taking notice.'

'No! What sort of sicko do you think I am?' Jamie shook his head. 'I wish we'd never moved here.'

'Why?' Meadows asked.

'Things were OK when it was just me and Mum. My Dad is a dick. He doesn't want me around and Mum is too wrapped up in looking after the baby to notice what he's doing.'

'What is it that you think your father is doing?' Meadows asked.

'Drugging her.'

'Who?'

'My Mum. She was fine until we moved back. Then suddenly she gets ill. Now she's so off her face half the time I don't think she'd notice if I disappeared. It's not the antidepressants. I tried a couple to see if I'd get high. They didn't do anything for me. He's giving her something. I'm sure.'

'Why would your father do that?' Meadows asked.

Jamie shrugged. 'All they do is argue. I've told you everything. Can I go now?'

'For now,' Blackwell said, 'while we decide whether or not to charge you with drugging the guests at the party. Meanwhile, I would strongly advise you to give a voluntary DNA sample, so we can eliminate you from Deryn Gibson's murder investigation.'

Meadows ended the interview and went back upstairs to the office. Valentine, Edris, and Paskin were waiting to hear the results of the interview.

'So, do you think he's guilty?' Edris asked.

'I can't see a motive,' Meadows said. 'Even if Deryn had called him out over the cake, he would have said Maisie was lying. I can't see him killing her.'

'He could have put Cora in the river,' Blackwell said. 'If he got that off his face, perhaps he and his mates thought it would be funny to float the baby down the river. Maybe one was supposed to catch her and missed.'

Edris nodded. 'If Deryn saw that, then it's something Jamie wouldn't want to be known.'

'He'd have to be pretty out of it to do something like that,' Valentine said.

'I think he's telling the truth,' Meadows said. 'He's just an unhappy teenager. One thing's for certain – he didn't kill Alex Morris. He was too young.'

'That doesn't mean anything,' Blackwell said. 'I am not sold on the cases being connected. It's just made things more complicated. Take away the house fire, Alex, and Ceri, and what are you left with? The kid is unhappy here. He doesn't get on with his dad. Now he's stuck with a new baby sister. He is reckless. He drugged his granny.'

'OK. Talk to his mates and let's see if he gives a DNA sample. Forensics are still processing the scene. Hopefully, they'll find something. Meanwhile, statements taken from anyone at the party can't be taken seriously. The whole lot of them were stoned.'

Edris huffed. 'That's just great.'

'Chris from tech called,' Paskin said. 'He has unlocked Deryn's phone. The last call she made was to a Mark

Jones. I've spoken to him. He's Deryn's son. He's coming in the morning to see his mother. I've arranged for you to meet him there.'

'Thanks,' Meadows said. 'It's late. I think you should all go home. Tomorrow, we need to check out where everyone was when Deryn was killed. Particularly the suspects in Cora's case. We also need to talk to Ceri's family. While I hate opening old wounds, I think we need to inform the family that we'll be treating her death as suspicious. It's possible that Ceri had concerns that she may have confided in her family.'

Meadows noticed that Edris had grabbed his coat and was heading out the door. Not even a goodbye. He hoped whatever was troubling him would be sorted out soon.

* * *

Edris was glad to get out of the office. He'd found it hard seeing Laura upset, and not being able to comfort her. It didn't help that Meadows had offered an opportunity to talk. He had been tempted but it was too late now. The moment had passed.

He knew he was digging himself deeper into trouble. His hopes for solving the case were slipping away. It just seemed to get more complicated. He realised he was gripping the steering wheel too hard, and his concentration was wandering. The last thing he needed now was to have an accident. He was glad when he pulled up outside Laura's house. He'd just unclipped his seatbelt when his phone bleeped with a message alert. He hoped it wasn't work, and was tempted to ignore it. The problem was that it may be Laura texting to say she had an unexpected visitor. It wouldn't be good to run into Gareth or anyone else involved in the investigation. He took his phone from his pocket and opened the messages. His stomach flipped.

Stay away from Laura if you know what's good for you. I'll be watching!

The message was from an unknown number. Edris looked around. There was no one walking on the pavement. He looked at each parked car. They appeared to be empty. He hit reply and started to type "Who is this?" then changed his mind. He'd ignore it for now and ask tech to trace the number. He got out of the car and knocked on the door.

When Laura opened the door, Edris could see she had been crying.

'I'm so sorry,' he said as he stepped inside and pulled her close.

'I still can't believe Mum is gone. It doesn't feel real.' Laura sobbed.

He could feel her body trembling as she clung to him. 'I wish there was something I could do. I felt so useless when you heard the news, and I could do nothing to comfort you.'

Laura pulled away from the embrace. 'It's not your fault. You're here now. That's what matters.'

'Is there anything I can do for you?'

'I don't know. To be honest, I can't think straight. Just keep me company. The children are staying with Beth tonight. I thought it best until I can pull myself together.'

'Have you eaten?'

Laura shook her head. 'I'm not hungry.'

'You need to eat something. I'll cook something light and maybe you could try and eat a little.'

Laura nodded.

While Edris made the omelettes, Laura sat on a stool by the worktop and opened a bottle of wine.

'It doesn't seem right drinking but I really need something.'

'There is no right or wrong in this situation,' Edris said. 'You need to do whatever it takes to get you through.'

'What happens now? Please, I want to know.'

Edris stopped grating cheese and turned around to face her. 'There will need to be a post-mortem, so it may be some time before you can lay her to rest.'

'I'm going to see her tomorrow. I want to go, but part of me is scared.'

'Is there someone who can go with you for support?'

'No. I'd rather do it by myself.'

Edris wondered why she couldn't call on her family members. He knew she at least had one brother, but this wasn't the time for questions. 'Have you been assigned a family liaison officer?'

'Yes, Brianna. I met her today.'

'I'm glad it's her. She's lovely.'

Laura nodded. 'She didn't give me any insight into the investigation.'

'That's normal, but if there are any developments, she will inform you.'

'You could tell me what's happening in the investigation.'

'I shouldn't really discuss that.' Edris turned back to the cooking.

'I know, but this is my mother.'

Edris could understand her need for information.

'At the moment we are looking at your mother's contacts and family. We are meeting with your brother tomorrow.' Edris turned to face Laura.

'Oh. I haven't seen him for years, but I don't want to go into that now. I'm not sure how much contact he had with Mum. I can't see that he'd be able to help.'

'It may be possible that she knew something about Alex's murder, or Cora's abduction, and talked to him about it.'

'If that's the case, I wish she would have talked to me.'

Laura became quiet as Edris continued cooking. When the omelettes were ready, he laid the kitchen table and served them up. She ate a few mouthfuls and washed it down with wine before refilling her glass.

'Is it OK?' Edris asked.

'Yes. I'm sorry, it just feels like every mouthful is sticking in my throat. It does taste good though. Maybe I'll try and eat a bit more later.'

'Why don't you take your wine into the sitting room? I'll clean up in here.'

'Thanks.' Laura stood up and kissed him before leaving the kitchen.

Edris washed up and then wiped the worktops down. He looked around. The kitchen wasn't up to his standard. He preferred clutter-free spaces, but he was trying his best to compromise. He turned off the light and went into the sitting room.

Laura was sitting on the sofa with her legs tucked underneath her. The wine glass was in her hand and she was rubbing the stem with her thumb and forefinger.

'How are you doing?' Edris asked as he took a seat next to her.

She leaned her head against his shoulder. 'Not good. I just can't believe that anyone would hurt my mother. She was in her home. A place where she should have been safe. I've been thinking, it had to be someone she trusted. I don't even want to think about how she must have felt, but I can't stop myself. I'm so scared.'

Edris took her hand. 'What are you scared of?'

'That I will be next.'

Edris' stomach clenched. For the first time, he felt like he had a future with someone. It wasn't perfect but he thought they had a chance of a life together. The idea that someone could hurt her made him feel sick.

'I'm not going to let anything happen to you. I'll take some time off work and stay with you until this is over.'

Laura shook her head. 'What if this never ends? You can't put your life on hold and neither can I. The best thing you can do is go to work and catch this bastard. Even better, stay away from me. I don't want anything to happen to you.' A tear tracked down Laura's cheek.

'Don't cry,' Edris said and pulled her close. 'Nothing is going to happen to me. I can take care of myself.'

'So could Alex. I'm better off on my own. That way, no one else will get hurt.'

'What do you mean?'

'I didn't want to tell you, but I've had text messages.'

'From whom?'

'I don't know.' Laura grabbed her phone from the coffee table, opened her messages, and handed it to Edris.

Edris felt anger spike in his veins as he read the messages that had been sent over the last week.

I know what you've been up to, you whore.

I've seen that detective going into your house.

I know where he lives.

He stayed the night again. Slut!

You better get rid of him before I do it for you.

'Have you had messages like this before?' Edris asked.

'Yeah, but I ignored them and blocked the number. It stopped for a while but then started up again. I changed my number and only gave it to close friends and family. I haven't had messages like this for a long time.'

'When was the last time you had a message before these ones?'

'About a year ago. I had started dating again. Each time I went out, I got a message the next day. They were all similar to what I'm getting now.'

'Is that when you changed your number?'

Laura nodded.

'Do you have any idea who is sending them?'

Laura shrugged.

'If you know, you need to tell me.'

'It's not that simple.'

'It is that simple. This could be the same person that killed your mother, and Alex. Just tell me what you know.'

'I can't.'

Edris felt his frustration building. 'Who are you protecting?'

'No one. You know too well if there is no evidence, nothing can be done. I'll either accuse someone innocent or I'll be in more danger because they'll know I talked.'

'I'll make sure your name stays out of it. You're obviously a target. If you don't do something now, then someone else close to you could get hurt. Actually, you don't have to do anything. I've had a text message. I'll take it to the boss in the morning.'

'How's that going to work? You'd have to say you've been seeing me. The same if I show the messages I received to the police, they'll want to know who I'm seeing. You'll lose your job.'

'I don't care about that now. I want to keep you safe.'

Laura shook her head. 'I'm not letting you throw your career away. There has to be another way.'

'Then give me a name or something to go on.'

Laura nodded. 'Take a look at what happened at Ogof y Cysg Eira. It's where I should have died.'

Chapter Twenty-three

The rain lashed against Meadows' back as he made a dash from his car to the police station. He pushed open the door, stepped inside, and pulled down his hood.

'Just the man I want,' Sergeant Folland called from the reception area.

As Meadows walked over to Folland, he noticed a woman was sitting on one of the plastic chairs. He could see her coat was wet and her hair damp. He guessed she'd also been caught in the heavy shower. On the chair next to her was a large recycling bag which looked to be full of clothes.

'This is Sally,' Folland said. 'She has some information for you.'

Meadows smiled at the woman. 'OK, come with me and I'll see if I can find us a cup of tea.'

Sally beamed. 'That would be lovely.'

'Room one is empty,' Folland said. 'I'll get one of the boys to fetch some tea.'

'Thanks.'

Meadows led Sally into the interview room and took her details. 'So you have some information for me?'

'I wanted to show you these.' Sally placed the recycling bag on the table. 'I work in a charity shop. The cat shelter, in Ystrad. Do you know it?'

'No.'

'Oh it's a great place and people are so generous. The cat shelter itself is up at Bryn Coch. It's sad how many cats we have to take in. Some people just move house and leave them, and don't get me started on neutering. We've just had six kittens dumped at the door in a box and...'

While Meadows liked cats, he had a feeling that Sally would happily talk about them for hours. He was glad when a uniformed officer brought in two cups of tea.

'Oh, thank you,' Sally said.

'You wanted to show me something in the bag,' Meadows said.

'Oh yes. I saw the appeal you put out asking for information on that man found in the cave.'

'Alex Morris.'

'Yes. Well, there was a picture of him, and a description of what he was wearing.'

Meadows tried not to smile. He imagined it would be easy to find a hiking outfit, similar to the one that Alex was wearing, in most charity shops in the area.

'So these are clothes donated to the shop that you think may be Alex's?'

'No, not the clothes. Well, some of them may be his.' She opened the bag and took out a box. 'I wanted to show you this.'

Meadows took the square box which was made of black faux leather. There was nothing unusual about it. Just the standard-size gift box that housed jewellery. He opened the box and saw a St Christopher nestled among the blue satin. He felt a flicker of excitement.

'His name is on the back with an inscription,' Sally said.

Meadows didn't want to turn it over without gloves. 'When did this come in?'

'Sometime yesterday. It was with this bag of clothes. People leave bags outside all the time. I didn't get around to opening it until this morning. I went in early to sort through some items. That's when I saw it. I thought I better bring it in along with the clothes.'

'Do you have CCTV outside the shop?'

Sally shook her head. 'It wouldn't have helped, as this was left around the back. There's access from the street behind. Sometimes people use that entrance if they have a lot of stuff – house clearances, that sort of thing.'

Meadows stood up. 'Thank you for bringing in these things. You've been very helpful.'

'I'm glad. It's such a pity. He looked like a nice boy.'

Sally drank her tea and Meadows saw her back to reception before taking the bag upstairs.

The team put on gloves and each item of clothing was taken from the bag, photographed, and put into labelled evidence bags. There was a mixture of men's and women's clothing along with a couple of woollen hats and scarves.

'Quite a coincidence that these appear outside the shop the same day Deryn Gibson is murdered,' Valentine said.

'Maybe she saw the necklace in someone's house and intended to tell someone about it,' Paskin said.

'Why not just report it?' Valentine asked.

Meadows looked along the line of bags. 'It could be that she wanted to protect someone and was seeking advice.'

'Yeah, well she chose the wrong person,' Edris said.

Blackwell peered at the St Christopher. 'Why keep it in the first place?'

'Why a charity shop?' Meadows asked. 'It would have been easier and safer to just throw it out with the rubbish. I think someone wanted us to find it. Let's get this stuff off to forensics.' He checked the time. 'We better get going. Mark Jones will be at the hospital soon.'

* * *

As they walked down the corridor, Meadows could see a man sitting on a chair outside the chapel of rest. A woman was standing in front of him. He recognised her as Daisy's assistant.

'That must be Mark Jones,' Meadows said.

'Poor bugger must be plucking up the courage to go in. I'm not sure I could do it,' Edris said.

As they neared the chapel, the door opened, and Laura stepped out. Mark shot out of the chair, grabbed Laura, and shoved her against the wall.

'Hey,' Edris shouted and moved quickly to grab Mark.

'You bitch,' Mark shouted. 'What did you do to her?'

Edris pulled Mark back and Meadows stepped in front of Laura.

'Whatever has gone on between you and your sister, now is not the time and place for accusations,' Meadows said.

Mark held up his hands and stepped back. 'This is her fault.'

Meadows looked at Laura. Her eyes were swimming with tears, and she looked afraid.

'Mark, please,' Laura said. 'I didn't know this was going to happen.'

'Don't try acting innocent with me. It won't work.' Mark turned to Meadows. 'Have you asked her where she was when my mother died?'

'She was at work. We've checked,' Edris said.

'Where were *you*, Mark?' Laura asked. 'When was the last time *you* visited her?'

'I think you both need to calm down,' Meadows said. 'I appreciate how upsetting this situation is, but this isn't helping.'

'You've no idea,' Mark said.

'Maybe you should go in now and spend some time with your mother,' Meadows said. 'We can talk after that.'

'As long as she isn't around.' Mark gave Laura a look of pure loathing, then walked into the chapel.

Meadows turned to Laura. 'Are you OK?'

Laura nodded. 'You can't choose your family. My parents divorced when we were young. I stayed with Mum, and Mark went with Dad. One child each.'

'That must have been difficult for the two of you,' Meadows said.

Laura gave him a wry smile. 'I didn't see much of Mark, or my father after the divorce. It started as birthday and Christmas visits, but that fizzled out. My mother never hid her anger and hate towards my father, and I guess it was the same for Mark. They turned us against each other. It was them and us. I never wanted that for my children. That's why Gareth and I work hard on our friendship. I did try to have a relationship with Mark and my father after Maisie was born. I wanted her to know her uncle and grandfather. They both got on with Alex, and for a while it was OK, but I guess too many years had passed and the poison ran too deep.'

Her eyes flicked towards the door of the chapel.

'Did Mark keep in contact with your mother?'

Laura nodded. 'I don't think they talked that often on the phone. He visited her once or twice at the most. Mum said they ended up arguing, and she felt she couldn't mention my name. I can understand why. I was a bitch to Mark. When we all lived together, I didn't want him playing with my toys or hanging around when my friends came to play. I saw having a little brother around as a nuisance. Then after the split, I was jealous of him. He'd talk about going on holiday with Dad and all the things they did together. I was secretly glad when the visits stopped. I guess now he thinks that I didn't take care of Mum, and I suppose he's right. I should have been there for her. I should have noticed that she was troubled.'

'I think you're being too hard on yourself,' Edris said. 'You had no way of knowing what was going to happen. I'm sure when Mark calms down, he will realise that himself.'

Laura shook her head. 'I can't see that happening. I better go before he comes out.'

'Before you do, would you mind looking at some photos? Alex's St Christopher was left outside a charity shop yesterday, along with some clothes.'

Laura's face registered surprise. 'Alex's parents had all his clothes. I'm sure I checked all the pockets. Maybe I missed the necklace. They'll be delighted to have it back. I guess they've held onto his things long enough and wanted a clear out.'

'It wasn't Alex's parents that left the items and we don't think any of them are Alex's clothes.'

'I don't understand.'

'We think someone was trying to get rid of the St Christopher. It is distinctive.' Edris took his phone from his pocket and showed the first photo.

Laura nodded. 'That's Alex's St Christopher. It should have an inscription on the back.'

Meadows saw Laura's eyes mist over as Edris showed her the next photo. There was no reaction to the next few. Laura kept shaking her head until she looked at one that showed a red, woman's top.

'Do you recognise that one?' Meadows asked.

'It looks familiar.' She bit her bottom lip. 'I'm not sure.'

'Take your time.'

'It looks like one that Ceri used to wear, but I can't be certain.'

Edris flicked through the rest of them.

'I'm sorry,' Laura said, 'I don't think I've seen the others before.'

'Thanks for looking,' Meadows said. 'We'll let you go.'

Laura walked away and Meadows and Edris sat in the chairs to wait for Mark.

'I'm sure I've seen that St Christopher somewhere,' Edris said.

'Alex is wearing it in the photo on the incident board,' Meadows said. 'Could it be that?'

Edris shook his head.

'OK. I'm sure someone wouldn't be so stupid to wear it, so it could have been lying around in one of the houses we've visited.'

'We've been in all the suspects' and witnesses' homes,' Edris replied. 'Henry had lots of weird stuff around his house.' His brow furrowed in concentration. 'No, I don't think it was there.'

'The night Cora went missing, we went upstairs to check the nursery and bedroom. Jenna's dressing table was covered in all sorts. Could it have been there?'

Edris sat up a little straighter. 'That may be it.'

'Well, we've got no chance of proving it now unless forensics find Jenna or Gareth's fingerprints on the necklace.' Meadows thought for a moment. 'What about all those teddy bears in Maisie's room? They had necklaces around their necks.'

'Maybe that's what Deryn was doing upstairs. She was going to show someone.'

'But if she did, then the killer would have taken the necklace before we arrived. It can't be there that you saw it, but if Maisie is in the habit of putting jewellery on toys, then it could have been in her room at Gareth's house. We did go in briefly. She could have taken it from anyone's jewellery box.'

Edris frowned as he concentrated. 'You know when something is lurking in the back of your mind? It's so frustrating.'

Before Meadows could respond, the door to the chapel opened and Mark stepped out.

'Would you like to grab a coffee?' Meadows asked.

'Yeah. Thanks.'

They walked to the cafeteria and chose a quiet corner. Edris went to fetch the drinks while Meadows took a seat opposite Mark.

'I'm sorry about earlier,' Mark said. 'I shouldn't have acted like that. You're right. It's not the time nor the place. I just hadn't prepared myself for the possibility of running into Laura so soon.'

'I understand. Emotions run high at times like this,' Meadows said. 'Did Laura call you, to tell you about your mother?'

Mark shook his head. 'She asked the family liaison officer to do it.'

'When was the last time you spoke to your mother?'

'The night before last. She wanted to talk to Dad, but I didn't want to give her his phone number without asking him first. He cut Mum and Laura out of his life for his well-being. They had caused him so much stress. He couldn't deal with it anymore. He's happy now, and I was worried about upsetting him. I told Mum that I would pass on a message to him, but she just asked that I get him to call.'

'Did you speak to your father?'

Mark shook his head. 'I guess I'm going to have to now.' He put his hand on the table and started tapping his fingers. 'Actually, maybe it's best I don't say anything. It's not like he would want to go to the funeral.'

'Had your mother asked you before for your father's number?'

'No. All she ever talked about was Laura.'

Edris joined them at the table and handed out the mugs of tea and coffee before sitting and taking out his notebook.

'Was your mother concerned about Laura?'

Mark laughed bitterly. 'No. It was all talk about how proud she was of her. What Laura had achieved. Laura's work. Laura's house. How bloody happy Laura was. Laura is a horrible person. She doesn't deserve to be happy. I thought she had changed when she got with Alex and had that brat. Alex was great. I tried to warn him about her, but he wouldn't listen. He indulged Laura and she could do no wrong. He just couldn't see through her act. She used him.'

'In what way?' Meadows asked.

'It's hard to explain. He'd give her anything she wanted. I remember one time, I visited and went to the fair. Laura wanted this huge teddy bear. Not for Maisie, but for herself. Alex spent so much money winning that bear for her. When we got home, Laura put it in her bedroom. You'd think she'd put it in the child's room.'

Mark took a sip of his coffee. 'It wasn't just that. Alex told me she was running up debts on credit cards and Mum would pay them off for her. He was embarrassed.'

'I understand you haven't seen Laura for some years,' Meadows said. 'Was there an argument? Or incident that made you break contact?'

'I just couldn't stand to be around her anymore. I tried to talk to my mother about her, but she took no notice. Laura was always leaving the brat with her. A mini Laura. Always demanding things. Just like her mother. The house was full of the child's shit. Mum just bought her anything she wanted. I just couldn't visit anymore. I did keep up contact. I phoned now and again, but it was a one-sided conversation. Mum's world revolved around Laura and Maisie. I could see history repeating itself. I feel so sorry for the boy, Ieuan. I've never met him, and I know nothing about him. I imagine that he's terrorised by Maisie. Just like me when I was a child. Well, neither of them will be getting any more from Mum.'

Mark drank the last of the coffee and set the mug down. He talked about growing up and some things Laura had done to him. Meadows could see how these little incidents had been lumped together and grown in his mind. Laura represented everything bad that had happened in his childhood. He even blamed her for his parents' divorce.

Mark stopped talking. 'There isn't anything else I can tell you.'

'Can you give me your father's details before you go?' Edris asked.

Mark shook his head. 'I'd rather you leave him out of it.' He pushed back the chair and stood up. 'I may sound like I've got some childhood chip on my shoulder, but if you saw the situation through my eyes, you'd understand. Don't be fooled by Laura.' Mark walked away.

'Interesting,' Meadows said.

Edris nodded but didn't comment.

Meadows thought he looked troubled again. 'You OK?'

'Yeah, just thinking. Is the guy a dick, or is there something to it?'

'He's grieving and angry. It sounds like there are a lot of unresolved issues in the family. I think it's worth digging deeper into Laura's background. Check her finances from five years ago. The question is, would she kill her partner and mother? It's not like she gained financially. Alex didn't have a life insurance policy, but I imagine she will get her mother's assets.'

'The brother also has a motive,' Edris said. 'You heard him say that Laura doesn't deserve to be happy. She lost her partner, her best friend, and now her mother.'

'What about Cora?'

'Maybe what happened to Cora has nothing to do with Alex, Ceri, and Deryn. Then again, Gareth is a co-owner of the vet practice and the father of Laura's son. Punish Gareth and make him step away from Laura.'

'What troubles me is why Deryn would try to contact her ex-husband. This is someone she hasn't had contact with for years. It sounds like it was a bitter divorce. The only reason I can see is it being about one of her children.'

'Maybe she was afraid of what Mark might do to Laura,' Edris said. 'He didn't hide his dislike for Maisie either. If he could say that to us about a ten-year-old child, then it makes you wonder how far that dislike runs.'

Meadows nodded. 'We need to look into Mark Jones and contact Laura's father. It's interesting that Mark doesn't want us to contact him. Maybe he's afraid of what he will tell us.'

Edris went to close his notebook. He stopped and flicked back the page. Worry flitted across his face.

'What is it?'

'Oh… erm… nothing. I was just checking back. Mark spouted so much stuff; I wanted to make sure I got all the key points.'

'Perhaps it would be a good idea to read back through all your notes. Something you wrote down may help you remember where you saw the St Christopher. We could do with a break.'

'I'll do my best,' Edris said.

'OK, let's go and see Ceri's parents.'

As they left the cafeteria, Meadows could see the tension in Edris. It was as if the world was crashing down on him, and he was trying to hold it up. He wished he'd open up so he could help him. He opened his mouth to say something but changed his mind. He'd give it a couple more days. Whether they solved the case or not, it was clear that an intervention was needed. How Meadows was going to go about that, he didn't know.

Chapter Twenty-four

Henry was sitting in his Land Rover, which was parked opposite the All Creatures veterinary practice. He knew Laura was inside. He'd been watching her for the past few days. He'd seen the police going into her home after Deryn had been found. He'd felt guilty then. When he wasn't watching Laura, he'd been following Gareth. The whole thing was getting exhausting.

'What should I do?' he asked out loud. He closed his eyes and heard a voice in his mind. He nodded. 'Speak to Laura, go and see Gareth, then go home and get some rest. Sounds like a good plan. I need to push them. One of them is bound to break.'

The door to the vet opened and he saw Laura step out. He jumped out of the Land Rover and was across the road before she reached her car.

'Laura!'

She looked over her shoulder. 'Henry, what are you doing here?'

'I heard about your mum. I had to come and see you. I'm so sorry. She was a lovely woman.' He leaned forward and hugged her.

Laura pulled away and he could see tears in her eyes. 'Thank you. At the moment it seems unreal.'

'What are you doing at work? You should be home.'

'I can't stay there. If I sit still too long, I think too much. I'm afraid if I start crying, I'll never stop. I thought coming here would be a distraction. Besides, Mark turned up at the hospital and I'm trying to avoid him. Do you remember my brother?'

'Not someone you can easily forget,' Henry said. He remembered how guarded Laura had been when her

167

brother visited. Constantly on edge. 'On the few occasions I met him, I got bad vibes. Really dark aura.'

'You're not wrong there.'

'I'm guessing things didn't go well when you saw him.'

Laura shook her head.

'I suppose it must be difficult for him as well,' Henry said.

'Yeah, I understand that, but I could do without the drama. I thought it best to stay away from the house until the coast was clear. Hopefully, he's on his way back home.'

'It sounds like you've had a tough day, and I hate to bring this up, but there's been talk.'

Laura frowned. 'What talk?'

'Among the spirits. Arthur says that–'

'Henry, don't, please. I know you are only trying to help but give me some time. If Mum has something to say to me, it can wait. I'm not strong enough to hear from her right now. I promise we will get together soon. Right now, I have to think about the funeral, sorting Mum's paperwork, and the police investigation. It's too much.' She touched Henry's arm. 'It will be better when my mind is clearer. I'll be more receptive.'

Henry felt torn. Laura had never mocked or judged him. He could see she wasn't in a good place, but neither was he. 'I'm sorry, this can't wait. I think what's happening now has something to do with what happened at...' He couldn't bring himself to say the name. 'At the cave. It's not over.'

Laura sighed. 'You need to let it go. Remember what happened last time? You don't want to go there again.'

'I'm fine. I'm in control this time.'

'Are you really?'

'Yes. I'm trying to help you. Or don't you want my help? What are you afraid of?'

'I'm not afraid.'

He heard her words, but her eyes told a different story. He could see the fear. Sense it. 'Maybe you *should* be afraid.

You know it should have been you that died that day, and Ceri–'

'What happened to Ceri was an accident.'

'–was wearing your coat.'

'It wouldn't have made a difference if she was wearing her own coat. She fell. Eira–'

'Don't,' Henry said. Just hearing her name pierced his heart. 'Even if you still believe Ceri's death was an accident, you know Alex was murdered. We need to go back to where this all started. We can hold a seance and get our answers.'

'No way. I'm not going back there.'

'You, me, and Gareth are the only ones left. I'm going to ask him to come with us.'

'No.'

'Why? Are you afraid of what he'll do? Or maybe you're afraid of what he'll tell me.'

'What's that supposed to mean? You know what, never mind. I have to go.' Laura opened the car door and climbed inside.

Henry grabbed hold of the door. 'You or Jenna could be next.'

'You're losing it,' Laura said.

'Am I? I've seen the way Jenna behaves. I know that look. She's rattling most of the time and doesn't know why. Think about it. If she's off her face, no one will listen to her.'

'You think that Gareth... No.'

Henry saw the doubt in her eyes. He was getting through.

'Henry, you need help,' Laura said. She grabbed the door and pulled it.

Henry watched her drive away. 'I tried,' he said. 'I really did.'

Chapter Twenty-five

Meadows took a sip of his tea and checked the time. He needed to start the briefing, but there was still no sign of Edris.

'I'll give him a call,' Valentine said.

Blackwell huffed. 'He's probably stayed the night with his latest fling, and slept in.'

'He's never late,' Paskin said.

Meadows had to agree. Edris was always punctual. Most of the time, he was in early.

'He's not answering,' Valentine said. She left a message asking him to call, then hung up.

'OK, we better start,' Meadows said. 'Initial reports from Deryn Gibson's post-mortem show the cause of death as asphyxiation. Fibers were found in her mouth and nostrils. Her other injuries are consistent with a fall down the stairs. Uniform have spoken to the neighbours. No reports of anyone, except Gareth, going into Deryn's house Monday morning.'

'Jamie Ford agreed to a voluntary DNA test,' Blackwell said. 'Forensics are testing it against any samples taken from Deryn's house.'

'We have reports from the schools,' Valentine said. 'Nothing of interest on Maisie. Polite, mixes well with the other children, and is educationally advanced for her age. Jamie, on the other hand, is disruptive, scoring below average on tests, and has poor attendance.'

'Jamie's prints weren't found at Deryn's house,' Meadows said. 'We already had Gareth and Maisie's samples from Cora's case. Laura provided a sample. Laura and Maisie's prints were found upstairs but not Gareth's, which is consistent with his story.'

'Only if he didn't touch anything upstairs,' Blackwell said. 'All he had to do was push her. Then he smothers her and gets rid of whatever he used before calling the police.'

Meadows nodded. 'It is a possibility, but we don't have enough to bring him in. Paskin, have you got anything on Mark Jones?'

Paskin nodded. 'Works at a recycling centre, single, and not active on social media. He's got previous – GBH. Fight in a pub got out of control and he glassed a man.'

'Nasty,' Blackwell commented.

'So we know he can be violent,' Meadows said. 'What about Laura and Mark's father?'

'Steve Jones,' Paskin said. 'He remarried three years ago. I've left messages for him to contact us, but he hasn't responded.'

'Are we going to bring in Mark Jones?' Blackwell asked. 'Sounds like he had a problem with his mother.'

Meadows thought for a moment. 'Let's see what forensics turn up. Mark was open with us about his dislike for Laura and Maisie. It could be domestic, but I can't see that he would take Cora.'

'It doesn't rule him out,' Valentine said. 'He could have killed his mother and Alex. We've got all the cases linked by family ties but that's the only link. The method is different for them all and the victims are all different ages. Deryn's only relationship with Cora is that her grandson is Cora's half-sibling.'

Meadows looked at the information on the incident board. 'Ceri's death was made to look like an accident. Deryn took a fall down the stairs. If she had died from the fall then it would have looked like an accident. The fire was ruled accidental, and Alex… erm… it was set up to look like he disappeared of his own accord. Cora is the only one that doesn't fit. You're right, it may well be that someone else took Cora.'

'Are you thinking Deryn knew something about Alex's death and not Cora's kidnapping?' Blackwell asked. 'It would make sense with the necklace turning up at the charity shop the same day she was killed.'

'We showed the photos of the items to Gareth and Jenna,' Valentine said. 'Both claimed that they didn't recognise any of them, but I saw a subtle shift in their body language on a couple of them.'

'Which ones?' Meadows asked.

'A man's burgundy hoodie and a woman's red top.'

'Interesting,' Meadows said. 'Laura thought that the red top could have been Ceri's. There were a lot of necklaces around teddy bears in Maisie's room. It may be that Maisie picked up the St Christopher and took it to Deryn's house.'

'Deryn saw it and called Gareth,' Blackwell said.

Valentine nodded. 'If that's the case, the only place Maisie could have found it was at Gareth's or Laura's house.'

'We know that Laura went straight to work after dropping Maisie off at school,' Meadows said. 'She had appointments first thing, and there is no way she could have slipped out. Gareth says he was at home before he went to Deryn's. Jenna says she went for a walk to clear her head before going to the hospital.'

'Beth and Joe Hendon were at home with Olwen,' Paskin said.

Meadows looked at the list of names. 'That leaves some of Gareth's work colleagues and Henry.'

'Henry had taken a group camping, and caving,' Paskin said.

'Anything on the haulage company?' Meadows asked.

Blackwell shook his head. 'Looks like they are clean.'

'Given where Alex was found, I still think this has something to do with caving,' Meadows said. 'Gareth, Laura, Jenna, Alex, Ceri, and Henry explored together. Two of that group are dead.'

'Do we know if Mark went caving with the group?' Blackwell asked. 'He was around at the time Alex went missing.'

'I'll see what I can find out,' Paskin said.

Meadows nodded. 'Even if he didn't go caving with the group, he could have asked Alex to show him a cave.'

'What about Ceri?' Valentine asked.

Meadows thought for a moment. 'Ceri was wearing Laura's coat. It would be easy to mistake one for the other. If Mark did kill Ceri, then perhaps Alex got suspicious. OK, we've got a lot of work to do.'

Meadows returned to his desk and the next couple of hours flew by. Now and again, he would look up to see Valentine checking her phone. He tried calling Edris, but the phone continued to ring until it went to voicemail. An uneasiness crept over him.

He pushed his chair back. 'I think we should check in with Edris' parents.'

'I'll do it,' Valentine said. 'I've met his mother on a few occasions. If you call, she might get worried.'

Meadows nodded.

Valentine made the call while the rest of the team listened. She kept it casual making it sound like she was trying to get hold of him for information on a case. She didn't mention that he hadn't turned up for work.

'She hasn't heard from him,' Valentine said when she ended the call. 'As you probably heard, she hasn't got a contact number for his girlfriend. Didn't know he was seeing anyone.'

'He hasn't called in sick,' Meadows said. 'Even if he slept in, the phone would have woken him by now.'

'Maybe he put it on silent,' Blackwell said.

Valentine shook her head. 'He was on call last night.'

Meadows grabbed his coat. 'It's nearly midday. I'm going to his flat.'

'I'm coming with you,' Valentine said.

* * *

Edris' flat was one of four in a block at the bottom of a dead-end street. To one side was a parking area with four garages. On the other side, tall sycamore trees lined a path to the back communal garden.

'His car isn't here,' Meadows said.

Valentine looked around. 'He sometimes parks it in the garage.'

The main entrance had an intercom system with flat numbers next to each buzzer. Valentine pressed flat three, which was located on the first floor. They waited a few moments, then Valentine keyed in a code.

'I've been here enough times,' she said.

Meadows followed her through the door and up the long flight of stairs. Outside Edris' flat was a large yucca tree and a doormat. He pressed the bell. Nothing.

'Edris!' He knocked on the door.

'Tristan. Are you in there?' Valentine called out. 'We're coming in.' She unzipped her handbag and took out a set of keys. 'We have each other's spares in case of emergency. I think this situation calls for me to use it.'

Meadows nodded and Valentine opened the door. They stepped into the hallway. It was painted white with two large modern prints framed in black. There wasn't a mark on the walls, and the wooden block flooring was spotless. There was a shoe rack near the door. It held several pairs of shoes and a pair of slippers. Directly ahead of them was a door.

'That's the bedroom,' Valentine said. She moved forward and put her hand on the handle. 'Tristan!' She hesitated for a moment then opened the door.

The curtains were open and the double bed in the centre of the room was made. The walls were decorated the same as the hallway. Grey curtains matched the duvet cover and pillowcases. The only furniture in the room was a glossy oak dresser and wardrobe. There was no clutter and no dust.

'Doesn't look like he slept here last night,' Meadows said.

'You know what a neat freak he is. He wouldn't have left the flat without making the bed.'

They left the bedroom and opened the door to the sitting room. More white walls and black-framed prints. The only colour in the room was a forest-green corner sofa with mustard-coloured cushions placed at equal distances. A laptop sat in the centre of an oak coffee table next to a stack of coasters and a TV remote control.

'He usually has his laptop with him,' Meadows said.

'At work, yes, but he wouldn't take it if he was going out for the evening.'

Meadows left the sitting room and checked out the kitchen. He wasn't surprised to find it as neat as the rest of the flat. The last place he checked was the bathroom.

'I don't think he's been here,' Meadows said. 'The shower and bath are bone dry, and there is no lingering smell of coffee or aftershave.'

'His garage keys are hanging up. Should we check it out?' Valentine asked.

Meadows nodded. They locked up the flat and walked around the side of the building to the garage. As expected, the car was missing. As they were locking up, a woman appeared.

'What are you doing?' she asked.

'We're looking for Tristan,' Valentine said. 'Have you seen him?'

Meadows could see suspicion in the woman's eyes. He took out his warrant card and showed it. 'We work with him.'

'Oh, right. Well, you can't be too careful. I thought you might be breaking in. I haven't seen him today.'

'What about last night?'

She shook her head. 'I didn't hear him come in. Come to think of it, I didn't hear him move around this morning.'

'What about his girlfriend? Have you seen her calling around?' Valentine asked.

'No, but I don't spend my time looking out of the window. I wave if I see him, and he always waves back or stops for a chat if I'm outside. He puts my rubbish out every week. He's such a sweetie. Is he OK?'

'I'm sure he's fine,' Meadows said.

The woman left and they returned to the car.

'I have a bad feeling about this,' Valentine said.

Meadows nodded. 'He hasn't been himself recently. Put out an APB on his car. We need to find him.'

Chapter Twenty-six

Cora's shrill cries woke Jenna up. Her head felt thick, and she wanted to curl up under the duvet and sleep. The crying intensified and seemed to penetrate Jenna's body. She checked the time, then jumped out of bed and picked up the baby. She couldn't believe she had slept so long. The crying stopped.

'Are you hungry?' Jenna kissed the top of Cora's head as she wiggled her feet into her slippers. As her head cleared, she realised that she hadn't heard Gareth come to bed. She'd been up until 3 a.m. and there had been no sign of him. She remembered taking a tablet after Cora had gone to sleep, and then nothing until she had woken a moment ago. She was glad she had moved Cora's cot into the bedroom. If she was that out of it, she needed to know that Cora was safe.

Jenna left the room. As she was walking downstairs, she suddenly recalled phoning Laura in the middle of the night. Her cheeks burned as she remembered the horrible message she had left. She had accused Laura of sleeping with Gareth. Demanded that she send him home to his children. She tried to chase away the anxiety that crawled at her insides as she walked into the kitchen.

She stopped. Gareth had a mop and bucket and was washing the floor.

'What are you doing?'

'Cleaning up the mess you made. Muddy footprints everywhere.'

'I haven't been anywhere.'

'Then it must have been Jamie.'

'Yeah, go ahead and blame him. Where the fuck were you last night?' Jenna opened the fridge and grabbed a baby bottle.

'I was out.'

Jenna put the bottle in the warmer. 'You were with her.'

Gareth sighed and put the mop in the bucket. 'I got drunk and slept in the summer house, but think what you like. Nothing I say makes any difference.' He rubbed his hands over his face. 'I can't deal with this anymore. I think you should move out.'

Jenna's stomach twisted and her mind began to race. She would be left on her own with a baby again. Cora started to cry, and Jenna's throat constricted with emotion as tears stung her eyes. She grabbed the bottle from the warmer as she tried to think. The milk hadn't reached the correct temperature, but she gave it to Cora anyway. Gareth had sat down at the kitchen table and put his head in his hands.

Jenna sat down opposite him. 'I can't move out. Where would I go? I can't believe you are throwing me and the children out so you can move Laura in.'

Gareth looked up. 'For fuck's sake. This has nothing to do with Laura. You saw the photos the police showed yesterday. The red top. The one you claimed was missing. It was found with Alex's necklace.'

'Along with *your* hoodie.'

'The one I put in the laundry for you to wash. The one you claimed mysteriously went missing. What do you expect me to think? You hated Alex and Ceri. All this shit has happened since you came back. You don't know what day of the week it is half the time. I'm not even sure you know what postcode you're in.'

'That's what you'd like me to think, isn't it? That I'm losing my mind. You're the one that moved Laura in here as soon as Alex went missing.'

Gareth jumped up from the chair. His eyes blazed. 'Is that what you think? That I… for crying out loud. I lost my best friend, my girlfriend, and Laura has lost her mother.'

'What about me? I was left pregnant and alone to raise our son. Someone set alight the house with me in it. And what about Cora?' Jenna looked down at the baby. 'We nearly lost her, or don't you care?'

'Of course I care. I love you and our children, but I can't deal with this shit anymore. I don't know who you are and I can't trust you.'

'I never stood a chance with Laura around.'

Gareth shook his head. 'There is nothing between Laura and me. We weren't together that long, and it didn't work out. We are just friends, and we have a child between us. You're the one who is letting jealousy get between us. This is never going to work.'

Jenna felt like her heart was splitting in two again. It was the same feeling she had at the church all those years ago. She opened her mouth, but couldn't find the words. Instead, she let herself cry.

Gareth sat down again and sighed. 'I don't expect you to leave the house right now. I'll go. All I ask is that you get some help. When you are better, we'll talk. You know I'll support you financially. I'll help you find somewhere to live.'

'Just go then,' Jenna sobbed.

Gareth left, and the house fell silent. Cora seemed oblivious to the turmoil around her. She'd finished her milk and was sleeping. Jenna grabbed two pills from the cupboard, swallowed them, and then carried Cora upstairs. She stopped outside Jamie's door.

'Are you awake?'

There was no answer, so she opened the door. The room was in a state and smelt of stale socks and sour body odour. The bed was empty so she guessed he must have got himself up for school. She'd have to talk to him when he got home.

She left Jamie's room, laid Cora in her cot, and climbed into bed. She curled into a tight ball and pulled the duvet over her head. She wanted to shut out the world and drift into oblivion where she didn't have to think. It didn't take long for the tablets to kick in and she fell into a deep sleep.

* * *

The screeching of the garage door awoke Jenna. She sat up and looked in the cot. Cora was still asleep. She checked the time. She had only been asleep for just over an hour. Gareth must have come back for something, she thought. Then it occurred to her that it was the second garage that had the squealing door. It was the one where Gareth kept the diving and caving equipment. He hadn't taken a trip since the fire. She couldn't believe he was going out and having some fun today. Not with everything going on. Then another thought struck her. Maybe he was taking Laura out. That would be just like him. He'd use the excuse that she needed cheering up, but it would really be a chance for them to be alone together. He'd tell her about all his problems and Laura would help him with a solution.

Jealousy erupted like lava in Jenna's stomach. It spread throughout her body, igniting a burning rage. She would catch them together and tell Laura exactly what she thought of her.

Careful not to make a noise, Jenna crept downstairs. She stopped at the bottom and listened. She could hear movement in the kitchen. She moved quickly and flung open the door.

Laura was standing with one hand in the kitchen cupboard. She pulled her hand away and turned around to face Jenna. Surprise on her face.

'What the fuck are you doing?' Jenna demanded.

'I erm… I was dropping off your herbal tablets. I didn't want to wake you.'

'Don't lie to me. Where's Gareth?'

'I don't know. I haven't seen him. Honestly.'

It was only then that Jenna noticed there was something off about Laura. She moved forward and took a closer look. Laura's make-up had worn off. There were smudges of mascara beneath her eyes. She looked like she'd been out partying all night, fallen into bed for a few hours, then not bothered to wash. Her hair was pulled back, but clumps had come loose. She was wearing a pair of jogging pants and a baggy sweatshirt. In her hand, she clutched a bottle of Jenna's tablets.

Jenna held out her hand. 'Give them to me.'

Laura shook her head. 'There's a new bottle in the cupboard. Look for yourself. This one is nearly empty. You don't want to run out.'

'There were plenty left.'

Jenna moved to snatch the bottle, but Laura was faster. She moved backwards and put her hand behind her back.

'What's going on?' Jenna asked.

Laura's eyes filled with tears and Jenna softened. She tried to think how she would feel if someone had murdered her mother. Maybe Laura was losing it.

'You look like shit,' Jenna said. 'Sit down and I'll make you a coffee.'

'I can't stay,' Laura said. 'I… I have to go.'

'No. Gareth doesn't come home all night, and you are sneaking around my house taking my tablets. I'm not stupid. You better tell me what's going on or I'm calling the police.'

'Please don't do that,' Laura begged. 'I can't explain right now. I thought my brother was... but... then Henry came. He said things. I don't know what to believe... and now... I don't have a choice.'

'Laura, you're not making any sense. What do you mean you don't have a choice? What are you going to do?'

'You need to let me leave. I have to take the tablets.' She dropped her voice to a whisper. 'I think you are being drugged. I need to find out. Please, you have to trust me. Take the children and go to your mother's. You're not safe here.'

Chapter Twenty-seven

Meadows ran upstairs to the office and found DCI Lester with the rest of his team. Lester was Meadows' boss and, most of the time, he was happy to let Meadows run the team without interference. He only showed up when there was a serious problem.

'I take it there is no sign of him,' Lester said.

'I've just come from Edris' parents' home,' said Meadows. 'We've contacted every other member of the family and his friends. No one has seen him. We need to act now. Track his phone as a matter of urgency. We don't have time to get a warrant.'

'I think you are being a bit hasty,' Lester said. 'It could be the case that he has gone AWOL with this girlfriend of his. There is nothing about your latest investigation that raises concerns. There have been no threats, I take it.'

This was not what Meadows expected. He needed Lester on his side and all the resources he could spare. 'No, but this is completely out of character.'

'You don't know how long he's been missing,' Lester said. 'If he decided to go out for the day at say 8 a.m., he's been gone less than twelve hours. Think about it. If you were called out for a missing person, with this information, you wouldn't be calling for a full-scale search. You would make initial enquiries, which you have done. He's not a missing child or a vulnerable adult. You know full well you have to demonstrate an immediate threat to life, or emergency, to access phone records without a warrant. We'd be breaking all sorts of privacy protocols.'

'Fine then. We'll get a warrant,' Meadows said.

'On what grounds?' Lester asked.

'He is a serving officer that may be in trouble.'

'Has his family expressed concerns for his safety?'

'They will,' Valentine said. 'We've tried not to alarm them, but I'm sure they will make an official missing person report. If that's what it takes, then I'll go and see them now.'

Lester whipped his head around to face Valentine. 'You'll do no such thing. I think the best thing to do is find out all you can about this girlfriend of his.'

'We don't know who she is and neither do his parents,' Meadows said.

'That's odd in itself,' Lester said. 'He could be seeing a married woman. Think how embarrassing it would be for him, and more importantly us, if we organise a search now. It's bad enough you jumped the gun and put out an APB.' He made a show of looking at the time. 'There is nothing more to be done this evening. I think we should wait until the morning. He'll probably turn up before then. Meanwhile, if there are any developments, let me know.'

Lester left the office and for a moment there was silence.

'Well, fuck that,' Blackwell said.

Meadows smiled. 'My thoughts exactly, but anything we do from now is on me.'

Valentine shook her head. 'If it were down to me, I'd go behind your back. Lester can't fire us all. We'll deal with the consequences later.'

Paskin and Blackwell nodded their agreement.

Meadows looked at his team and he knew they would stand by him whatever decision he made. 'Paskin, can you organise a warrant for Edris' call data? Valentine, go back to Edris' flat and pick up his laptop. He may have been working on some theories outside of work. Take it to Chris Harley in tech. Blackwell, I want you to break into his locker and get his notebook. I'm going to make some calls to see how many officers I can get to help us search.'

Everyone sprang to action. Meadows called Folland who was coming back in. He would round up uniform and wait for instructions. He made a few more calls, and just as Blackwell returned with Edris' notebook, his phone rang. The call display showed it was PC Matt Hanes. Meadows answered.

'We've found Edris' car,' Hanes said.

Meadows turned to Blackwell. 'Let's go.'

He ran down the stairs and out to the car with Blackwell close behind. As Blackwell updated Valentine, Meadows drove out of the car park, put on his blue light, and headed for the mountain road.

'What the bloody hell is he doing in Pen Arthur Forest?' Blackwell said.

Meadows gripped the steering wheel. 'There is no reason for him to be there. Even if he went for a walk, he'd be back by now. He's got enough sense not to walk in the forest after dark.'

Blackwell didn't respond and Meadows concentrated on his driving. There was nothing to be said.

As darkness fell, the headlights illuminated the studs that guided drivers on the twisting road. The Black Mountain rose ominously, like a giant shadow. Meadows pulled the car around the bends. He knew the road so well he could afford to keep the speed up. They reached the top of the mountain, drove down the other side, and then past the area where Alex's car had been found. If Edris had been in the passenger seat, he would have been spouting out theories of the proximity of the two cars, and what it may mean. Blackwell wasn't one for keeping up a conversation, so Meadows filled the silence.

'It's the same road as where Alex's car was found.'

'You think Edris found something out and went off on his own?'

'No, I can't see it.'

'Then this is something else.'

Further down the road, Meadows spotted blue flashing lights. He pulled up behind the police car and jumped out. Hanes was waiting for him.

'You can see why I had to leave the car on the road,' Hanes said. He indicated the car parked lengthways across the entrance to the track. Near the car was a sign for Pen Arthur Forest.

'Natural Resources Wales had a report about the car blocking the way. A few hikers wanted to walk the trail. It took them some time to send someone out. They thought it was a walker, but when it started to get dark and no one returned, they called us.'

'OK, let's take a look.'

'It's locked,' Hanes said.

Meadows grabbed a torch and shined it through the driver's window. Blackwell did the same on the passenger side. The torch beams picked up a stain on the passenger-seat headrest.

Meadows moved to the other side of the car to take a closer look.

'It looks like it could be blood,' he said.

Blackwell nodded. 'Hanes, have you got something to jemmy the boot?

Meadows saw a look of understanding on Hanes' face and felt a sickness in his stomach. Hanes went to the police car and came back carrying a tool. He hesitated by the boot of Edris' car.

'I'll do it,' Blackwell said. He grabbed the tool and set about opening the boot.

There was a click and Meadows held his breath. A knot had formed in his stomach, and he had to force himself to keep looking. The boot sprang upwards and all three looked inside. It was empty.

Meadows released his breath. 'Call Paskin and ask her to request phone data urgently. Threat to life.'

* * *

Mountain rescue arrived along with another two police cars, and a tow truck. Meadows watched as Edris' car was put on a truck and taken to forensics. Word was spreading and he knew more officers would come to join the search, but he feared that time was against them. He moved to join Valentine and Blackwell who were talking to Eddy from mountain rescue.

'We've got over four miles of forest stretching upwards,' Eddy said as he trailed his torch over an area on the map. 'It's a strenuous walk up until it opens to a viewpoint. It's not waymarked. Added to that, the forest stretches for miles in both directions. Then you have the Afon Sawdde across the road. I don't have to tell you how fast that river is flowing. To be honest, there is not a lot we can do tonight. The forest is dense in parts with thick undergrowth. The phone signal is sporadic. It's just too dangerous. We can stick to the track and spread out to cover each side. That will take a few hours. Then we can ramp up the search at first light.'

'I've requested the dog unit,' Blackwell said.

'We're still waiting on the phone data,' Meadows said. 'Once the phone is triangulated, we may have a better idea of his location.'

'How long will that take?' Eddy asked.

Meadows shrugged. 'Minutes to hours.'

'OK, let's make a start,' Eddy said.

The search party formed a line and kept around two metres between them. Meadows positioned himself at one end. It meant he was continually moving around trees. A line of light lit the way, but beyond that was inky darkness. Periodically, they called out then stood still and listened. They were met by an eerie silence. The track split in two. Half the party went to the left. Meadows joined Blackwell, Valentine, and Eddy, and proceeded right and upwards.

Progress was slow as those who were not on the track were hindered by low branches, brambles and tree roots. Each bump in the ground took on the form of a body. The tree branches were like hands reaching out. The forest had turned from tranquil to sinister. Meadows could almost feel the darkness pressing on his back.

They were all weary when they finally reached the top and turned to look at the silhouette of the mountain. Blackwell was breathing heavily.

'You can pick up the Beacons Way from here,' Eddy said. 'That covers miles. I think we should call it a night. If he was injured and came in here of his own accord or… well, logically he would have stuck to the track.'

'There is no logic about it,' Blackwell said. 'If he was injured and left in his car, he would have called for help.'

'Maybe he had no signal and was trying to get to higher ground,' Valentine said. 'Or he could have escaped and ran into the forest and got lost.'

Blackwell shook his head. 'You're clutching at straws.'

'I just don't want to think the worst.'

Blackwell put his hand on Valentine's shoulder. 'None of us do, but it's not looking good. Come on, let's get moving. I'm bloody freezing.'

'We're not giving up on him yet,' Meadows said. 'I've been thinking about his car. There's something odd about the way it was left.'

'What do you mean?' Blackwell asked.

'It wasn't just driven in and left. It was parked across the track. I think whoever put it there wanted to cause a disruption. They wanted us to find the car.'

'That could be a good thing,' Valentine said. 'Whoever drove him here wanted him to get help.'

'Whoever drove him here would also need a way of getting home,' Blackwell said.

Valentine stopped. 'That's worse. If two people came here with him, they could have put him anywhere.'

Meadows' phone rang and he pulled it from his pocket. 'It's Paskin.' He listened for a moment then ended the call. 'Edris' phone had been triangulated. It's nowhere near here.'

Chapter Twenty-eight

Meadows spread the map on the desk and circled the area in red.

'That's near the cycle path,' Blackwell said.

Meadows nodded. 'It's also close to Gareth and Jenna's house. Let's go.'

'Hold up,' Lester said. 'You can't go barging in there in the middle of the night.'

'I think we have good cause to search the property,' Meadows said. 'If you had listened to my concerns, we could have had the phone's location hours ago.'

Lester glared at Meadows. While fully dressed in a suit and tie, he looked like he had been dragged out of bed.

'You haven't got an exact location for the phone. Someone could have thrown it anywhere in this area.' Lester pointed to the map.

'What are the odds of the phone happening to be within fifty metres of the house?' Meadows said.

'So now you're thinking that Edris' disappearance is directly related to the case?' Lester sighed. 'I'll organise a warrant. I suggest you all go home and get some rest. At least go and get something to eat. I'll call as soon as the warrant is issued.'

Meadows looked at his team. They all looked exhausted. He nodded. 'Let's take a break. None of us can do any more here. Daylight is only a few hours away and the search can resume.'

Reluctantly, the team left and Meadows drove home through the silent villages. He had told Daisy not to wait up for him, so he was surprised to see a light in the kitchen when he stepped through his front door.

'What are you still doing up?' he said as he hung up his coat.

His mother appeared in the kitchen doorway and put her fingers to her lips. She was dressed in a long colourful skirt and a Baja hoodie. As usual, her feet were bare.

Meadows' stomach flipped. 'What are you doing here in the middle of the night? Is Daisy OK?'

'She's fine,' Fern said. 'Just worried about Tristan. I came to keep her company while she waited for news. She fell asleep on the sofa, so I covered her with a blanket.'

'Thanks.' He kissed his mother on the cheek before sitting at the kitchen table and filling her in on the latest developments. 'I wish I'd pushed him a little more. I knew something was wrong.'

'I doubt it would have made a difference,' Fern said. 'It sounds like his disappearance has more to do with the case than his personal life.'

Meadows nodded. 'Although, I can't figure out why he would be a target. Unless his personal life has got entangled with the case.'

'You know what it's like in the valleys. Everyone is related to each other to some degree.'

'A relative, a friend, or a girlfriend,' Meadows said. 'When I think about it, he was fine until the baby went missing. Since then, his mood has been up and down. He's been working hard to solve the case and is frustrated by the lack of progress.' He rubbed his hand over his face. 'I don't know. There are a lot of things that don't add up about this case. I can't see a motive for any of it.'

'You're worn out,' Fern said. 'Why don't you try and sleep.'

Meadows shook his head. 'I'll take a shower and get into fresh clothes. Maybe that will wake me up.'

When Meadows came down from the shower, he checked on Daisy. She was sleeping peacefully. He sat in the armchair, put his head back, and closed his eyes. He only meant to rest for a moment but he drifted off to sleep. The alarm going off on Daisy's phone awoke him.

Daisy sat up. 'When did you get back?'

Meadows yawned. 'Very late.'

'Any news?'

Meadows shook his head.

Daisy got up from the sofa and put her arms around him. He pulled her onto his lap and told her about his night and the investigation.

'Do you think Edris is involved with these people?'

'I don't know, but until we find his phone, I have no reason to put this on the team. Besides, Lester will pitch a fit.'

Daisy rested her head against his shoulder, and they sat in silence for a few moments. The smell of hot buttered toast drifted into the room along with hushed voices. A lot of them.

'What's going on?' Daisy asked.

'Let's go and see.'

When Meadows walked into the kitchen, he found a group of people. All of them had mugs in their hands and a few were eating toast.

'We didn't wake you, did we?' Rain asked as he moved forward and hugged Meadows.

Meadows hugged his brother tightly and then moved to greet the rest of the group. They were all from the commune, and people that he considered family.

'What are you all doing here?'

'I called your brother,' Fern said.

Rain nodded. 'Mum filled us in. We've come to help look for Tristan. Pen Arthur Forest has a lot of ground to cover. More are on their way.'

Meadows could feel the emotion gathering in his eyes. 'Thank you. I'll give search and rescue a call, and tell them to expect you.'

Fern placed a plate of toast on the table. 'Eat up, then you can be on your way. I'll bake some cakes, make sandwiches, and bring them to the woods at lunchtime.'

'I think you should get some sleep, Mum,' Meadows said.

'I'll have plenty of rest when I'm dead. I can't traipse around the forest, but I can help keep up the strength of those searching. Daisy love, you better get ready for work. I'll cook you some breakfast.'

'Thanks, but I'm not hungry.'

'You're not going to work on an empty stomach, and only a few hours' sleep. You need to look after yourself.'

'I wouldn't argue with her,' Rain said.

Daisy smiled. 'OK, thanks, Mum.' She pecked Fern on the cheek and left the room.

Meadows stepped closer to Fern. 'What was that all about?'

'What?'

'Fussing over Daisy. Is there something I should know?'

'No. I'm just looking after her. The way her mother would have if she was alive. Daisy works hard. You both do.'

Meadows wasn't convinced, but he knew if there was something to worry about, his mother would tell him. His phone beeped, indicating a message. He opened it and saw the warrant had been granted.

'I've got to go.'

He heard his mother complaining that he hadn't eaten as he hurried off. He sent a message to his team before driving to Gareth and Jenna's house. It was only two villages away from his home, so he was the first to arrive. Hanes was waiting for him.

'No sign that anyone is up yet,' Hanes said. 'Gareth's car isn't here, but he could have put it in the garage overnight.'

A van pulled up with more uniformed officers, and then Blackwell and Valentine arrived.

'OK, let's go,' Meadows said. He marched up to the front door and pushed the bell. He kept the button pressed down, then started hammering the door. 'Police! Open the door.'

'Do you want us to break it down?' Hanes asked.

'Hold on.' Meadows put his ear to the door. 'I think someone is coming.' He knocked again.

He heard Jenna shout from inside. 'OK, I'm coming.'

The door opened and Jenna appeared in her dressing gown.

'We have a warrant to search the premises,' Meadows said.

'What!'

Meadows thrust the paperwork at her. 'Move aside please.'

Jenna looked bewildered as she stepped back. The team of officers entered and spread out.

'Wait,' Jenna said. 'Cora and Jamie are sleeping upstairs.'

'Go and fetch them both, and come into the sitting room,' Meadows said. 'Detective Valentine will go with you.' He snapped on gloves and joined Blackwell in the sitting room.

Drawers were opened, furniture turned up, and cushions moved. By the time Jenna had prepared a bottle for Cora, and was escorted in by Valentine, the room had been cleared.

'What the fuck!' Jamie said.

'Sit down,' Blackwell snarled. 'Any problems from you and I won't hesitate to arrest you.'

'Do as he says,' Jenna said.

Jamie sat in the armchair with a look of pure loathing on his face.

'Where are the keys to the garages?' Blackwell asked.

'Hanging up in the kitchen,' Jenna said.

Blackwell left the room and Jenna turned to Meadows. 'Would you mind explaining what is going on?'

'Where is Gareth?'

'I don't know.'

'What time did he leave this morning?'

Jenna hesitated.

'We need to know where Gareth is. You can answer questions here or down at the station.'

Tears filled Jenna's eyes. 'I don't know. He didn't come home last night. He hasn't slept here for the last two nights. We had an argument.'

'When was the last time you saw him?'

'Yesterday morning.'

Jamie leaned forward in the chair. 'Why are you asking about Dad?'

'We just need to talk to him,' Valentine said. 'Do you know where he is?'

Jamie shook his head, and his legs jiggled up and down.

'What happened yesterday morning?' Meadows asked.

Jenna rocked Cora and she fed her. 'Nothing. When I got up with Cora, he was in the kitchen. We argued and he left again.'

'What did you argue about?'

Jenna's eyes narrowed. 'Bloody Laura, as usual. I think that's where he spent the night. Has this got anything to do with her creeping around the house? I knew she was up to something.'

'What do you mean?' Meadows asked.

'I caught her in the kitchen yesterday. It was about an hour after Gareth left. She was doing something with my tablets.'

Meadows sat forward. 'Did you ask her about it?'

'Yeah. She said I wasn't safe. She wasn't making much sense. She was in a state. Her hair was all over the place and she looked like she'd slept in her make-up or not slept at all. She said something about Henry, and getting the tablets tested. I think she was implying that Gareth was drugging me. She took the tablets and left.'

Jamie glared at Meadows. 'I told you about the drugs.'

'What do you mean?' Jenna asked.

'I told them I think Dad has been drugging you since we moved in here.'

Jenna's eyes widened. 'Why would he do that?'

'Jenna,' Meadows said, 'would you be willing to give a blood sample so we can test it for the presence of drugs?'

'Gareth wouldn't do that. He's the one who keeps insisting I'm losing it.' Jenna looked down at Cora who was sleeping in her arms. 'He thinks that I'm not fit to look after her.' Tears welled up in her eyes. 'Unless…'

'Unless what?' Meadows asked.

'They are in it together. I heard them on the phone arguing. Gareth was telling Laura to keep her mouth shut. He said something like "She doesn't know." What if they were talking about me? I don't know what to think anymore.'

'The only way to be certain is to take the blood test,' Valentine said.

'Do it, Mum,' Jamie said.

Jenna grimaced. 'OK.'

'Jamie, you can go with your mother,' Meadows said.

'Can I at least get dressed first?' Jenna asked.

Meadows nodded. 'One more thing. Did Detective Edris call here?'

'The one that was with you last time?'

'Yes.'

'No, I haven't seen him.'

Valentine left with Jenna and Meadows made some calls before going to the garage to talk to Blackwell.

'This place is full of diving and climbing equipment,' Blackwell said. 'So far we've turned up nothing.'

Meadows filled him in on the conversation with Jenna.

'Neither Gareth nor Laura are at work. They weren't in yesterday. We need to find them both,' Blackwell said.

Hanes shouted out and they both turned.

'I've found his phone,' Hanes said.

Chapter Twenty-nine

Meadows was standing behind Chris Harley in the tech department, watching the screen. He had handed over Edris' phone and, without question, Chris had started work to retrieve the data. Valentine was sitting next to Chris and Meadows could see the tension on her face. There were dark circles beneath her eyes, which were missing their usual sparkle.

'I helped him set up the security on this,' Chris said.

'Can you get in?' Meadows asked.

Chris nodded. 'Just need a little time.'

Time we haven't got, Meadows thought, but he didn't say anything. They were all feeling the pressure, and added to that was the uncomfortable feeling of invading Edris' privacy, but they had no choice.

The door to the office opened and Blackwell came in. 'Anything yet?'

Meadows shook his head.

Blackwell pulled up a chair next to Chris. 'We found Gareth Hendon in a pup. Pissed as a trout.'

Valentine frowned. 'At this time of the day?'

Blackwell nodded. 'Looks like he's been on a bender. I doubt it would've taken much to top him up. He got a bit aggressive so I arrested him. I put him in a cell to sober up. Folland is drip-feeding him coffee. No sign of Laura. The last person to see her was Jenna, yesterday. She dropped the children off at school but didn't pick them up. Gareth's mother, Beth, got a call. The children are staying with her. I told her to call if Laura shows up.'

'Did you speak to Henry Tay?'

Blackwell shook his head. 'He's not home and his phone is going to voicemail.'

'I'm in,' Chris said. 'What do you want to look at first?'

'Text messages,' Meadows said.

Chris clicked the keyboard, and a list of contacts appeared on the screen. 'These are the recent ones.'

The name on the top of the list was Laura.

'Can you open all the messages from the top contact, please?' Meadows asked.

The screen filled up with messages sent between Edris and Laura. There were so many that Chris had to scroll down.

'That's... he...' Valentine looked at Meadows.

'Tossing idiot,' Blackwell said. 'What the hell was he thinking? Did either of you know?'

Valentine shook her head.

'I thought he may have been involved with someone related to the case, but I didn't expect this,' Meadows said.

'When did the messages start?' Valentine asked.

Chris scrolled up. 'Two months ago.'

'Start from Tuesday night,' Meadows said.

Chris called up the messages.

Edris: I need to see you tonight.

Laura: OK. I should be home by 6 xx

Edris: Any chance you can get off earlier?

Laura: I'll try. Is everything OK? xx

Edris: Something came up and I need to talk to you about it x

Laura: See you later xxx

Meadows looked at the time stamp. 'That was sent just after we talked to Mark.' He continued reading.

Laura: Sorry I got held up by Henry xx

Edris: I'm only just leaving work x

Laura: If you get there before me, let yourself in. I'm on my way.

There was nothing until 7.30 p.m.

Laura: Are you still coming over? xx

Laura: It's getting late. I have to be up early.

Laura: Is everything OK? Call me xxx

There were no more messages.

'Go back to the contact list,' Meadows said. He looked at the screen. 'Can you open the messages from the unknown number?'

Chris nodded.

Meadows waited for the messages to show. The first one had been the day Deryn was murdered.

Unknown: Stay away from Laura if you know what's good for you. I'll be watching!

'Hold on a sec,' Chris said. He called up a file on a second screen. 'Yeah, that's the one. Edris asked me to trace that number, the day after the message was received – burner phone.'

Meadows looked away from the screen. 'We need to trace Laura's phone.'

'I'll get on to it,' Chris said.

'Any luck with Edris' laptop?' Meadows asked.

'I'm working on it. I'll call you as soon as I have a breakthrough.'

Meadows turned to Blackwell. 'Get over to Laura's house. Break the door down if you have to.'

Blackwell nodded and left.

'Valentine, can I leave you to go through the rest of the text messages? See if anything stands out. I'm going to check in with search and rescue, then interview Gareth Hendon.'

Meadows left the office with anxiety churning his stomach.

* * *

It took a long time for Gareth to sober up, and then there was a delay with his solicitor. Meadows was sitting at his desk reading through Edris' notebook from the beginning of the investigation. He got to the interview notes with Mark Jones, then flipped back to the day Deryn Gibson had been found. He put the notebook down.

'Anything?' Paskin asked.

'I don't know,' Meadows said. 'The notes he took when we talked to Mark are more detailed. I mean, he doesn't usually write information verbatim. Just the key points. Unless word for word is required.'

'Did he write everything Mark said?'

'He wrote "Teddy bear in the bedroom" and underlined it. Mark told us a story of when Alex won a bear for Laura at the fair and she put it in her bedroom. It's not an important fact, so why write it down?'

'I'm guessing he saw the bear and was surprised she kept it.'

Meadows shook his head. 'Edris was fixated on the St Christoper. He was sure he'd seen it somewhere. Perhaps Maisie got hold of it and put it on the bear. Maybe Edris was going to ask Laura about it. There are only two places she could have got the necklace. Laura's house or Gareth's house. If Laura did see the St Christopher, then why not tell us?'

'She's guilty or she's protecting someone,' Paskin said.

Blackwell walked in and Meadows didn't need to ask if he had found Laura or Henry.

'Lester's downstairs talking to Folland,' Blackwell said. 'What does he know?'

Meadows ran a hand through his hair. 'I haven't told him about Laura and Edris. I don't want his reputation tarnished.'

Blackwell nodded. 'It will have to come out at some point.'

'Let's give him the chance to explain.'

'What if… Well, hopefully, we can minimise the damage.'

Mike Fielding walked into the office. 'How are you all holding up?'

Paskin shook her head and turned her attention to the screen.

'It's not good news,' Mike said. 'The blood found in the car is a match to Edris. No fingerprints, other than his, were found on the steering wheel. We did find mud in the driver's footwell. The soil sample doesn't match that found in Pen Arthur Wood. We've called in an expert to see if they can narrow down an area from the sample. One small bit of good news. A pair of size ten and a pair of size six hiking boots were taken from Gareth Hendon's garage. Both had soil which matches that found in the car.' He handed Meadows the test results.

Meadows stood up. 'That's something to work with, thanks.'

'There were also traces of lubricant found in the boot. The type used on bike chains.'

'Does Edris have a bike?' Blackwell asked.

Meadows shook his head. 'It explains how someone could dump Edris' car and get away quickly. Just put a folding bike in the boot.'

Mike headed for the door. 'Oh, the blood test results from Jenna Ford show ketamine in her system. I'll keep you posted on any further developments.'

Meadows turned to Paskin. 'Better send someone to tell Jenna the results. Right, Gareth Hendon has had enough time with his solicitor. Let's see what he has to say about the phone, boots, and drugs. Want to sit in?'

'Yeah,' Blackwell said.

* * *

Gareth was already waiting in the interview room with his solicitor. His eyes were bloodshot, and his hair was sticking up at various angles. He didn't look like he had changed his clothes in days.

Blackwell started the recording and noted the time, date, and those present.

'We've prepared a statement,' the solicitor said and slid a sheet of paper across the table.

Meadows read it then handed it to Blackwell.

Blackwell skimmed over the paper and grunted. 'You say you were drinking in the Half Moon pub with Henry on Tuesday night, and slept in the summer house.'

'Yeah,' Gareth said.

Blackwell sat back and folded his arms. 'We haven't been able to locate Henry to corroborate your story. The pub landlord says you left at 10.30 p.m. That's not particularly late. Why sleep in the summerhouse?'

Gareth shifted in his seat. 'Jenna and I had argued.'

'What about?' Meadows asked.

'The usual stuff. Laura and the children.'

'Were Jenna or Jamie still up when you went in the summer house?'

Gareth shrugged.

'I'm sure one of them would have seen you go in the summer house or at least seen a light. I take it you weren't stumbling around in the dark,' Meadows said. 'There is a clear view of the garden from the kitchen. We will be checking with Jenna and Jamie.'

'No one was up. I didn't go home straight after the pub. It was around 2 a.m. Something like that. I don't remember.'

'What did you do from the time you left the pub until you got home?' Meadows asked.

'I picked up a bottle of vodka from the off-licence. Henry stayed with me for a while but he wasn't drinking. He'd been drinking lemonade all evening. I had to get pissed.' Gareth laughed. 'It's the only way to understand Henry. After a while, I zoned out. Henry left and I sat by the river and drank the bottle.'

Meadows took out a photo of Edris and pushed it towards Gareth. 'Do you know this man?'

'Yeah. He's the other detective that came to the house the night Cora was taken, and a couple of times after.'

'He's missing,' Blackwell said.

'That's nothing to do with me,' Gareth said. 'I don't know the guy.'

'Detective Edris' phone was found in your garage,' Meadows said.

'I didn't put it there. I'm being set up.'

'Who is setting you up?' Meadows asked.

Gareth didn't answer.

Meadows took a sheet of paper from the folder and slid it across the table, along with a photograph. 'Two pairs of hiking boots were found in your garage. A size ten and a size six. Do you recognise these boots?'

Gareth looked at the photo. 'They look like my boots and probably Jenna's.'

'Soil samples taken from these boots match soil samples found in Detective Edris' car.'

Gareth paled.

The solicitor picked up the sheet of paper and viewed the results. 'My client is known to hike in the area. He would likely have picked up the same soil sample. Just take the area around the cycle path near my client's home for example. My client was searching for his daughter the night she went missing. As was Detective Edris. They both would have had the same soil beneath their boots.'

'That doesn't explain the phone,' Blackwell snapped. 'It was found in a locked garage.'

The solicitor looked at Gareth and nodded.

'OK. Jenna isn't well,' Gareth said. 'She's suffering from depression, but I think it may be more than that. She's not been herself. It's like she's had a personality change. When I went into the house yesterday morning, she was in bed and muddy footprints were all over the kitchen. When she got up, she denied walking mud into the house. I honestly think she doesn't remember.'

'Are you saying Jenna is somehow responsible for Detective Edris' disappearance?' Meadows asked. 'That she was the one to hide his phone in the garage?'

'No… I don't know. I don't want to believe that she would hurt anyone.' Gareth looked at Blackwell. 'When you showed us the photographs of the clothes that had been left at the charity shop, I recognised Jenna's red top. She was complaining that it was missing a few days before. That's what we were arguing about yesterday morning.'

'Do you think Jenna had something to do with Alex's murder?' Meadows asked.

'She blamed him for our break-up.'

'What about Ceri's death?'

'That was an accident,' Gareth said.

Meadows shook his head. 'We are looking into the original investigation. It appears that she may have been pushed.'

Gareth put his head in his hands.

'It's very convenient to blame Jenna,' Meadows said.

Gareth looked up. 'What do you mean?'

'She has a history of depression and mood swings and a motive to kill Alex and Ceri. The thing is, so do you. With Ceri and Alex out of the way, you were free to pursue a relationship with Laura.'

'You think I would kill my girlfriend and best friend?'

'Why did you and Laura break up?'

'I don't think that's relevant,' the solicitor said.

Meadows looked at Blackwell. If they brought up Laura's relationship with a serving officer, working the case, they would be open to all sorts of questions. The IOPC would get involved and they couldn't afford any delays. Let alone having the case taken from them.

'If Jenna were to be charged with abduction and murder, then that would leave your client free to rekindle his relationship with Laura. I should also add that we haven't been able to locate Laura.'

'I broke up with Laura,' Gareth said. 'I didn't love her in that way. Laura and I would never have worked. I love Jenna and I wanted it to work. Do you think I want to sit here and tell you I don't trust Jenna? That she may have done something awful? She's not well. She needs help.'

Meadows leaned forward. 'Jenna isn't ill and she will get the help she needs. We asked her to take a blood test this morning. The results showed ketamine in her system.'

Gareth's eyes widened. 'She's been taking drugs? I knew she was off her face most of the time, but she denied taking anything. If she had a problem, she could have told me.'

'Jenna wasn't aware that she was taking drugs,' Blackwell said. 'She told us that Laura took her herbal tablets to get them tested. Laura told Jenna to leave the house as it wasn't safe.'

'Laura was the one who was giving Jenna the tablets. She picked them up whenever Jenna ran out,' Gareth said.

'Easy to switch them out,' Blackwell said.

'Why would I drug Jenna? I'm hardly going to do that and leave her in charge of the children.'

'Maybe you wanted to make her believe she was losing it,' Blackwell said. 'Throw suspicion on her.'

'This is so fucked up,' Gareth said. 'I'm not the only one that had access to those tablets. People are in and out of the house all the time. I told you someone is messing with me. It has to be Henry. He's the one that…'

'That what?' Meadows asked.

Gareth sat back and shook his head.

'Why would Henry be messing with you?'

'I'm not saying any more,' Gareth said. 'I've answered all your questions. If you're stupid enough to believe that I would drug Jenna, kill Ceri and Alex, and do fuck knows what to this missing detective, and hide his phone in my garage, then that's your problem.'

All other questions were met with a "no comment". Meadows could see the frustration on Blackwell's face and time was galloping by. He ended the interview and went back to the office.

'Are we going to charge him?' Blackwell asked.

'We don't have enough evidence, and besides which, I don't think he's involved in Edris' disappearance. He's not stupid. If he wanted to get rid of the phone, he could have thrown it in the river. It's only metres from his house. Same with the boots. I think we're being played.'

'By whom?' Paskin asked.

'Edris either found out something about Laura or he was trying to protect her. Her brother said she couldn't be trusted. Then there's Henry. Gareth thinks Henry is messing with him but wouldn't say why.'

'It has to be something they were both involved in,' Blackwell said. 'If Gareth tells us, then he implicates himself. Why else would he clam up?'

'Any news on Henry?' Meadows asked.

Paskin shook her head. 'Hanes is looking for him, and I asked Taylor to talk to Jenna. She couldn't locate her. The kids are with Beth. Jenna left them there a few hours ago. Beth said she was in a hurry, and didn't say where she was going.'

'Oh that's just great,' Blackwell said. 'She could be in it with Gareth for all we know.'

'Or she's the one playing games,' Paskin said.

Meadows nodded. 'She could be acting the victim. Gareth hasn't been home so she could have been out of the house without anyone noticing. Her boots also had mud, but–'

Meadows was interrupted by Chris who rushed into the office followed by Valentine. 'I managed to get into Edris' laptop,' he said.

'We found something interesting,' Valentine said.

Chris sat down and opened the screen. The team gathered around.

'OK. First, I took a look at Edris' search history.' Chris tapped the keys.

'Ogof y Cysg Eira. The cave of the sleeping snow,' Valentine said.

'Eira,' Paskin said. 'Same name as the waterfall. The one in the photo where Ceri looked upset.'

Valentine nodded. 'There is a connection.' She looked at Chris. 'Go on.'

'Nothing was coming back on the searches,' Chris said. 'He's also got a file of the same name. Here.' He opened the file. 'Not a lot in it.'

Meadows read the document. 'OK, so it's a cave that was found by Alex, Laura, Gareth, Ceri, Henry, and Eira Thomas.'

'Who is Eira Thomas?' Blackwell asked.

'That's who Edris was looking into,' Valentine said. 'He requested her death certificate and an inquest report. She died on the 20th of May 2018 in a caving accident. Drowned.'

'Why the fuck would he keep this information to himself?' Blackwell asked.

'I'm guessing because he couldn't reveal his source of information,' Meadows said.

Valentine sighed. 'Laura.'

'If he had found a record of the cave, then he could have brought it to us. I'd asked him to check out caves in the area to see if there had been any incidents,' Meadows said.

Valentine nodded. 'He put in a request to cave rescue for records of accidents in that year. I guess he didn't want to be specific. There is a record, but the cave is not named. It's listed as unnamed and no mention of the others. Doesn't even give the exact location.'

Paskin, who had been typing away on her keyboard, called them over. 'I found Eira Thomas' obituary.' She read aloud. 'Eira Thomas beloved daughter of May and Craig Thomas. Much-loved little sister to Daniel and Stephen, and loving fiancée of Henry Tay.'

The pieces all slotted together, and a coldness crept over Meadows. 'We need to find him. Now.'

Chapter Thirty

Another drop of water fell on Edris' head. It tracked down his wet hair and ran into his eye. He felt so cold and it was difficult to wake up. He forced his eyes to open. Nothing. He blinked. Still nothing. He was in complete darkness.

He tried to move his hands to wipe his eyes, but they were bound behind his back. He struggled for a moment, but it was no use. It was then that he became aware of the pain. Pain in his head. Pain in his arms and legs. Pain in his back. Everything hurt and his mouth was dry.

He tried to focus and work out where he was. He was going to Laura's house. Did he get there? What was he doing before that? He tried to call out, but only a croaking sound left his mouth. Another drip fell on his head. He tilted his head back as far as it would go and waited. He was rewarded with a drop of water. It wasn't enough. He kept his mouth open, waiting. The only thing he could think about now was his thirst. He could hear running water nearby. It sounded like a stream, but he didn't know how far away it was, and if he had the strength to get there. It seemed to take forever just for the drips of water to wet his tongue enough for him to swallow. Still, there was no relief for his throat. The water was crisp and cold with an earthy taste and his thoughts turned to his location. It was hard to think through the fog of his mind, but snippets were coming back to him.

A necklace. A St Christopher. He'd been looking for it. He had to get somewhere. Where was he going? Another memory surfaced. Walking in the dark. Someone leading him. A voice. "We need to hide." It disappeared like a wisp of smoke.

He tried to move his feet now. The rough surface scraped at his heels. He didn't recall taking off his shoes. He stretched out his fingers. The surface was hard and cold. More memories were coming back. Leaving work. A hot shower. Getting in the car. Pain in his head. Someone had hit him. He needed to move and get some help.

He shifted his legs to the right then shuffled over, then again. The third time, his feet hit freezing water and sank. He quickly shuffled back.

'Help! Is anyone there?'

His voice echoed in the darkness, and then his mind cleared. The dripping, the freezing water, the echo, and the absolute darkness. He was underground. Panic gripped him like a vice, and he screamed.

Chapter Thirty-one

Meadows looked out of the station window. The wind had picked up and was bending the trees. Dark clouds swirled in the sky and a flock of crows were heading to roost before the oncoming storm hit.

He turned away from the window. 'When did Hanes call?'

'Fifteen minutes ago,' Valentine said. 'He should arrive any minute with Henry. He said he was going to blue-light it.'

'They're not going to be able to keep up the search if the storm hits,' Blackwell said.

'Let's just hope it blows over,' Meadows said. He turned back to the window. 'They're here. We'll give Hanes a few moments to book in, then we'll speak to Henry. With a bit of luck, we won't have to wait for a solicitor.'

Paskin swivelled around in her chair. 'Data from Laura's phone has come through. Calls and text messages. The phone is still turned off, so they haven't been able to triangulate it yet.'

Meadows joined Blackwell and Valentine at Paskin's desk. 'Look at the last messages Laura sent.'

'It's the same unknown number that was coming up on Edris' phone,' Valentine said.

Meadows read the messages.

> Unknown: If you want to see your lover again, you need to do exactly what I say.

Laura: What have you done?

Unknown: Stay in the house and don't call anyone.

Laura: Why are you doing this? I didn't tell the police.

Laura: Please, he doesn't know anything.

Unknown: Take the kids to school in the morning as usual. Don't talk to anyone. Go straight back home and I'll tell you what to do next. I'll be watching.

Laura: I've done what you asked. The kids are in school.

Unknown: There's a phone and a bottle of tablets in the dustbin outside your house. Switch Jenna's tablets and get rid of the bottle. Leave the phone in the garage behind the oxygen tanks. Then meet me at Herbert's Quarry.

'Look at the time stamp between the texts,' Paskin said. 'She had to wait all night before receiving instructions.'

'She must have been going out of her mind,' Valentine said. 'Jenna did say she looked in a state.'

Meadows re-read the messages. 'She appears to know the sender. She never asks who it is.'

Valentine nodded. 'It's clear she knows something by her reference to not talking to the police.'

'The question is, why keep that information when your mother has been murdered?'

'Probably frightened for her own life,' Paskin said.

'I'm not so sure,' said Meadows. 'She told Edris about the cave. OK, Henry's had enough time. Let's go and speak to him.'

'He's probably going to spout some mumbo jumbo about spirits and plead insanity,' Blackwell said.

'At the moment we have no evidence against Henry,' Meadows said. 'Our best bet now is to appear open-minded. I don't care if we have to speak to his spirit guide to get the answers.'

'Fine, I'll just get a Ouija board,' Blackwell said.

'Don't be a dick,' Valentine snapped.

Meadows sighed. 'It could be Henry's way of protecting himself. Perhaps he can't deal with the reality of losing his fiancée. Going in hard is likely to make him clam up. We need to play along. Valentine, you better sit in with me. Blackwell, go to Herbert's Quarry and see if Laura's car is there.'

Meadows grabbed a file and headed downstairs with Valentine. Hanes was standing with a group of uniformed officers by the custody desk.

'I've put him in interview room one,' Hanes said. 'He came quietly, but I had to listen to all sorts of bollocks on the way back. I could barely bring myself to look at him.'

'We're not sure it's him, yet,' Valentine said.

Meadows could see the stress on Hanes' face. All the officers were tired from searching the forest, and morale was low. Edris was well liked in the station and often went out with Hanes. There was nothing he could say to them. He left the group and headed for the interview room.

Henry was wearing a dirty boiler suit. He'd slung his jacket over the back of the chair.

Meadows waited for Valentine to set up the recording before he started.

'Henry, at this stage, you are not under arrest. However, this is a formal interview, and you are entitled to representation.'

'I'll take my advice from Arthur,' Henry said.

It was the response Meadows had hoped for. They didn't have time to wait for a solicitor. 'Arthur is your spirit guide, is that correct?'

'Yes.'

'That's fine. Just let us know when you need a moment to communicate.'

Henry looked at Meadows and smiled.

'You're a difficult man to find. Do you mind telling us where you've been for the last two days?' Meadows asked.

'I took a group out camping, gorge walking, and caving. Young offenders. It's part of their rehabilitation. You know, they get really into it. You can see a change in them when they achieve something. Everyone deserves a second chance, don't you think?'

'Yes,' Meadows said. 'You weren't away with the group for the whole time, though.'

'When we got back, I decided to go to Ogof Ffynnon Ddu. Have you been?'

Meadows shook his head. 'I'm not that adventurous.'

Henry nodded. 'It's the second longest cave in Wales and the deepest in the UK. I can't take a group of novices down there. It's too dangerous. Sometimes I like to go off on my own.'

Meadows gave Valentine a nod.

Valentine took out a photo of Edris and moved it towards Henry. 'That's Detective Tristan Edris. He's been missing for two nights.'

Henry looked at the photo and then at Meadows. 'He's your partner.'

'Yes,' Meadows said.

'You must be very worried. The last time I saw him, he was going into Laura's house. Three nights ago.'

Meadows hadn't expected this response and wasn't too happy about it being on record. He took a sheet of paper from the file and handed it to Henry. 'Did you send this text?'

Henry looked at the paper and frowned. 'No, why would I? It's none of my business what people get up to in their spare time.'

'What were you doing outside Laura's house?'

'I was just checking to see if she was OK. With everything that's been going on, I was worried about her.'

'When was the last time you saw Laura?'

'I spoke to her outside the vet's, Tuesday evening.'

'What did you talk about?'

'I wanted to offer my condolences and warn her.'

Meadows sat forward. 'Warn her?'

Henry nodded. 'I told her I had messages for her, but she didn't want to know. Is she in trouble?'

'We haven't been able to contact her. Were these messages from Arthur?'

'No, not as such. From others. Arthur helps me communicate with the others. He also protects me from evil spirits. He's a kind of filter.'

'What was it that the others wanted you to tell Laura?'

'They wanted to warn her; let her know she was in trouble.'

'Do you often get messages like that?'

Henry nodded. 'The problem is, people don't want to believe. Like that missing detective. Do you remember when you came to my house? I told him he had a dark aura. He didn't take it seriously.'

'If you asked for a message now, do you think the spirits would help? Maybe they can locate him.'

'I can try,' Henry said. He sat back and closed his eyes.

Meadows and Valentine watched. Nothing happened for a moment, then Henry nodded and opened his eyes.

'He's still in this world, but not for much longer,' Henry said. 'The problem is, he's not receptive. He won't open his mind. Arthur is going to keep trying.'

If Henry is guilty, then that's his way of saying Edris is still alive, Meadows thought. He just had to play along and hope he got more information.

'OK,' Meadows said. 'We appreciate that.' He gave Valentine a nod.

Valentine folded her hands and placed them on the table. 'We heard about what happened to your fiancée, Eira. I'm sorry, that must have been very hard for you.'

Meadows saw Henry stiffen.

Valentine leaned forward. 'I understand how difficult it must be for you to talk about, but it's important that we know what happened that day.'

'What's the point?' Henry said. 'I told them all it wasn't an accident. I even said it at the inquest.'

'We're listening now,' Meadows said.

Valentine nodded.

'The six of us used to go hiking and looking for unexplored caves.'

'The six being Alex, Laura, Gareth, Ceri, Eira, and yourself?' Meadows asked.

Henry nodded.

'There's something magical about being in a place no one has ever seen. We found a few small caves, but nothing major. Sometimes we would go off alone or in pairs. It was Alex who discovered the cave. He took a quick look, then took us all to see for ourselves. We explored the first cavern but we needed our diving equipment to go further. The left- and right-hand passages both led to sumps. That's a flooded area of the cave. The one on the right led to a resurgence pool. We knew it was going to be a difficult dive. We explored that one first. The pool was about seven metres deep with ledges and an undercurrent. It led to a second cavern. That's as far as we got on that visit, and the same in the other passage. We laid down guidelines and then went back a third time.

'We decided to split into two groups. Alex, Ceri, and Eira took the right-hand passages. Laura, Gareth, and I took the left. I should have gone with Eira, but I had a close call the week before. I lost my nerve. I'd got stuck under a ledge when we were laying the guideline on that side. It's deeper and has a strong undercurrent. Eira was a good diver. The best out of all of us, so I wasn't overly worried.

'The three of us went down the left-hand passage. It was when we were about to enter the water that Laura realised she had picked up Ceri's gear. She wanted to go back, but we thought the others would already be in the water. There was no difference with the equipment. It's just Ceri's SPG was a twin console.'

'What's an SPG?' Valentine asked.

'Submersible pressure gauge. Ceri's had a compass. Laura was comfortable using a single, but she was worried about Ceri. Ceri had a fear of getting lost. You can't afford to get distracted when you're underwater. We waited about ten minutes and decided Ceri must have gone ahead with the dive.

'We completed the second passage and found a third cavern. It was on the way back that we met with Ceri. She said there had been a rockfall, and Eira was trapped. We went back to the first cavern. We had brought extra tanks of air for emergencies. Gareth and I took an extra tank each. By the time we reached the second cavern, Alex had pulled Eira from the water. He was doing CPR, but it was too late.

'Alex said he had managed to free Eira, and she was following him back. When he got out of the water, he waited a few minutes for her to surface. When she didn't, he realised something was wrong. He found her floating in the water. Her regulator had come free from her mouth.'

'Did you blame Alex for not going back sooner?' Meadows asked.

'No. Not then, at least. I was in shock. When I started to think about it, I knew it was no accident. Eira was the most experienced diver among us. Then I started getting messages and I knew she wasn't at peace. She was trying to tell me something.'

Meadows leaned a little closer. 'What was she trying to tell you?'

'That one of the others had killed her.'

'I don't understand,' Valentine said.

'I spoke to Ceri first. She was in a state. When she realised she had Laura's equipment, she didn't want to go through with the dive. Eira had a twin SPG, so they swapped. Not the SPG, the whole outfit. You can't mess around with tanks in a dark cave. Ceri was happy with that. They took the first sump, and they were all OK. The second sump was where Ceri was supposed to take the lead, but she asked Eira to go first. They were about thirty minutes in when Eira got stuck. Ceri got caught up in the guideline and Alex had to cut it. He took Ceri back to the second cavern and sent her to get help.

'I know Eira wouldn't have panicked. She would be sticking to the rule of thirds. A third of air on the way in, a third on the way back, and a third spare. If she had realised she had used over a third of her air, she would have signalled to Alex that she was getting low when he freed her. When I spoke to Alex, he said she had signalled for him to go ahead.'

Henry looked from Valentine to Meadows. 'Don't you get it? Alex got out with no problems. He had gone back to help Eira, twice, and still had enough air to get back to the first cavern. There was an investigation and Eira's equipment was checked out. Her SPG was broken. It could have happened when she got stuck. Even so, she would have calculated her air supply by the amount of time they had been in the water. She always did it. She would have checked her watch before the SPG.'

'So you're saying that Eira had less air in the tanks than the rest of you,' Meadows said.

Henry nodded. 'The tanks were all supposed to be full, and don't forget it was Laura's gear.'

'Do you think Laura tampered with the equipment?' Valentine asked.

'No, she couldn't have. The group were together the whole time. She was the one meant to die.'

'Don't you check the equipment before diving?' Meadows asked.

Henry nodded. 'Buoyancy, weights, releases, and air. The last thing she would have done is purge the regulator. None of this would have shown the tanks weren't full if the SPG was broken. All the equipment had been checked the night before. We kept all the gear in Gareth's garage, as he had the space. We were all working at the time. We would take turns to set everything up the night before and load the van. That trip was Gareth and Alex's turn. We all met up at the quarry that morning. I thought one, or both of them, messed up and didn't want to admit it. Then when Ceri died, I knew that what happened to Eira wasn't an accident. Again no one would listen. To be honest, I had lost my shit by then. I was drinking and taking all sorts of stuff. It was easy to let things in, if you know what I mean. I was more in the spirit world than this one. Without Arthur, I would have permanently crossed over. You get the ones who encourage you. I tried to get my life back together and find some peace. Then Alex was found. Six people went into that cave and only three are left. That's why I was trying to warn Laura. She's escaped death twice. First in the cave, then the second time when she switched coats with Ceri. I think Laura was meant to go over that waterfall.'

'Who do you think is trying to kill Laura?'

Henry closed his eyes.

Valentine looked at Meadows and raised her eyebrows.

'OK,' Henry said. 'Yes, I know.' He opened his eyes and looked at Meadows. 'I believe you have an open mind and I can trust you.'

'Yes,' Meadows said.

Henry nodded. 'Eira. She won't stop until the truth is out.'

Meadows struggled to keep the frustration from his face. 'Eira acting through somebody?'

'That's possible,' Henry said.

'If Eira wanted to hurt Laura, where would she take her?'

Henry leaned forward. 'The cave.'

'In that case, I think Laura is in trouble. Can you give us the location of Ogof y Cysg Eira?'

'I don't want her disturbed.'

'We'll be very respectful,' Meadows said. 'Don't you want answers? Don't you want Eira to be at peace?'

'Yes. I'll tell you the location when Gareth tells the truth. You won't find the cave without me. I doubt Gareth will remember how to get there. It was supposed to be our discovery. We would have all been given credit. They let me name the cave. They always planned to go back and finish the exploration, but Eira would never allow that. The name of the cave and the location weren't made public. As soon as Gareth tells you what happened, I'll take you there myself. You have my word.'

Meadows left the interview room and slammed his hand against the wall. 'Damn it!'

'Are you OK?' Valentine asked.

Meadows took a deep breath and reminded himself that anger never solved anything. He nodded.

Hanes came over to join them.

'What is it? Is it Edris?'

Meadows shook his head. 'Hanes, get Gareth Hendon out of the cell. I've had enough of these games. He's going to talk or we charge him.'

Chapter Thirty-two

Gareth plonked himself down in the chair and folded his arms. 'I already told you, I've got nothing more to say. You can't just haul me in here without my solicitor.'

Valentine took a seat and switched on the recording.

Meadows remained standing. 'Your solicitor is on the way. While we wait, I want to talk to you about Ogof y Cysg Eira.'

Gareth paled.

'I'd like you to give me the location.'

'I don't know it.'

'You are very fond of Laura,' Meadows said.

Gareth nodded.

'Then help her.'

'I can't. It's been over six years since I went to the cave. Alex was the one that led the way.'

'Henry told us what happened there,' Meadows said.

Gareth huffed. 'Henry has lost the plot. He wanted me and Laura to go there and have a seance.'

'If Laura is in that cave, she doesn't have much time,' Meadows said. 'If she has no access to water…' He let the sentence hang in the air.

'She could be injured,' Valentine added.

'Henry knows the location,' Meadows said. 'He won't tell us until he learns the truth. At the moment, you are looking at a charge for the abduction of a police officer, and a possible charge for the murder of Alex and Ceri. Detective Edris' phone was found in your garage. At the very least, you are obstructing an investigation by withholding information. Information that could save two lives.' Meadows sat down. 'You can choose to wait for your solicitor and waste more time, or you can tell us what you know.'

Gareth rubbed his hands over his face. 'OK. It was just an accident. Alex and I were supposed to set up the equipment and load the van. When Alex didn't turn up, I started without him. Ceri was helping me. We'd got two done when Laura showed up with Maisie. She said Alex had a flat battery and she needed to go and give him a jump start. She asked if I had a set of leads. I got them from the jeep. She asked Ceri to take Maisie to Deryn's to save time. They all went off and I carried on. By the time they came back, I'd finished.'

'Go on,' Meadows said.

'We were all in shock after it happened. Henry was in a hell of a state. Ceri and Alex blamed themselves because they were with Eira. Laura and I tried to stay strong and help them. We all went back to my place. We didn't want to leave Henry alone. Laura was worried about leaving the rest of the equipment in the van. She didn't want Henry to see it the next morning, so we went to empty it.

'We always stacked the used tanks on the right and the new ones on the left,' Gareth continued. 'There should have been six sets of doubles on the left and six sets ready to refill on the right. There were only four sets on the right. We checked the left and found seven sets. I must have taken the tanks from the wrong side after I got the jump leads for Laura. I just don't understand how I could have done that, and then not noticed. I'm sure all the SPGs showed full. I would have checked, but it's one of those things you do automatically. When I tried to think back, I started to doubt myself. The only other explanation is that the SPG was broken before the dive, and not damaged when Eira got stuck. I know from the inquest that Eira's isolation switch was open, and both tanks were empty.'

Meadows could well imagine the guilt Gareth had felt at the time.

'I couldn't face Henry, and I asked Laura not to say anything. She agreed as it wouldn't have made a difference. After Ceri died, I thought about coming clean. Henry's talk of spirits made me think it may have been some sort of payback. Laura convinced me to stay quiet. She said she looked into it, and I could get charged with manslaughter, especially after not speaking up at the inquest.'

'Did Ceri know about this?'

'No, only me and Laura.'

Meadows stood. 'Thank you.' He rushed to see Henry and repeated what Gareth had told him.

Henry sobbed.

Meadows could see the years of not knowing and not having anyone listen, come crashing down. Henry's body shook as tears ran down his face.

'Henry,' Meadows said gently. 'We need the location of the cave.'

Henry nodded. 'Give me a pen and paper.'

Valentine took a pen from her pocket and tore a sheet of paper from her pad. Henry started scribbling and then handed the sheet to Meadows.

'It will be better if I come with you. It's dangerous.'

'I can't let you do that,' Meadows said.

'I guessed as much. Stick to the instructions. Whatever you do, don't go in the water.'

Chapter Thirty-three

'Are you out of your mind?' Lester said. 'There is a reason that the search helicopter is grounded. Look.' He pointed to the window.

Meadows didn't need to look. He could hear the rain pounding against the glass. It didn't matter. He'd made up his mind.

Lester continued. 'There's not enough daylight left for search and rescue to locate the cave. It's over a two-hour hike at best. They will resume the search at daybreak, by which time the storm will have cleared. The helicopter can drop them near the location.'

'Edris and Laura may not have until daybreak,' Meadows said. 'It's approaching forty-eight hours since he was last seen. If he's had no access to water, then—'

Lester cut in. 'You don't even know he is in that cave.'

'This whole case has been about the cave. Gareth told us that Henry wanted them to go there to perform a seance. Henry's alibi checks out for the evening Edris went missing. He was miles away with a camping group but he might not have been working alone. Eira has two brothers that Paskin is trying to trace. On top of that, Jenna is missing. She could be working with Henry. To be honest, we can't even be sure Henry is guilty.'

'Then you don't know what you will face when you enter that cave.'

'I'm prepared for that.'

Blackwell and Valentine were leaning against a desk, listening to the exchange. So far, they hadn't commented. Meadows wasn't sure if they agreed with Lester or not. He knew they would be torn.

Lester moved in front of him. 'I'm sorry, I can't let you go wandering the mountains alone in a storm. That's my final word.'

'Right, well I'm off duty,' Meadows said. 'I'm well over my hours, so this is on my own time.'

'I… you…' Lester grew red in the face. 'I'm giving you a direct order.'

'I haven't got time for this,' Meadows said. 'You can suspend me or fire me. It makes no difference.'

'Yeah, me too,' Blackwell said.

'I'm no longer on duty,' Valentine added.

'Oh. No,' Meadows said. 'I can't ask you to do that.'

'You didn't,' Valentine said.

'You can't stop us, any more than we can stop you,' Blackwell said. 'You didn't think I was letting you go alone.'

Meadows nodded. 'Go home and grab some warm clothes and waterproofs. We also need plenty of water.'

'I'll coordinate with search and rescue,' Paskin said. 'As soon the storm moves, I'll get them to assist you.'

'Bloody idiots,' Lester said and marched out of the office.

* * *

The rain was driving into their faces as they battled against the wind. Search and rescue had provided them with rope, head torches, and a handheld GPS device. Meadows' backpack was filled with bottled water, a flask of hot tea, and food. Valentine carried a first aid kit, and

Blackwell had foil blankets. Each of them had a handheld torch and handcuffs. They were taking no chances.

'It has to be Henry,' Valentine shouted above the wind. 'Someone is helping him.'

Meadows nodded. 'He didn't deny it, but I didn't ask him outright. We needed to gain his trust.'

'Don't know how you kept your patience,' Blackwell said. 'Then again, I've never seen you lose it.'

'He did tell Lester where to get off,' Valentine said.

Blackwell laughed. 'I thought he was going to burst a blood vessel. Now he's going to be in a conundrum. He can't fire us all.'

'Don't be too sure,' Meadows said.

'Let's just hope we find this knobhead,' Blackwell said. 'The only reason I'm with you is because I would have looked like a right pussy if I let you two go alone.'

Meadows knew this wasn't true, but Blackwell would never let on that he also cared about Edris.

'If it is Henry, I can't figure out why he would take a defenceless baby and put her in the river,' Valentine said. 'The baby had nothing to do with what happened to Eira.'

'I guess he wanted to make Gareth suffer. Lose someone close to him,' Blackwell said.

Meadows rubbed the rain from his eyes. 'Gareth had already lost Ceri. Then there's Deryn's murder. There is no record of her calling Henry and, if she suspected him, she wouldn't have let him into the house. Logically, she would have called the police, not Gareth. All I know is that we were meant to find this cave. Just as we were meant to find Edris' car and phone. The question is, what are we going to find there?'

They became silent as they battled their way across the mountain. There was no let-up in the wind, but the rain had slowed. Darkness had fallen by the time they reached a ravine with a wide stream cutting through it.

'We need to get down,' Meadows said. He took his torch from his backpack and pointed it downwards.

There was a steep drop to the bottom. Large rocks jutted out from the water.

'Hell no,' Blackwell said.

'We'll walk further along and see if we can find a safer way down,' Meadows said.

They tracked alongside the ravine until Meadows spotted a rocky area. He stopped and checked the GPS. 'We're getting too far off course. We'll use the ropes. I can bear the weight when the two of you go down.'

'How are you going to get down?' Valentine asked.

'I can do it,' Meadows said.

They sent Blackwell down first so that Valentine could help support his weight. Meadows kept his feet apart and used the rock to anchor himself. With a lot of cursing, Blackwell reached the bottom. Valentine was faster to get down. Meadows let the rope drop and scrambled down on his backside. He was sliding out of control by the time he reached the bottom, and was grateful that Blackwell and Valentine caught him before he went into the water.

Blackwell shined his torch into the stream. 'Now what?'

Meadows started unlacing his boots. 'We have to wade across. We're not going to find a bridge.' He took off his socks and placed them in his pocket before stepping into the icy water.

The stones were slippery and moved under Meadows' feet. He stopped and held out his hand to Valentine. 'Be careful. You're going to have to feel your way across. Try and find the smaller stones.'

Blackwell stepped into the water. 'Fucking hell! I'm going to lose my toes.'

Meadows couldn't help smiling despite the situation. He was glad that Blackwell and Valentine were with him. Halfway across the stream, they were up to their thighs in fast-flowing water, and he couldn't feel his toes. He was first to reach the bank and pulled the other two out.

'I can't get my bastard socks on,' Blackwell said.

'Stop bitching,' Valentine said. 'Roll them on.'

Blackwell grunted but managed to get his boots back on.

The climb back up was difficult. Blackwell struggled and kept sliding back down. Meadows had to pull him most of the way, and by the time they reached the top, they were exhausted. It was difficult to see now, as heavy clouds hid the moonlight. They pushed on, too tired to talk. Each time they reached the top of a hill, another one appeared in front of them.

When they thought they had faced the worst, lightning cracked the sky and illuminated the mountain. Wild horses scattered and sheep bleated.

'We should find shelter,' Blackwell said. 'If we get hit by the lightning, we're fucked.'

'Don't worry,' Meadows said. 'It will hit the highest point first.'

Valentine laughed. 'That will be you then.'

Meadows checked the GPS. 'We're nearly there.'

He picked up speed with Blackwell huffing behind him. Twenty minutes later, he stopped. It's around here somewhere. Henry said it's between the rocks.'

Blackwell swept his torch around. The beam picked up a large rocky area. 'Like that's going to help.'

They began searching between the rocks, but it was slow-going.

'When we find the entrance, we'll have to go in quietly. If someone is in there with Laura and Edris, I don't want to give them a chance to act.'

'I'm so done,' Blackwell said. He sat on a rock and took out his flask.

Meadows continued searching with Valentine. He was cold, wet, and tired, but there was no way he was giving up. He moved further down and stopped and listened.

'I can hear the stream,' he said. 'Henry said the water comes out at some point below the cave entrance.'

'Oi!' Blackwell called out.

Meadows turned and saw Blackwell pointing the beam of his torch down the side of the rock he was sitting on. 'Found the bugger.'

Chapter Thirty-four

Meadows entered the cave first and felt the drop in temperature.

'I didn't think it could get any colder,' Blackwell whispered.

Meadows didn't answer. He wasn't sure how far their voices would carry. He moved along, keeping his head low, and torch trained on the floor. The passage narrowed and Meadows had to turn sideways.

'No way,' Blackwell hissed. 'I'm not going to get through there.'

'Stay here,' Meadows said. 'We don't know how deep we have to go. If we find him, we'll shout. You can get outside quickly and call for help. I think the worst of the storm is over. They should be able to get the helicopter down somewhere nearby. If we're not out in an hour... well, it's your call.'

Blackwell nodded.

Meadows and Valentine continued. The floor sloped downwards, and they had to squeeze through some parts. The ceiling glistened in the light, and the only sound came from the drips of water that plinked as they hit the floor.

A sudden noise made them freeze. It sounded like an object had been dropped and had bounced as it went downhill. The clattering sound echoed around them. Next came a scrabbling noise.

Meadows put his finger to his lips and moved on. He quickened his pace, putting his hand against the rock to keep himself steady. The passageway opened into a cavern and the floor changed to a pile of loose stones sloping downwards. His torch lit a pair of eyes and he heard Valentine gasp behind him.

Laura was crouched on the floor. Her hair was wild and her face dirty. She whimpered and backed away.

'Laura, it's OK. We're police,' Valentine said.

Laura got slowly to her feet. A sob escaped her mouth and she ran towards Meadows. She put her arms around his waist and sobbed against him. 'I didn't think anyone would find me down here.'

Meadows could feel her body trembling. He gently pulled her arms from his body and took a step back. 'Laura, I understand how distressing this is for you but we need to find Tristan.'

'He's not here.'

Meadows' stomach plummeted. 'You need to tell us what happened.'

Laura nodded. 'Just get me out of this place.'

'We will. I promise, but we need to know what happened.'

'Tristan was supposed to come to my house. He didn't show up and then I got a message.'

'We know about the text messages,' Meadows said. 'What happened when you got to the quarry car park?'

'Tristan's car was there with a note on the windscreen. The note said to come here. It took me so long to find it. When I got inside, someone grabbed me from behind. They tied my hands behind my back and pushed me further in. I thought they were going to throw me in the water. Then I felt a scratch on my side. I don't remember anything after that except waking up in the dark. I managed to get my hands loose and was trying to get out.'

'Who did this?' Valentine asked.

'I don't know, but I think... I think it was Gareth. Please, can we just go?'

Meadows nodded. 'Go with Detective Valentine.' He turned to Valentine. 'I'm going to keep looking for Edris. He may have been taken down one of the passages.'

'No!' Laura grabbed Meadows' arm. 'You can't go down there. It's too dangerous.'

Valentine took Laura's arm. 'Come on. Help is on the way.'

As Meadows moved forward, his light reflected off a piece of glass. He moved the beam and saw a broken torch. 'Hang on.'

Valentine stopped, and Laura turned around. Her eyes followed the beam of light.

It happened very quickly. It took Meadows seconds to process what he was seeing. The clatter they heard must have been the torch falling. Laura wasn't crawling out; she was scrabbling around for the torch. She knew the cave and said there was water ahead. She knew the way out. Even in the dark, she would know which direction to go.

'You were never–'

Laura grabbed the torch from Meadows' hand and took off.

Meadows only had the head torch but took off after Laura. His feet slid on the stones, and he leapt from the bottom onto solid ground. Laura was quick. She was smaller and had the advantage of knowing the cave.

Meadows could hear Valentine close behind. Her torch swung up and down as she ran, casting long shadows on the cave wall. He was gaining on Laura when a low-hanging rock struck his head. It knocked him backwards into Valentine.

In the seconds it took for Meadows to regain his balance, Laura had careered to the right. Meadows knew what was down that way. The pool that Henry had warned him about. He could hear the stream now. That meant they were close to the pool where the water gathered before spilling out and forcing its way through the rocks to create an underground passage.

He took off again.

'Careful,' he said as he wiped the blood that was running down into his eye.

Valentine's light caught the rippling water in the pool and to Meadows' horror, he saw Laura pushing a slumped figure into the water.

'No!' Valentine screamed.

Laura shoved and Edris disappeared head first into the pool. Meadows dived forward and managed to grab Edris' ankles before he completely went under. Valentine dropped to her knees beside him and gripped Edris' leg. Both began pulling.

'Watch out!' Valentine yelled.

Meadows turned his head in time to see Laura aim a syringe at his arm. Valentine let go of Edris and launched herself at Laura. Edris' weight pulled Meadows forward, plunging his hands into the freezing water. He had no idea if Edris was alive. If he was, there wasn't much time. He dug his heels into the floor and pulled with all his strength. He could hear the struggle going on behind him. He risked a look.

Laura was on Valentine's back with the syringe still grasped in her hand. Meadows could see the needle getting dangerously close to Valentine's neck. He had seconds to make a decision. If he let go of Edris, he would sink into the depths. They would have no chance of getting him back. If he didn't help Valentine, then whatever was in the syringe could kill her.

'Get off me, you crazy bitch,' Valentine shouted. She clenched her hand and thrust her arm up and over her shoulder. Her fist collided with Laura's nose.

Meadows heard Laura scream out in pain and turned back to Edris. He grabbed hold of his belt and with one final heave, he pulled him clear of the water. He looked across and saw Valentine straddling Laura and placing her hands in cuffs. He tilted Edris' head to the side, put his hands on his abdomen, and thrust upwards. Water sluiced from Edris' mouth.

Valentine came to kneel beside Edris. She removed her coat and put it over him before laying her head against his chest. 'He's so cold and I don't think he's breathing.'

Chapter Thirty-five

Meadows' head throbbed from where he'd hit it against the jagged rock. He'd received stitches in the hospital while they had waited for news of Edris. It was daylight by the time they all went home. Edris was still unconscious, and all they could do was wait.

After a quick shower, he'd come into the office. He was hoping for a few moments to gather his thoughts before interviewing Laura but had an unexpected visitor to the station.

Laura's father, Steve Jones, was sitting in the interview room and cradling a cup of tea.

Meadows took a seat. 'I'm sorry to have kept you waiting.'

'That's OK. I should have called first, but I thought it best to do this in person.'

'Are you aware we have your daughter in custody?'

Steve nodded. 'Laura is no daughter of mine. If I had known, well, even if I did, would any of you have believed what she is capable of? Mark tried to warn you. I never thought it would go this far. She needs to be locked up. If you need me to testify, then I'm more than happy to do that. She's very clever and manipulative. Even if you think you've got a case against her, I'm sure she'll find a way out.'

Meadows was all too aware that they had no physical evidence to tie Laura to the murder of Alex, Eira, and Ceri.

As for the murder of Deryn, she had an alibi. Only he and Valentine were witnesses to what happened in the cave. Laura did have a needle mark upon examination. All she had to do was claim that she was drugged and didn't know what she was doing. Their only hope was for Edris to wake up and tell them what happened. Added to that, Laura had put in a complaint about Valentine. He needed all the help he could get.

'Did you suspect that Laura had killed Alex?'

Steve shook his head. 'I thought he'd realised what she was like and got the hell out of there.'

'What about Deryn?'

'Mark said Laura had an alibi for when Deryn was killed.'

Meadows nodded. 'Given recent events, we're going back over all the statements to see if there is any way she could have been involved. Why do you think Deryn tried to contact you before she died? Could it be that she suspected Laura of killing Alex?'

'It's possible, but even if she knew for certain, she would never have turned Laura in. It was always like that. She made excuses and covered for her.'

'I take it Laura has been in trouble before.'

Steve took a sip of his tea. 'She was always a demanding child and quickly learned how to get her own way. She would play me and Deryn off against each other. When Mark was born, she was jealous of any attention we gave him. She used to hurt him. Not just pinching. She locked him in a cupboard, pushed him down the stairs, and tried to drown him in the bath. You had to constantly watch her. Deryn said it was normal for older siblings to be jealous, and she would grow out of it.' He shook his head.

'The final straw came when we attended a family wedding. We were all staying at a country hotel. My brother, his wife, and his two children were there. Laura was seven at the time. My niece Emily was five, a sweet little thing. During the evening, all the children were playing and Emily went missing. She was found face down in the swimming pool. I saw Laura watching her get pulled out. She had a satisfied smirk on her face. I don't mind telling you that she scared me.'

Meadows could visualise the scene. The screams and the chaos. A coldness crept over him. 'You're saying Laura pushed her cousin in the pool?'

Steve shrugged. 'I can't be certain, but she never showed any emotion. The other children were crying. At the funeral, Laura never shed a tear. That's what she was like. She never showed love, empathy, or compassion. There was always a callousness about her.'

'Did you talk to Deryn about it?'

'Yeah, but Deryn wouldn't have any of it. In the end, I was so frightened for Mark that I left and took him with me. It wasn't easy but I managed. I did take Mark to visit his mother. I wanted them to have a relationship, but Mark was terrified of Laura. It was easier to stay away. Just a quick visit on birthdays and Christmases.'

Steve took another sip of his tea and then set the cup down.

'As Laura got older, she learned to mimic emotions. She could turn on the charm, but I knew what lay beneath. I did try again. Both Mark and I did. I liked Alex and I thought that Laura had at least learned to control herself. I wanted to be a grandfather to Maisie but I couldn't stand being around Laura. All that pretence. The fake smile. And when I looked at Maisie, I saw Laura. I couldn't do it anymore. I felt sick every time I went there, and my health started to suffer. I decided to cut all ties.'

Steve stood up. 'Make sure she's locked up where she can't hurt anyone else.'

'Thank you for coming in,' Meadows said. 'It can't have been easy.'

'Actually, it's a relief,' Steve said.

* * *

Laura was sitting in the interview room with her hands resting on her lap. No one had been in to bring her fresh clothes. She wore the grey joggers and sweatshirt she had been given when her clothes were taken to forensics. Her nose was swollen, and she had a dark bruise under each eye.

Blackwell set up the recording and reminded Laura that she was entitled to legal representation. Again she refused. It didn't surprise Meadows. He felt it was part of her plan to get off the charges. He knew they would have to play it carefully to get answers.

Laura smiled sweetly at them. 'Are you ready to take my statement? As you can see, it was a vicious attack.' She pointed to her nose.

'Is that where you want to start?' Meadows asked. 'I agree it was a vicious attack you inflicted on Detective Reena Valentine.'

Laura's smile disappeared. 'Is that what she is saying?'

'I'm stating a fact,' Meadows said. 'You tried to inject Detective Valentine with a lethal dose of Pentobarsol.'

Laura shrugged. 'If you say so. Is this the part where you offer me a deal to tell you everything?'

'We don't need your cooperation,' Blackwell said. 'We have enough evidence.'

Laura raised her eyebrows. 'Really?'

Meadows sat forward. 'You may be interested to know that Detective Tristan Edris survived, and is expected to make a full recovery.'

'Oh that's a shame,' Laura said. 'The thing is, I just can't help myself. It's not like I could ask someone's advice or seek medical attention. I was afraid of being locked up.'

Meadows saw Blackwell stiffen. He knew where Laura was going with this. She would plead insanity and possibly be remanded to the hospital with an order for treatment. He knew that patients in high-security hospitals had a chance of rehabilitation and release. What he had to do was play to her ego. Let her talk her way into a prison sentence. At the very least, he needed her to confirm that she had murdered Alex, Ceri, and Eira. There was also the abduction and the attempted murder of Cora.

Meadows sat back. 'We understand your situation,' he said. 'There can be so much judgement around certain illnesses.'

'Exactly,' Laura said.

'Do you think there is something that triggers you?'

Laura shrugged. 'It's hard to explain. When I want something, it kind of takes over. I have to have it, no matter the cost.'

'Is that why you broke up Jenna and Gareth? Because you wanted Gareth.'

Laura laughed. 'I never wanted Gareth. I just didn't want him to marry Jenna. There was such a fuss. Everyone talking about the wedding. Then there were the engagement presents, the wedding present list, and the wedding dress. The bridesmaids. It's all Jenna and Ceri talked about. It was all about Jenna, and it started to really upset me, so I started a rumour.' She smirked.

'I put on the tears for Ceri. Told her I couldn't bear to be the one to tell Gareth. Ceri was torn, as she secretly liked Gareth. I made her think it was her idea to tell Alex. Alex then told Gareth. You should have seen Jenna's face at the church when Alex turned up and said Gareth wasn't coming.' Laura grinned. 'That was the first time I met Alex. I had heard everything about him from Ceri, but he didn't go to the same school as us. When I saw him, I decided he would do.'

'Do for what?' Blackwell asked.

'A husband. I'd be the one to get all the fuss. The one to wear the wedding dress. It didn't work out that way. He never proposed. There was always some excuse for us not to get married. He wanted to save up for a house, and stuff like that. Then I got pregnant, and I was stuck with that little bitch. Do you know how exhausting it is to pretend to love something? Worse than that, I saw Ceri get everything. She'd moved in with Gareth, then he inherited the money and built that big house. He spoilt Ceri – new clothes, jewellery, even a new car.'

'You wanted her life,' Meadows said.

'Yeah. It wasn't easy to plan and some of it was down to luck.'

'How did you manage to sabotage the oxygen tanks?'

Laura leaned forward. Her eyes danced with excitement. Meadows hoped this was where she could trip up and demonstrate that her actions were not impulsive, but were meticulously planned.

'I had to work first on the SPG. Ceri had a double unit. I got a few second-hand ones to try out but it was difficult. I needed the needle to indicate a full tank and the unit had to be watertight. I managed it with a single unit and just adjusted my plans.'

Blackwell had caught on. 'It must have taken you a long time.'

Laura nodded. 'Then I had to wait for an opportunity. Alex was the one who found the cave and showed the rest of us. I went there alone to explore and to time the dive. I needed the oxygen to run out at just the right time. Somewhere in the middle of the sump, so there was no chance of getting out. Then I fixed the air supply to just the right amount. The night before the dive, Alex was supposed to help Gareth set up. I had a little fun with Alex's car when it was in his work car park. When it was time to leave, he found that he had a flat battery.' Laura giggled.

'Alex was useless with cars. He called me and I said I would come with jump leads. It was enough of an excuse to distract Gareth. He was in the garage setting up with Ceri. I asked Ceri to take Maisie to my mother's house to save time, then I asked Gareth for a set of jump leads. He obliged. When everyone was asleep that night, I changed over Ceri's tanks for the half-filled ones. Later, I convinced Gareth that he must have picked up a set of tanks from the used side, after he helped me with the jump leads. Eira was the one that spoilt everything by swapping out with Ceri.'

Meadows glanced at Blackwell who was struggling to hide his disgust.

'You had to try again,' Meadows said.

Laura tucked her hair behind her ear. 'I couldn't do it straight away. Ceri wouldn't dive after what happened to Eira, so I convinced her to take up hiking. We did a few hikes and took photos. I even got her to change coats. I needed it to look like I was the target if there was any suspicion. It was easy. She was taking a bunch of selfies, and I just pushed her off the edge.

'I ran back towards the car park. Halfway there, I put my foot against a root to trip. I only meant to sprain my ankle, not break the bloody thing. I was in agony, and I had to wait for some walkers to come along. I suppose it looked better in the end.'

'Then you had to get rid of Alex,' Blackwell said.

'That didn't take much effort,' Laura said. 'I told him I wanted to go to one of the easier caves, to get my confidence back. We set off early. When he was securing the ropes, I injected him with Pentobarsol. Enough to put down a horse. It is painless, and the most humane way. Then I pushed him down the hole. I dragged him further into the cave so he wouldn't be easily seen. Just in case someone took a peek down the hole. No one ever goes down that cave.'

Laura talked matter-of-factly and showed no signs of remorse. Meadows was finding it increasingly difficult to listen to her.

'I think work suspected me of taking the drugs,' she continued. 'They had no proof, but they found a way of getting rid of me. I didn't care as I wanted my own practice.'

'And you got it with Gareth,' Blackwell said.

'Yeah, but Gareth wasn't so easy to control. Most men do as I want, but not him. I even got pregnant to keep him tied to me. I don't think he was in love with me.'

'I'm guessing you didn't expect him to get back with Jenna,' Blackwell said.

Laura frowned. 'Jenna wanted it all her own way. She complained about Gareth giving me money and about looking after the brats. She was trying to persuade him to sell his share of the vet practice. I couldn't have that. He put up most of the money and I wouldn't have been able to buy him out. She wasn't so easy to get rid of. I started giving her all sorts of drugs. I'd put them in smoothies and told her it would help her lose the pounds she'd put on over the years. I gave her levothyroxine to mimic a problem with her thyroid, nitarsone… that one increases weight gain in poultry. There were a few others I tried. It was fun to experiment and see the results. I finally got her hooked on ketamine.' Laura grinned. 'I filled capsules with the powder. I gave her the first lot and told her they were herbal tablets that I'd ordered. I said they had really helped me. Once she tried them, she couldn't get enough. The stuff isn't cheap but it was worth every penny.'

Laura leaned forward. 'I moved things around the house. I even took clothes, keys, and her driving licence. I wanted to make her think she was losing her mind.'

'You set fire to the house,' Meadows said.

Laura shook her head.

'You put Cora in the river though.'

'I'd love to take credit for that one. Genius idea, but that wasn't me. Neither did I kill my mother, before you ask. Why would I? Who is going to look after the brats? On the upside, I'll get the house.'

'I doubt you'll see a penny,' Blackwell said.

Laura glared at him.

'I'm curious as to why you tried to kill Detective Edris,' Meadows said. 'You kept him alive in the cave for nearly three nights.'

'Tristan was fun, and he knew how to treat a woman. When Alex was found, I thought it might be useful to keep him around. That way I would know what was happening in the case. I could also feed him information, and steer the investigation in the direction I wanted. Of course, I made a show of breaking it off for his benefit. My plan was to pin it all on Henry. It would have been easy for you to believe that Henry was on some revenge mission for his dead fiancée. That's why I told Tristan about the cave.'

Laura sighed. 'Then he had to spoil it all by snooping around my house. I couldn't have that. I hit him over the head. I thought he was never going to come around. I could have killed him straight away, but I needed to know what he knew. I had to think fast after that. I came up with an even better plan. Blame it on Gareth. He'd be put away and I'd have the vet practice to myself. Gareth has keys to the practice and access to all the drugs, so it wouldn't be hard to make him look guilty. I drugged Tristan and took him to the cave. It was hard-going. He didn't know where he was half the time. I kept telling him we needed to hide. All I had to do was get back and set everything up.

'I kept him alive in the cave for company. I knew it would take you a couple of days to piece things together and get Henry to give you the location. I kept an eye out. I'd planned on giving Tristan a lethal dose and putting him in the water. You would have found me tied up and drugged.'

Meadows saw Blackwell clench his jaw and guessed he was finding it hard not to comment.

'I'd practised injecting myself and fixing cable ties before I passed out. I had it down to perfection. I didn't expect you to turn up in a storm. I thought I heard a noise and was coming to check when I tripped and dropped the torch. Then you found me. If I'd got the needle in you, I could have dumped you in the water as well. Then do the same to that bitch. I'm sure I would have come up with an alternative plan.'

Meadows had heard enough. He got up and left the interview room. Blackwell followed.

'Do you think she's telling the truth about Deryn and Cora?' Blackwell asked.

'Yeah. She has no reason to lie at this stage.'

DCI Lester joined them. 'Good result all around,' he said.

'I wouldn't say that,' Meadows replied. 'Three people dead, one unsolved murder, and an unsolved abduction, and attempted murder of a baby. We still can't locate Jenna. Her phone is turned off. She had opportunity to kill Deryn and put Cora in the river. She's unstable and who knows what she may do?'

Lester's face fell. 'Right, well, I'll get a substitute team to take over for now. There will be a full investigation into Valentine's and Edris' conduct. As for you two, there will need to be a formal discipline. Insubordination cannot be tolerated.'

'OK,' Meadows said.

'OK? Is that all you've got to say for yourself?'

'Yeah. I'm going to the hospital then I'm going home. I'll return when my team has been reinstated.'

Before Lester had a chance to respond, Meadows walked out.

Chapter Thirty-six

Edris was sitting up in bed when Meadows arrived at the hospital. He still looked deathly pale and was hooked up to a drip, but it was the broken look in his eyes that Meadows found disturbing. He knew Edris' fear of being underground, and that, coupled with lying in his own filth, being injected with ketamine, and thrown in the water, would understandably break his spirit.

'You look like shit,' Blackwell said and plonked himself down in a seat next to the bed.

'You don't look so hot yourself,' Valentine retorted from where she was perched on the end of the bed.

Meadows looked at his team. They all looked worse for wear. Valentine was covered in scratches and had a bruise on her cheek, Blackwell looked like he hadn't slept for a week, and he knew they were eyeing the cut and bruise on his forehead.

Meadows moved a chair closer to the bed and sat down. 'At least you look better than when we pulled you out of the water. I thought we'd lost you for a minute.'

'I'm sorry. I feel like a right twat,' Edris said.

Blackwell folded his arms. 'That's because you are. Valentine has been suspended and you got "Mr Peace to the People" telling the boss where to stick his job.'

Edris looked at Meadows. 'You didn't, did you?'

'Not in so many words,' Meadows said.

Edris sighed. 'Valentine filled me in on what happened. I'm so very sorry. I don't know what to say. All of you risked your lives to come and find me.'

Blackwell snorted. 'Not me. I only went to make sure these two didn't get in trouble. If it were up to me, I would have left your sorry arse to rot in that cave. What the hell were you thinking?'

'I… I fucked up.'

Blackwell shook his head. 'Yeah, Golden Boy, you did.'

'I should have said something about Laura the night Cora went missing, but the baby was found and it looked like there was no case. Then Alex was found.' He looked at Meadows. 'I nearly told you then but… I don't know. Laura didn't react when we went to see her, and it looked like Alex had likely had an accident. I thought it would all blow over. Then we found out it wasn't Olwen who took Cora, and it didn't look like Alex's death was an accident. I panicked. It was too late to say anything then. I never thought Laura was involved.' A tear slid down his cheek and he wiped it away.

'Stop being a wimp,' Blackwell said. 'You need to get out of here, face the music, and get back to work. I expect payback. You can take my "on call" for the next six months.'

'Make the tea and coffee for the rest of your life,' Valentine added.

'Write up all the reports,' Paskin said from the doorway. She stepped inside. 'I think you should also supply cake.'

Valentine nodded. 'And chocolate.'

Meadows knew the team were trying to make light of the situation, but he imagined the guilt Edris felt wouldn't be easily abated. Maybe talking about the experience would help, and there were a few things Meadows needed to know.

'It was the St Christopher that made you suspect Laura, wasn't it?'

Edris nodded. 'When Mark talked about the teddy bear Alex had won for Laura at the fair, I remembered seeing it in her bedroom. The St Christopher was around the bear's neck. Just like the jewellery on the toys in Maisie's bedroom. I still didn't want to believe that Laura was involved. I thought maybe she had one of her own or something similar. I waited until she had gone for a bath then started to look around. Of course, there was nothing on the bear. I checked her jewellery box and there was nothing like a St Christopher in there. I did a general search. I don't know what I was looking for, but I guess I had an uneasy feeling. The next thing, I woke up on the floor. It's a bit hazy after that. I only remember bits.'

Edris picked up a glass of water from the bedside table and took a sip.

'Laura talked a lot when we were in the cave. She said Maisie had put the St Christopher around the teddy bear and…'

The rest of Edris' story faded out as something struck Meadows. He jumped up from the chair.

'I think I know who put Cora in the river. I need to check something.'

He rushed out of the hospital and drove to the station. He was sitting at his desk reading through Edris' notes when Blackwell came in.

'I thought you were going home,' Meadows said.

'I was, but you can't just say "I think I've solved the case" then fuck off.'

Meadows smiled. 'Oh, sorry. I needed to be sure. I would have sent you all a message. Hold on a minute.' He scanned through the notes until he found what he was looking for, then typed a question into Google. He read the answer and then sat back. 'It's Maisie.'

'What?' Blackwell laughed. 'You think she put her baby sister in the river and then killed her grandmother. She's just a little girl.'

'So was Laura when she pushed her five-year-old cousin into a pool. When Edris talked about the St Christopher, he said that Laura had bribed Maisie to keep her quiet.'

'That doesn't make her a killer.'

'No, but it says something about Maisie's character. Steve Jones said that when he looked at Maisie, he saw Laura. I thought he meant in looks at the time. The child does look like her mother, but that's not what he meant. I think he saw the same traits. When Olwen was looking out of the window, on the day of the christening, I think she saw Maisie with Cora. She told us she saw Miriam.'

Blackwell shook his head. 'That doesn't make any sense.'

'It does if you think about what Olwen said that day. She talked about the baby boys being thrown into the River Nile. Miriam was Moses' sister. That's what Olwen was trying to tell us.'

'Shit.'

'Deryn said to Gareth, "I can't believe this is happening again." She had to mean that Maisie was turning out the same as Laura.'

'That's why she tried to talk to her ex-husband,' Blackwell said. 'She wanted his help as she couldn't bring herself to turn in Maisie.'

'Where is Maisie now?' Meadows asked.

'With Gareth,' Blackwell said.

'And Cora. We need to go.'

Chapter Thirty-seven

Meadows was standing in an observation room, in the hospital, with Blackwell and Valentine. Through the glass, he could see what looked like a sitting room. There were lime-green comfy chairs, a thick cream rug, and colourful prints on the walls.

'Are you sure it's OK me being here?' Valentine asked.

Meadows nodded. 'I don't think there is any danger of Lester showing his face. Anyway, you need to see this as much as the rest of us.'

A woman entered the room. She was dressed casually and had soft brown eyes and an open friendly face. She introduced herself as Caroline.

'I've been working with Maisie for the past few days,' Caroline said. 'She has classic signs of an anti-social personality disorder.'

'You mean she's a psychopath,' Blackwell said.

'We don't tend to use that label anymore, and it's difficult to diagnose a child with such a disorder. What I have observed is callous and unemotional behaviour.'

'Could that have been learned from her mother?' Meadows asked.

'Her upbringing could have been a contributory factor, although I think these traits run deeper. She is bright, and aware of the trouble she is in, but has a total lack of concern. She shows no remorse or regret. On the contrary, she finds it funny.'

'Forensic tech have looked at her phone and tablet,' Meadows said. 'There were no parental controls and some of the videos she's watched have graphic violence and sexual content. Her history also showed a particular interest in true crime.'

'That doesn't surprise me,' Caroline said. 'She is likely to have found those types of videos entertaining, rather than frightening or disturbing. They'll be bringing in Maisie soon, so I better go into the room.'

The three of them turned to the window. Meadows observed the child being brought in. Her hair was in two braids and she wore a pink dress, white woollen tights, and pink ankle boots. She looked a picture of innocence.

Caroline talked to her for a few moments and then asked her about the house fire. Maisie smiled and tucked her feet up on the chair.

'Did you want to hurt Jenna?' Caroline asked.

'I wanted her to die,' Maisie said. 'Everything was good until she moved in. She stopped Daddy buying me things and wouldn't let me watch what I wanted.'

'What about Cora? I've seen pictures of the two of you together. You looked happy to have a baby sister, and I know you helped take care of her.'

Maisie mimicked sticking her finger down her throat and being sick. 'I was pretending. I hate babies. This one was worse. I knew Daddy would love it more than me. I know he's not my real dad.'

'But there's Ieuan. Your Dad loved you both the same.'

Maisie shook her head. 'I was his favourite. He called me his little princess, then I heard him call Cora that.'

'Tell me about the christening,' Caroline said.

The smirk on Maisie's face gave Meadows goosebumps.

'There was a lot of fuss, a party and presents. I didn't get a christening.'

'That's because God would have incinerated her before she stepped through the church door,' Blackwell said.

'Everyone was busy with the baby,' Maisie continued. 'No one was taking any notice of me. I went to Nanna's house and grabbed a plastic box from my bedroom and put it by the river. I knew Cora would be put in her cot at some time. When Jenna took her up, I waited a while, then I told Nanna I was going to the park. I took Cora, put her in the box, and threw it in the river.' Maisie giggled. 'I watched her float away, then I went to call for my friend and we played in the park.'

'What did you think would happen to Cora?'

'I thought she would end up in the sea.'

'Did your grandmother find out?' Caroline asked.

Maisie nodded. 'Only because the red box was missing. I heard her on the phone to Dad and I knew she was going to tell him, so I pushed her down the stairs. She didn't die. I had to put a pillow over her head and kneel on it. I put the pillow in a black bag, then ran to the bottom of the garden. I jumped over the wall, and crept up Mrs Pugh's garden and around the side of the house. I put the bag in her dustbin. I know you've got to get rid of evidence.' Maisie beamed. 'I am clever.'

'This child is creeping me out,' Blackwell said.

'I think we've heard enough,' Meadows said. 'I'll see you both at work.' He turned to Valentine. 'Don't worry about the inquiry. You risked your life to save a colleague. If anything, they should be giving you a medal.'

Valentine smiled. 'Thank you.'

As Meadows was leaving the hospital, he met with Jenna who was pushing Cora in a pram.

'How are you feeling?' Meadows asked.

'Much better,' Jenna said. 'I'm having help with the withdrawal symptoms, but it's much easier now I know.

Up here.' She pointed to her head. 'I'm starting to feel like my old self.'

Meadows smiled. He could already see a difference. Her hair was washed and styled, but more than that, the anger had gone from her eyes. 'I'm glad. You had us worried when we couldn't find you.'

'I'm sorry about that. At the time, I thought I'd been living with a killer that had been drugging me. I had to get away. I went to a friend's house and turned off my phone. I just needed some space. I feel bad that I thought Gareth was capable of doing those things. We're going to make a go of it. I think we'll be all right.'

'I hope everything turns out well for you all. Take care of yourself.'

'Thank you.'

Meadows stepped outside to where the sun was breaking through the clouds. The smell of autumn was in the air. It was usually his favourite time of year, with the colours and the crisp air, but all he felt was heaviness. All of his previous cases had a clear motive. Individuals who had been victims themselves, but this one was different. When he interviewed Laura, it was like being in the presence of someone without a soul. He guessed what it was. No conscience or morals. It was the same with Maisie. He felt as though his world was out of kilter.

When he arrived home, he spotted Daisy's car outside the cottage. He wasn't expecting her to be home and worry instantly gnawed at his stomach. He opened the door and called out.

'Oh, good. You're back,' Daisy said.

'You're home early. Is everything OK?'

Daisy nodded.

'I asked Valentine to give me the heads-up when you were on your way. Come sit down and tell me how it went at the hospital.'

Meadows filled her in.

Daisy shook her head. 'It's hard to believe, but at least both mother and daughter can't hurt anyone else. I know you've been down and this case has got on top of you. That's why I wanted to wait to give you some news.'

'Please let it be good,' Meadows said.

'I'm pregnant.'

A smile spread across Meadows' face. 'I'm going to be a father.' Suddenly the world didn't seem like such a bad place after all.

List of characters

Joe Hendon – Gareth's father
Jenna Ford – Gareth's partner
Jamie Ford – Gareth and Jenna's son
Cora Hendon – Gareth and Jenna's baby daughter
Ceri Rees – caving club member
Eira Thomas – caving club member
Henry Tay – caving club member

If you enjoyed this book, please let others know by leaving a quick review on Amazon. Also, if you spot anything untoward in the paperback, get in touch. We strive for the best quality and appreciate reader feedback.

editor@thebookfolks.com

www.thebookfolks.com

Also in this series:

THE SILENT QUARRY (Book 1)

Following a fall and a bang to the head, a woman's
memories come flooding back about an incident that
occurred twenty years ago in which her friend was
murdered. As she pieces together the events and tells the
police, she begins to fear repercussions. DI Winter
Meadows must work out the identity of the killer before
they strike again.

FROZEN MINDS (Book 2)

When the boss of a care home for mentally challenged
adults is murdered, the residents are not the most reliable
of witnesses. DI Winter Meadows draws on his soft nature
to gain the trust of an individual he believes saw the crime.
But without unravelling the mystery and finding the
evidence, the case will freeze over.

SUFFER THE CHILDREN (Book 3)

When a toddler goes missing from the family home, the
police and community come out in force to find her.
However, with few traces found after an extensive search,
DI Winter Meadows fears the child has been abducted.
But someone knows something, and when a man is found
dead, the race is on to solve the puzzle.

A KNOT OF SPARROWS (Book 4)

When local teenage troublemaker and ne'er-do-well Stacey Evans is found dead, locals in a small Welsh village couldn't give a monkey's. That gives nice guy cop DI Winter Meadows a headache. Can he win over their trust and catch a killer in their midst?

LIES OF MINE (Book 5)

A body is found in an old mine in a secluded spot in the Welsh hills. There are no signs of struggle so DI Winter Meadows suspects that the victim, youth worker David Harris, knew his killer. But when the detective discovers it is not the first murder in the area, he must dig deep to join up the dots.

RISE TO THE FLY (Book 6)

When the bodies of a retired couple are found by a reservoir, the police are concerned to discover fishing flies have been impaled on their tongues. After they find nothing in the couple's past to indicate a reason for the murder, they begin to look local. What will they turn up in this dark and secluded corner of Wales?

WINTER'S CRY (Book 7)

When a farmer clears some trees from a field, he unearths a corpse. Suspicion immediately falls upon the neighbouring commune, a collection of makeshift huts and tents which house a reclusive group of people. Having grown up there, DI Winter Meadows goes to talk to its members, who are wary of the police. But what he finds will have him questioning everything he knows about his past.

HARBOUR NO SECRETS (Book 8)

A young woman is found in a Welsh lake, murdered. Detectives find seaside trinkets placed in her home. Are they a message from the killer? DI Winter Meadows becomes convinced that the perp might be lurking within the victim's circle of friends. Who is bearing a grudge and who might be targeted next?

THE CRIMSON HARVEST (Book 9)

Unflappable cop DI Winter Meadows has his wedding plans interrupted when bodies begin to turn up on his patch. The Welsh police have a serial killer on their hands and no stone is left unturned in the hunt. But only a detective who truly understands the community will be able to catch a killer in their midst.

All available FREE with Kindle Unlimited and in paperback.

More fiction by the author:

BLUE HOLLOW

When a family friend is murdered, a journalist begins to
probe into his past. What she finds there makes her
question everything about her life. Should she bury his
secrets with him, or become the next victim of
Blue Hollow?

Other titles of interest:

MURDER IN THE NEW FOREST by Carol Cole

When a woman's body is found on the ground next to her
horse, it seems an unfortunate accident had occurred.
However, DI Callum MacLean, newly arrived in the
picturesque New Forest from Glasgow, suspects
differently. But hunting a killer in this close-knit
community, suspicious of outsiders, will be tough.
Especially when not everyone in his team is on side.

THAT CARE FORGOT by James Warren

Junior attorney Rebecca Holt isn't too happy when given
the pro bono case of a convicted murderer. Yet Nick
Malone isn't really interested in his parole hearing, rather
he is obsessed with a serial killer who terrorized New
Orleans in the 1990s. When Malone reveals his secrets,
Rebecca is faced with a life-changing decision.

*Sign up to our mailing list to find out about new releases
and special offers!*

www.thebookfolks.com

Printed in Dunstable, United Kingdom